HEALED TO DEATH

HEALED TO DEATH

KENZIE KIRSCH MEDICAL THRILLERS
BOOK TWELVE

P.D. WORKMAN

ISBN: 9781774687925 (KDP Paperback)
ISBN: 9781774687932 (KDP Hardcover)
ISBN: 9781774687956 (Lulu Paperback)
ISBN: 9781774687949 (Large Print)
ISBN: 9781774687963 (Digital)
ISBN: 9781774687970 (Auto-narrated audiobook)

ALSO BY P.D. WORKMAN

FIND MORE BOOKS AT PDWORKMAN.COM

Kenzie Kirsch Medical Thrillers

Unlawful Harvest

Doctored Death

Dosed to Death

Gentle Angel

Rushin' Death

Posed for Death

Death of a Corpse

Endowed with Death

Shattered to Death

Captured in Death

Currying Death

Healed to Death

Death's Charm (Coming Soon)

Zachary Goldman Mysteries

Private Investigator

She Wore Mourning

His Hands Were Quiet

She Was Dying Anyway

He Was Walking Alone

They Thought He was Safe

He Was Not There

Her Work Was Everything

She Told a Lie

He Never Forgot

She Was At Risk

He Drowned in Memory

Their Walls Were Empty

They Came for Him

They Sought Vengeance

She Was Their Target

His Fear Was Real

She Was Out of Reach

He Was Deceived

She Once Vanished

Bleeding Hearts Valley Thrillers

An Abrupt Departure

High-Tech Crime Solvers Series

Virtually Harmless

Cowritten with D. D. VanDyke

California Corwin P. I. Mystery Series

The Girl in the Morgue

Stand Alone Suspense Novels

Looking Over Your Shoulder

Lion Within

Pursued by the Past

In the Tick of Time

Loose the Dogs

AND MORE AT PDWORKMAN.COM

*To those who make a difference
despite the odds*

1

Kenzie's phone started ringing loudly on the side table, jarring her awake. She grabbed it and tried to silence the noise, her fingers clumsy with sleep. She wanted the noise to end as quickly as possible, but finding the button to mute it took precious seconds. She considered getting out of bed and stepping out into the hallway to take the call so that her voice would not disturb Zachary's sleep but, by the time she had formed the thought, she knew there was no use. Zachary woke more quickly than she did and, if he were awakened at night, it was pretty much guaranteed that he would stay that way. Even if Kenzie could go back to sleep after the sound of that klaxon, there was no way Zachary would.

So she saved herself the risk of stubbing her toes or other accidents that might occur stumbling around in the dark—or blinding herself by turning on a light—by staying in bed. She blinked a couple of times to clear her vision, then swiped the screen to accept the call.

"Dr. Kirsch," she acknowledged. "Sorry, took me a minute there."

"Good morning, Dr. Kirsch," the operator at the other end of the line greeted pleasantly. "I'm afraid I have a callout for you."

"Sure," Kenzie agreed. "Where are the remains? Any details about the situation?"

The operator gave her an address and directed her to an alley, which was not particularly surprising. Kenzie thumbed the address into a note on her phone and read it back. The operator confirmed.

"Police have secured the scene."

"Great, thanks."

"Have a great day, doctor," the operator told her pleasantly and disconnected.

Kenzie looked at the window. Though the blinds were pulled, she could still see through the crack between them. It was dark—streetlights shining. Though the dispatcher had wished her a good morning and told her to have a good day, it was still in the middle of the night. Kenzie looked at the time on her phone screen.

Two o'clock in the morning.

At least she had a few hours of sleep under her belt. She wouldn't be getting any more. While in theory, she could go back to sleep, and the police would hold the scene until it was *actually* morning, she would never do that. With her heart hammering after being startled out of sound sleep, she wouldn't be able to get back to sleep if she wanted to, and she wouldn't make the law enforcement officers who had secured the scene stand around for hours waiting for her. That would just be rude and would guarantee she would not get the friendly cooperation she was used to from the police force in the future.

She took a few deep breaths to settle her heart and try to get the oxygen to her brain to help her wake up and focus on the business at hand.

"Got a callout?" Zachary asked in a quiet, calm voice intended not to startle her.

Kenzie stretched and turned partway around to look at him. She couldn't see much in the darkness of the room, just his shape beside her. Her brain filled in what her eyes could not see—his very short, dark hair, a scruff of several days' growth of whiskers, the mixture of concern and reassurance on his face.

"Yup," she agreed, "body in a back alley. Those are always nice."

He chuckled. "Who knows, it could just be a heart attack. A businessman who went out for a breath of fresh air."

"It's never just a heart attack," Kenzie countered. If it were earlier or later, it could be. A businessman having a nightcap before bed, or an early morning heart attack on his commute to work. But two in the morning was rarely anything so benign.

Of course, he might have died hours or even days before. No one had said that he had died within the last hour or two.

In her experience, it would not be pretty.

Zachary stirred beside her. He untangled himself from the blankets and got out of bed, stopping momentarily to feel around for some clothing. "Do you want me to make coffee?" he asked. He was already moving, heading toward the door. There was no point in telling him no. He'd already made up his mind. He'd be making coffee for himself. She might as well take advantage of it.

"Sure," she agreed, "that would be nice. But just regular strength. None of that high-test stuff."

"You sure you don't need an extra boost?"

"If I need more caffeine, I'll drink another cup."

"Aye-aye," he agreed.

Kenzie rubbed her eyes and got moving. She didn't want to keep the police waiting longer than necessary.

By the time she had splashed water on her face, combed her curly hair, and finished making herself presentable, the smell of coffee was wafting through the house. On her arrival in the kitchen, Zachary handed her a large travel mug filled with the fresh brew. He leaned in for a kiss, bristly, still smelling of sweat and musk.

"Have a good day," he told her. "Shoot me a text or call me over lunch and let me know how it is going."

"Will do," Kenzie agreed. She slipped on her jacket and shoes, grabbed her purse, and entered the garage where her "baby"—a sporty red convertible—awaited her. Her small scene-of-crime kit was stowed in the trunk as usual. If she found she needed additional equipment when she got to the scene, she would have Carlos bring it to her when he drove the medical examiner's van to the scene for transportation.

2

Despite the fact that it was not yet a decent hour of the morning, it was not lonely and creepy in the back alley where the remains had been found. A police perimeter had been set up and large lights banished all thoughts of night. Kenzie was happy to see that the police mostly stayed outside the perimeter until she and the forensic unit gathered the evidence they needed and turned the scene over. They did not need a scene that had been trampled all over. She pulled on the prescribed protective gear and approached the scene.

"Morning, everyone," Kenzie greeted. "What've we got?"

A detective had arrived ahead of her and was patiently waiting with his own cup of coffee, an extra-large from the nearest coffee shop. He took a sip, considering her. He had wavy, sandy-colored hair and was young for a detective. He looked as if he, like Kenzie, had been woken up by the call. His name bar gave his name as Samuels.

Kenzie knew she wasn't what most people pictured when the title "Assistant Medical Examiner" was mentioned. Most people expected a gray-haired man, not Kenzie, with her wild dark curls and bright red lipstick. Her red sports car didn't advertise that she was from the medical examiner's office either, although, if Samuels got close enough, he would be able to see her medical examiner parking pass hanging from the mirror. Kenzie smiled and nodded, indicating the identification on the lanyard around her neck in case he doubted who she was. He cleared his throat and nodded.

"Just an old homeless guy," Samuels told her. "No sign of violence or anything out of place."

Kenzie nodded. "Great. This should be quick, then."

He escorted her to the officer who was logging the visitors to the scene and Kenzie signed in. The detective pointed to the body in case she couldn't see it, which she could, and suggested that she walk around the edges to preserve any evidence. Kenzie didn't push back on being told how to preserve the crime scene. She was happy to have them cordoning it off and controlling foot traffic in and out of the scene as they were supposed to. It didn't always turn out that way and she was never happy to arrive at a crime scene where people were just wandering around or, even worse, had touched or moved the body for one reason or another.

Kenzie walked as close to the brick wall of the building on her right as she could, shining a flashlight ahead of her at an angle to detect any footprints, fluids, pocket debris, or other piece of evidence before she stepped on it. When she reached the body, she checked the ground carefully before setting down her kit and leaning in to examine the body.

The first matter of business was to confirm that he was, in fact, deceased. That was apparent just by looking at him. Yellow, waxy skin and lifeless eyes. But she checked for a carotid pulse anyway and shifted his jaw slightly. Either he didn't yet smell, or the other smells of the alley were overwhelming the beginnings of decomposition. It had not been long since he had passed.

"Who found him?" Kenzie asked, projecting her voice toward Detective Samuels, standing outside the tape.

"Another homeless guy."

"You got him? To get a full statement?"

"Didn't seem like he knew anything. We got his details in case we need to reach him again."

The homeless did have the unfortunate habit of disappearing

when the police were looking for them. They had the ability to disappear without a trace for long periods of time, swallowed up by the streets, with no address and often no phone number to reach them at. Kenzie wished she'd had a chance to talk to the homeless man before he had been allowed to leave.

"What did he have to say?"

"Just that he knew his friend was sleeping close by and was looking for him. Found him here, deceased, and called it in."

"He is very recently deceased. No rigor. Are you sure he was already dead when the friend arrived?"

Samuels frowned, a crease appearing between his eyes. "Why would he call it in as a death if he was still alive? He would call 9-1-1."

Kenzie nodded slowly. Usually, people went with 9-1-1 even when calling in a dead body. Sometimes, they thought the person could be saved, even if they knew their hopes were most likely unfounded. They wanted to do *something*, and preserved the hope of revival long after it was reasonable.

"I would like to talk to him, if you would please be sure to include his contact information in your report."

"Of course," he agreed.

"If you have his friend, then I assume you also have his identity? A name for our victim?"

"John Lane. Jack. A longtime resident of these mean streets."

Kenzie nodded, not surprised. The man's clothing and rough-looking appearance suggested that he was not new to homeless life. She looked around for his possessions but did not see a shopping cart or stash anywhere close by. He might live some distance from there, maybe in a tent or other shelter, and that was where his belongings were.

She looked at his hands and fingers for any sign of what he had been doing recently. They were stained yellow, making it obvious that he had been a smoker of many years. She could smell alcohol and vomit on him. She pushed up one of his sleeves. No tattoos. No track marks. But there was something.

"There is an IV puncture mark here," she observed. "Would you call the hospital and find out what he was being treated for?"

"Sure," Detective Samuels agreed. He pulled out his phone and tapped the screen a few times. Like most other first responders in town, he had one or more of the hospitals' numbers in his contact list. He called Admitting and talked to them while Kenzie made her next few observations.

There were bloody stains on the collar of his shirt. Kenzie leaned in closer. There were no cuts on his throat or face. That fact, combined with the smell of vomit, told her that he had likely been throwing up blood.

Certainly not unheard of for an alcoholic. Long-term alcohol use did terrible things to the digestive tract. And alcoholics just kept drinking despite the pain. His skin and eyes were yellow. Jaundice. The elevated bilirubin told her there was liver damage.

The detective was probably right. He had probably died of natural causes, the destructive effects of long-term alcoholism, and not any street violence.

She examined the rest of the victim's limbs as far as his clothing would allow and checked his torso, front and back. There was some bruising, which was concerning, but she didn't think he had been beaten up. More than likely, it was just another sign of impending organ failure. He had been pretty hard on his body for some years.

"Okay," Kenzie called over to Samuels. "I'm going to call for transport and see how long we are waiting on the forensic team."

"Hospital says he was not admitted."

"Not admitted? But he was treated."

He shook his head. "They don't have any records of him being there. Not recently, and I assume you meant the IV mark was new."

"Yes. It's fresh. The IV was just pulled out in the last few hours. He *must* have been at the hospital."

"Maybe some kind of private clinic?" Samuels suggested.

A clinic. Kenzie nodded slowly. What kind of clinic was nearby that might have treated Mr. Lane? Someone might have noticed that he was dehydrated after throwing up. A doctor's office, rehab center, or some mobile clinic or outreach center that treated the homeless.

"We'll have to find out where he was being treated. Or maybe he was admitted to the hospital as a John Doe if he wouldn't give his name or was unconscious when he was taken there."

"Already asked that. No John Does treated in the last week. Few patients that meet his demographic.'"

"Hmm. We'll have to check around. Where was he living? Was he in a shelter?"

"More than likely. Ninety-five percent of the homeless population in Vermont is sheltered. We'll make a few calls around. I'm sure it won't take long to find out where he was being treated and for what."

"I can tell you the what. Alcoholism and ulcers in the upper GI. Vomiting, dehydrated, throwing up blood. It wouldn't have been pretty."

He sniffed and nodded in agreement.

"Wherever it was, he shouldn't have been released in this condition," Kenzie pointed out.

"He probably snuck out or signed an AMA."

"Against Medical Advice," Kenzie agreed, sighing. And there wasn't really anything anyone could do about it. They could try to have him declared incompetent and to put him under some kind of conservatorship but, other than a locked ward in a nursing home, there weren't many places that would physically prevent him from walking away if he wanted to leave.

Most doctors and social workers would shrug and let him leave if he insisted. Choosing to live a high-risk lifestyle was not cause to have someone declared incompetent. If he knew the likely consequences of his behavior and was coherent, it was pretty hard to convince a court to take away his freedom.

3

There wasn't any point in going home after having Mr. Lane transported to the medical examiner's office. There wouldn't be enough time to go back to sleep before having to get up again. Instead, Kenzie followed the transport van to the office and helped move the body into autopsy to prepare it for the postmortem. She didn't have a lot of other cases on her roster, so she would be able to do the post that morning.

She went over the clothing and body for any trace evidence and carefully packaged and labeled everything.

Mr. Lane was even more yellow under the bright white lights of the autopsy than he had been outside under the floodlights. After a careful examination of the body under a magnifying lens, Kenzie took a few swabs for trace evidence and then washed the body.

By the time Dr. Cook arrived, Kenzie had sorted through her email and was ready to begin the postmortem. Interoffice mail from the police department, postal mail, and lab reports would not come in until later in the morning.

"You're ready to start on our new guest?" Dr. Cook asked, reading Kenzie's body language.

"Yes. Do you want to join me? I can do it alone if you have other things."

"I would rather be in on the autopsy. I can catch up on other work later. Go ahead and suit up, and I'll be in as soon as I drop these things in my office." He indicated his briefcase and the raincoat that was folded over his arm.

"Great, see you in a few minutes."

Kenzie locked her computer and the desk drawers and posted a sign that she would be back at her desk later. They didn't get much foot traffic and most requests could be made online if people discovered she wasn't at her desk. Or they could leave her a message that she would deal with later.

She wasn't sure why she was quite so eager to start on the postmortem. Something aside from her usual eagerness to solve the puzzle of life and death was driving her. Her curiosity about the IV puncture? The desire to do something with her hands instead of sitting in front of a computer screen? The significant amount of caffeine she had consumed since waking up early that morning?

Something elusive and intangible lay just out of her grasp.

Kenzie clicked the foot button and dictated the date, file number, John Lane's name, and her name and Dr. Cook's. He joined her by the time she had finished the introductions and stood gazing at the body, wondering what they were going to find. Would there be any surprises, or would it all be routine? A man who had succeeded in drinking himself to death.

She described the body to the record, taking his weight and height measurements from the scales on the table. "Patient has significant jaundice. Some bruising on abdomen and limbs." Dr. Cook took pictures of each of the bruises with a scale beside each to document its size. They were blue and purple, deep bruises. No yellow or green to indicate that they were starting to break down and heal.

"A single puncture mark is observed in the left antecubital fossa, approximately two centimeters proximal to the median cubital vein. The puncture mark is approximately five millimeters in diameter. Suggestive of an intravenous drip."

"Have you interfaced with the hospital?" Dr. Cook asked.

"The detective already talked to them. He was not a patient at the hospital. Must have been treated in some clinic. He's looking into it."

Dr. Cook raised one eyebrow. "Really. Okay. I imagine he'll be able to find something. There aren't many professionals in Roxboro that would have given him an IV outside of the hospital."

Kenzie nodded. "That's what I figured."

She gave a brief description of the stains on Lane's clothing and her conclusion that the stains were consistent with hematemesis. She would circle back to a more detailed description of the clothing and any marks or stains at the end of the autopsy.

She looked over the body with a clinical eye. There were various other minor notes to be made regarding old scars, a rash that suggested vitamin deficiency, and the general wear and tear on the body. She looked at Dr. Cook. "Anything else?"

He shook his head. "I think that covers it."

"Do you want to do the incision?"

Dr. Cook shrugged and moved into position. Without further discussion, he performed the Y-incision and retracted the skin and tissue necessary to visualize the thoracic cavity. Lane was thin, with little adipose tissue. His organs were pale.

"Assuming the bleeding was caused by chronic alcoholism, we should examine the mediastinal structures first," Kenzie suggested. Dr. Cook moved aside, and she dissected the tissues around Lane's throat.

The most likely cause of his throwing up blood was the rupture of enlarged vessels around the esophagus, bleeding in the stomach, or the tearing of membranes between the stomach and esophagus due to severe retching or vomiting.

Kenzie carefully exposed the esophagus and confirmed her findings on the recording as Dr. Cook photographed the enlarged vessels. "Presence of esophageal varices confirmed. Evidence of significant bleeding."

"Don't forget to check for Mallory-Weiss Tears," Dr. Cook advised.

Kenzie nodded without looking up and, in a few minutes, could also confirm tears in the membranes.

"Possible death by exsanguination?" Dr. Cook suggested. "If he was presenting with hematemesis, he was in need of immediate medical attention. If he was alone or his street friends would not take him to the emergency room, it would not have taken him long to bleed out."

"But he *did* have medical attention," Kenzie pointed out. "He'd had an IV within the last few hours."

Cook nodded slowly, pondering this. "But where was he treated? And if he was treated for hematemesis, how did he end up back on the street, dead within hours?"

"They thought it had stopped bleeding and he eloped..." Kenzie suggested. "I don't know. He should have been closely supervised, but even a patient who is being watched can sneak off."

Dr. Cook agreed. "Yes, true. If he's not feeling well and decides he needs a drink... he knows he's not going to get one in the hospital. He's no longer throwing up, so he thinks he is fine. But then after he leaves..."

Kenzie frowned, a headache gathering in the front of her head. "It would make sense that he goes off on his own and then has another crisis and bleeds out," she agreed. "Only... he was lying on bare pavement."

Cook gave her a quizzical look. "Meaning...?"

"If he had bled out... he should have been in a pool of blood. But he wasn't. His clothes were stained, but dry. He was on bare pavement, no blood around him. It was a very clean scene... for a back alley."

4

Without the answers to these questions, they went on with the autopsy. Kenzie hoped they would come up with some more answers as they investigated further. Dr. Cook removed the heart, noting fatty deposits in the muscle tissue and increased thickness in the walls of the left ventricle. Neither sign came as a surprise. Alcoholism affected almost all organs and systems in the body in some way.

Other than appearing pale, the lungs were unremarkable. Kenzie weighed them and took tissue samples for microscopic examination lab tests. The liver and spleen were exposed.

Kenzie leaned in for a closer look. The liver looked like the worst case of cirrhosis she had ever seen in a textbook. Discolored, lumpy, and shrunken. It barely even looked like a liver anymore.

"I don't think Mr. Lane had very long, even if he had survived the GI bleed," Dr. Cook observed, shaking his head.

"No kidding." Dr. Cook positioned the camera and took a number of shots. "It's a good teaching case," he observed. "You want to show students what alcoholism does to the body... what you have here shows all of the classic signs."

"Yeah." Kenzie carefully cut the liver free and removed it,

weighing it and documenting it for the record. She took several tissue samples for histology.

She had been focused on the liver and was surprised when she looked back at the body and saw the spleen.

"The spleen is huge! I don't think I've ever seen one so big. That's not typical for alcoholism, is it?"

"Not usually, no," Dr. Cook replied. "Splenomegaly can be associated with cirrhosis due to portal hypertension, but there are other more common causes, such as infection or parasites, both of which are common in indigent patients."

They worked together to free the enlarged spleen and to document and examine it as they had the liver. Kenzie labeled tissue samples and marked the tests they needed on the lab request control sheets.

The gastrointestinal tract was now fully visible. Even before they removed the stomach, Kenzie could see that it was in bad shape. When she emptied the stomach of its contents, it seemed to contain nothing but blood and alcohol. Kenzie dissected it on a tray. The entire lining was inflamed, with erosions that had clearly been bleeding.

"Quite possibly our cause of death," Dr. Cook said. "It looks as though his entire upper GI was eroded. He must have been in terrible pain. No doctor could have done much to help him. Some heavy painkillers and... palliative care."

Kenzie sighed. "But it doesn't look like that's what he got. Or what he wanted."

"It can be hard to get people off the streets, no matter how many outreach programs you've got. There are always those who resist it no matter what you try. Or, given alcoholism or mental illness, who cannot find their way back even if they do want it."

Kenzie felt a shiver of anxiety, as she often did when people talked about the possibly dire effects of mental illness. Since she had gotten involved with Zachary, her eyes had been opened to the pervasiveness and seriousness of mental illness. Although some of Zachary's issues could not be concealed, there were many other people who suffered in silence. People who were afraid to talk about what they were going through or to seek the help they needed. People who had no access to care or the other resources they needed. People like Zachary, who, even when treated consistently by caring, capable professionals, still ended up hospitalized when things went off the rails.

She was afraid that he was always just one step away from homelessness. He had been there before, when he aged out of foster care. He had nearly been there again when his apartment had been destroyed by fire. She could see it happening again if a traumatic or psychotic episode overcame his defenses. She thought of all of the schizophrenics and addicts and others who were suffering and couldn't get their lives back, no matter how hard their families and loved ones tried to help.

Zachary's younger brother, Tyrrell, had ended up on the skids due to alcoholism more than once, disappearing off the radar for weeks or months at a time. He had been clean since his last drug rehab program, but they all feared that it was only a peaceful interlude and, when things got too hard, his illness would again overwhelm him.

"Dr. Kirsch? Kenzie?"

"Sorry." Kenzie refocused on her work. "The stomach was badly diseased," she summed up. "We should also check for ulcerations in the small and large intestines."

Dr. Cook agreed, and they continued to run the rest of the digestive tract. While the intestines looked better than the stomach, they were still not in good shape. The paleness of all the organs made Kenzie wonder just how much blood Lane had lost.

"This is interesting."

Kenzie followed Dr. Cook's scalpel, pointing to the kidneys. After all of the rest of the damage she had seen throughout Mr. Lane's body, she was not expecting to see healthy organs, and she was right. The kidneys were significantly swollen and dark brown in color rather than red.

"Hemoglobinuria," she remembered.

Dr. Cook agreed. "Very good. What tests should we be running on the kidneys?"

Kenzie cast her mind back on all of the checkboxes applicable to kidneys on the lab request sheets, and she listed the various tests that might help to reveal the cause of the kidney damage.

"And…?"

Kenzie thought about what she might have missed.

"Coombs test."

"I agree. The signs of acute kidney injury, together with the enlarged spleen, are suggestive of issues unrelated to blood loss. It may be related to an infection or medication he was on. Maybe due to some toxic chemical he consumed, such as methanol or ethylene glycol. Not unheard of in alcoholics."

Kenzie brought up the lab request forms and checked each of the appropriate boxes.

"Whatever the proximate cause," Dr. Cook said, "I think we can agree that this was a natural death. The severe damage done by his alcoholism started the ball rolling, and whether the kidneys, liver, or bleeding actually killed him, it was the natural result of his addiction."

Kenzie nodded. "It's very sobering to see a case like this. I would hope that our society would be so much further advanced in its treatment of addiction. Something like this… it's a sad reminder of where we are."

"Sometimes people fall through the cracks. Or refuse the help they are offered."

"But he had friends; someone who knew him by name called the police. The detective said that he was known. People knew… but still…"

"It's a difficult disease to treat. Many different facets."

Kenzie knew that Tyrrell's alcoholism was not just a physical addiction, but was tied up in the traumas that he had gone through as a child. The same traumas that had triggered a lifetime of cyclical depression, anxiety, PTSD, and sleep trouble for Zachary. Add responsibilities like trying to take care of a wife and kids on top of that, and it could be overwhelming. And it had overwhelmed Tyrrell multiple times.

"I'm just sorry no one was able to help Mr. Lane."

"Try to maintain some distance. You need to be able to look at our patients clinically. Save the empathy for the people in your life. What we do here is about… giving answers to their families and trying to inform the system of things we can do to improve quality of life."

Kenzie took a deep breath. She knew Dr. Cook was right and she had to be careful about how much emotion she allowed herself to feel for the deceased and their families. She didn't need to take all that burden home with her at the end of the day, where it would affect not only her mood but also Zachary's.

5

Since Kenzie had been up so early and working at the office well before her usual start time, she was ready to go home by early afternoon. She had no intention of staying until the close of business as she normally would. After a postmortem, her muscles were always sore; she felt sweaty, gritty, and in dire need of a long shower followed by comfy pajamas.

It was probably too early in the day to contemplate pajamas, but she thought she deserved them, considering what time she'd had to put on adult clothes and go out to work. Zachary would never question the need to slip into comfy clothes, no matter the time of day. His usual work-from-home clothes were sweats or shorts and a t-shirt, only changing into khakis and a collared shirt if he had to go to a client meeting, lunch, or maybe to visit Kenzie's parents, or into a hoodie and blue jeans or other nondescript clothes if he were going out on surveillance.

Kenzie made sure that all the samples from the Lane postmortem were in the fridge and properly labeled for when the lab runner arrived to pick them up. Then she let Dr. Cook know she was on her way out.

He didn't object, of course, just gave her a little wave and told her to catch up on her sleep. She would not be on call again tonight so that she could get an uninterrupted night of sleep. Hopefully, she would not have any dreams about Mr. Lane or be repeating the autopsy in her sleep. Sometimes, if she didn't manage to relax and put it out of her mind, her work managed to worm its way into her dreams.

Leaving it all behind, Kenzie took the elevator to the parking garage and drove home. The weather was lovely and warm, and it was still light outside. She felt a little like she was playing hooky, and it felt good. She gave her baby a little extra burst of speed on a couple of straightaways on her way home, then pulled sedately into the garage, humming to herself.

Zachary was sitting on the couch working on his computer when she walked into the kitchen from the garage and looked through the doorway at him.

"Hey. Nice to see you're home early." He stretched and looked around. "Everything is okay?"

"Yes, everything is fine. I just decided I'd put in enough hours today and it was time to come home."

"Great." He looked at his phone, probably to check the time. "Are you going to shower?"

"You know me too well even to ask."

He grinned. "Great. That will give me time to finish this, and then I'll cut it off, and we'll spend some time together. Did you want to go out, or are you going to put on your pajamas?"

"It's time for jammies. Obviously."

"Obviously," he agreed. He hesitated, looking around the room. "And you're not going to be ready for supper yet when you get out, so should we... watch a movie? Give your mom a call? Do something else?"

Kenzie thought about her mother. It had been a few days since they had spoken, and Kenzie was trying to keep in better contact with her. But she didn't think she had the mental defenses to have a discussion with Lisa Cole Kirsch yet. Maybe later. Maybe tomorrow. Or the next day.

"Why don't you find a movie? I know that's just being lazy, and we should probably find something more active to do, but..."

"You were up at two o'clock. That's asking a bit much."

"Are you telling me that *you* weren't up at two o'clock too? You didn't go back to sleep again, did you?"

She knew he worried when she was out on a call in the middle of the night. Even though she was probably safer there, surrounded by cops, than anywhere else.

He shrugged. "No. But that isn't unusual for me."

"Then I think we can both be excused from doing anything that takes too many physical or mental faculties today."

Zachary nodded. "Okay. It's a deal, then. Vegging in front of the TV. Nothing that takes any brain cells."

6

They had a leisurely breakfast the next morning. In contrast to her early callout the day before, Kenzie savored the chance to just sit down, sip her coffee, nibble at her toast and marmalade, and enjoy a visit with Zachary. It was those little things that mattered. The relationship. The little rituals that kept everything glued together.

"So, you didn't have much to say about your call out yesterday," Zachary pointed out. "Was it anything interesting?"

Kenzie considered it, her stomach tightening. "Well, now that you ask… it was a pretty sad case. Homeless alcoholic. Bad GI bleeds, cirrhosis, and kidney injury. We'll see what comes back in the lab tests before making a guess about which one it was that actually killed him, but he had a lot of bad stuff going on."

"Natural causes, then?"

"Yes. Unless you want to call it suicide, the way his death resulted from his own decisions." She held up a hand. "I know addiction wasn't something he chose, but if he had accepted help, managed to stop or reduce the amount he was drinking… things might have been different."

Zachary shrugged. "It's hard to know how responsible he was

for the choices he made while he was addicted. But I guess he paid the price."

"He did." Kenzie sighed. "There were a couple of *interesting* things, though."

She took another bite of her toast, thinking about it. Zachary cocked his head, interested.

"No," Kenzie decided. "A couple of *inconsistencies*. Nothing that really points to anything but an accident."

"What? I won't hold you to it."

Kenzie hesitated. She knew she was teasing him and that she would eventually tell him. But she was also telling herself that they were nothing.

There were always unanswered questions in an investigation. Things didn't wrap up neatly with a bow. There was always some unexplained medical issue, evidence, or witness statement. Something that just didn't quite fit with everything else. But that didn't mean every death was an episode of Unsolved Mysteries.

The majority of the evidence would point in one direction, and that is the direction they would rule. They would close the file, and go on to the next one.

"Come on, you want to tell me," Zachary coaxed.

"Well… I just don't know if they mean anything."

"I'm listening." He drummed his fingers on the table.

Kenzie chuckled. "If you insist. He did have medical treatment sometime in the hours before his death. But we don't know where, or what was done, or why he left. Whether he was released or just wandered off."

"How do you know he had medical treatment?"

"He had an IV puncture in his arm. Fresh."

"But the hospital doesn't have any record of treating him? Maybe it was under a different name?"

"The detective checked. No one by his description was treated in the twelve hours before his death. And he'd been treated far more recently than that."

"Then he must have been treated at some other clinic or doctor's office."

"Exactly. So we're looking for some record of that. Trying to find out where he was treated and for what. Make sure there was no medical malpractice with him being released and then dying. Sometimes that happens. People are sent home too early, told that everything is fine, and then they die."

"I know," Zachary agreed. He had a spoonful of yogurt, eating very slowly while he considered the possibilities. "Could have been someone who wasn't a doctor, too. Nurses can put in lines. Vets. It could be someone who was just trying to help him, not in a hospital, but then it turned out that he was a lot sicker than they thought."

"Could be. Or a nursing home or palliative care facility, but he didn't have a bracelet on. *Someone* was trying to help him right before he died. Maybe they can tell us what happened."

"They might be afraid to come forward if they know that he died."

"Wouldn't you be?"

"I sure would," he agreed vehemently. "I wouldn't want someone's death hanging over my head. I wouldn't want to have to tell anyone that I had not understood how sick he was and given him the wrong treatment and didn't call an ambulance."

Kenzie agreed. She sipped her coffee, drawing out breakfast as long as possible. She wasn't ready to go back into the office quite yet.

"And what was the other thing?" Zachary asked. "You said there were a *couple* of inconsistencies."

"Well... the postmortem showed that he had been vomiting blood. He had quite severe blood loss, which might have been the cause of death."

Zachary nodded for her to go on, waiting for the rest.

"But there was no blood at the scene! If that was what killed him, I would expect there to have been a large pool of bloody emesis around him. But there was nothing. The pavement was clear. His shirt was stained, but not soaked."

"So he threw up somewhere else."

"Yes. And if he lost that much blood, he didn't go far. He bled out and would have been too weak to travel any distance."

Zachary slurped a spoonful of yogurt. "So… he was dumped there."

Kenzie nodded.

"After receiving medical treatment."

"Yes," she confirmed.

"Well… that sounds more like malpractice than accidental death."

"We need to find out a lot more information before making that determination."

"What did Dr. Cook have to say about it?"

"Not much," Kenzie admitted. "We talked around it a bit during the post, but I didn't really put it all together until afterward, thinking in the shower."

"I get some of my best ideas in the shower," Zachary laughed. "Are you going to talk to him about it today, then?"

"Yes." Kenzie had to admit that she wasn't looking forward to it. She frowned. Dr. Cook was a great pathologist, very smart, and she was surprised he hadn't focused more on the possibility of medical malpractice.

But they didn't know yet where he had been treated and what for. Until they had a better idea of what had transpired in the hours before his death, it would be difficult to make that kind of determination.

"You don't sound too eager."

"No. We were pretty focused on it being natural causes, and the tragedy of alcoholism. I didn't really put together the IV mark and the possibility of his being dumped until later."

"Maybe he will have realized the same thing."

Kenzie hadn't considered that possibility, and her spirits lifted. "Yeah, maybe. Or he may be waiting to see if I get there on my own. Testing me."

"Does he do that a lot?"

"Not exactly, but he does ask a lot of questions to see where my investigation leads. Both he and Dr. Wiltshire follow a Socratic questioning model. Asking me questions to prompt me to look into something further, to figure out what things mean."

Kenzie took the last couple of bites of her toast and marmalade.

"I'll need to talk to the detective on the case, too. We need to see if we can find some answers about what happened *before* Lane's death."

"You're going to talk to friends and family?"

"Well... normally, yes. But I'm a bit in the dark on who his family and friends are."

"Homeless."

"Yes."

"But he still would have had friends on the street. And maybe even have been in contact with his family. We tend to assume that because someone is living *unhomed*, his family doesn't know where he is. But sometimes they do; they just can't do anything about it."

"Does that happen a lot?" As Zachary had suggested, Kenzie had assumed that if Jack Lane was living on the street, no one from his previous life knew where he was or was in contact with him. That he was isolated and had left his former life behind completely.

"More than you would think." Zachary nodded. "There are people who cut all ties and just disappear, but there are probably more who are in and out of their loved ones' lives. Bouncing back and forth between street life and home visits, or in phone or internet contact with their family members. They just don't want to live with them, for one reason or another."

"Because of addiction. Their family has had to enforce boundaries, telling them they can't live there anymore..."

"Sometimes. People don't want drugs or drunks around their kids. Or they have stolen or hocked their valuables. Sometimes precious family memories."

It couldn't be easy to live with someone like that. But it would be incredibly difficult to have to tell them to leave. Especially knowing they didn't have anywhere else to go and would be on the street.

"They might have put him in rehab and he left the facility,"

Zachary said. "Maybe he didn't want his family to see him that way. And then there is schizophrenia…"

"A large proportion of the homeless population is mentally ill."

"And you've got your runaways, don't forget. But I gather your patient was not a kid."

"No, luckily. The cases with kids are always that much more difficult."

"Try not to take too much on yourself."

"I know. That's what Dr. Cook told me. Keep my clinical distance. You have to have a certain amount of professional detachment and not get too wrapped up in cases. And I know that. I just… was tired yesterday and got to feeling a bit melancholy."

7

Kenzie took her time working through her email processing and filing of various reports before tracking down Dr. Cook to talk to him about the Lane autopsy.

They ended up in the breakroom together while Kenzie brewed a fresh pot of coffee to replace the one Dr. Cook had put on early that morning.

"You know, I was thinking about the Jack Lane case…" Kenzie started.

"Uh-huh?"

"The two things that bothered me about the case were the fact that he has an IV puncture and we don't know where he was treated, and that he might have been moved into that alley from somewhere else."

"I don't think either one has a lot of bearing on our role here, which is to determine how he died. For that, we can lean into the information that we do have. We don't have to worry about reconciling every stray piece of information that doesn't directly speak to how he died."

"But if he was treated and then dumped, it is possible that he died while under medical care and someone dumped him to hide that fact."

Dr. Cook pondered this and then shook his head. "That doesn't seem likely. I wouldn't want to jump to that conclusion."

"We know he was receiving medical care within a couple of hours of his death. And that he was moved after he died, because he was throwing up blood, and that blood is nowhere to be seen. If we say that he died of exsanguination, then where is the blood? It's not possible to bleed to death without leaving any trace of blood at the scene."

"But we don't have any proof that he died while in medical care or that it was a medical professional who moved the body. It is just as likely that he voluntarily left whatever medical care that he was under. He subsequently passed, and someone moved the body. Maybe the friend who called it in was hoping to get him to some other location, but when that didn't work, and they found transporting the body was too difficult, they called for help."

"Why would his friend move the body?"

"I don't know. People often act irrationally, especially after a tragedy; surely you've witnessed such behavior. Maybe they hoped to take him home. Maybe they thought they could cremate him in a nearby furnace and dispose of the ashes. Maybe they thought they would take him on a road trip like in that movie. Or transport him to wherever his family is. We don't know the reason and can't assign it any nefarious purpose. All we know is the fact. He was likely moved away from the scene of death. That is the only conclusion we can draw from the fact that there was no bloody emesis where he was found. Anything else is up to the detective assigned to the case. And he will only be investigating if we say it was homicide, which it was not."

Kenzie frowned. She did not like Cook's answer, but she had to consider it. He was her senior and had more experience than she had. He would have to sign off on any report she produced. If she concluded that it was not natural causes, he would have to approve the issuance of that report. And she wasn't sure that he would.

"I'll have a chat with Detective Samuels about it," she offered. "He can let me know what his thinking is and what evidence they have been able to discover. Things may be more clear once we know his perspective."

Cook grimaced as if he didn't like this answer, but he nodded and didn't argue with her suggestion. "I'm sure he will tell you the same as I have. That in the absence of anything that definitively shows that someone caused Mr. Lane's death by action or neglect, we have to assume it was natural causes. We have budgetary constraints, as I'm sure Dr. Wiltshire has told you in the past. We need to be careful not to put extra time, money, and resources into an unfortunate natural death when it might be needed down the line for a homicide investigation."

Kenzie poured herself a mug of coffee. It was too hot to drink, but she brought it up to her face and breathed in the rich-smelling steam.

"You are *not* telling me that a homeless man's death is not important enough for us to investigate."

"Of course not. Didn't I put in a couple of hours with you yesterday attending to the postmortem of that homeless man? If I didn't think it was important, I could have left it for you to do by yourself. Even told you that a full dissection was not required and you should just chalk it up to cirrhosis of the liver based on his jaundice and chronic alcoholism."

It was true. Dr. Cook could have done much less. She had never experienced any pushback from him on doing a full dissection, either on the Lane case or on any other indigent person's death. She had not been told not to explore all of the possibilities or that she was doing too much when she chose a full dissection.

"Okay. I just wanted to make sure we were on the same page."

Dr. Cook looked at her steadily, his dreamy blue eyes thoughtful. "I'm not sure we are on the same page," he said slowly. "But I think we are at least in the same book. Let's stay on top of this. Keep me apprised of your activities, okay? I don't want any surprises."

Kenzie nodded her agreement. She did not want to get crosswise with Dr. Cook. He was not telling her not to complete her investigation. Just to keep him in the loop and to be careful not to put more resources into it than the situation warranted. Her time was valuable to the medical examiner's office as well as to her personally. He didn't want her to waste it chasing shadows.

8

Detective Samuels was brusque at first. He told Kenzie just to email her initial findings, and sounded irritated when she said she wanted to review them in person. Kenzie reminded herself that he probably had a number of other files he was working on, and he didn't have unlimited time. He wanted to budget his time just as she did. He might have a wife and children to go home to at the end of the day. He might have some really big cases on his desk right now. She just didn't know what his challenges were. So she needed to be patient with him and not be offended by a few short words.

When she pressed, Samuels agreed that she could come upstairs to see him and review the results, but warned her he didn't have very much time. Kenzie headed immediately for the elevator, not wanting to waste any of that time. They might be interrupted at any time. She needed to get her point across quickly.

The Officer of the Day at the front desk escorted her down the hall for a few steps, indicating an office just down the corridor. "Second door there, on the right."

Kenzie approached. She knocked on the doorframe and waited for Samuels to look up from his computer and motion to the guest chair before entering his office. Several piles of papers and files competed with the computer for space on his desk.

"Sorry for the interruption. Thank you for making the time."

"Of course, Dr. Kirsch. So, this is your report?" He reached for the stapled pages she handed him.

"This is just preliminary findings. We are still waiting for a number of lab tests, need to ask questions of family, friends, doctors who treated him, and so on."

"I'm not sure you'll be able to do that. Is there any question of what he died of?"

"There are several possibilities."

"All of them natural."

"We have some concerns about possible medical malpractice," Kenzie said slowly. She elected to use "we" to give it more weight and hoped Dr. Cook would back her up if asked. "If there was medical malpractice, that changes it from natural causes to accidental."

"But not to homicide," he stated.

"It depends on how he was treated. If he was treated for hematemesis and then released, then that would be more than just malpractice. Whoever treated him might be guilty of manslaughter or worse."

"What is hemate-whatsit?"

"Throwing up blood. He had quite a bit of bleeding in his upper GI tract. In fact, he bled so much that all of his organs were pale. He might have thrown up two liters of blood. If a doctor saw that and released him…"

The detective stared at her. "Who releases a man who had just thrown up two liters of blood?"

"That's exactly my point. He had been under a doctor's care. We know that from the IV. Or that he had, at least, been under some kind of medical care. We don't know whether or not it was a board-certified doctor at this point. But within an hour or two, Lane is dead on the street."

Samuels ran his fingers through his disorderly, wavy hair.

"Okay… you've got my attention. Could anything have been done for him?"

"If they acted quickly enough… possibly. Give him enough fluids and enough blood, get him into surgery to stop the bleeds… *maybe* they could have saved him. But he certainly should not have been out of his hospital bed."

"Or his bed wherever it was. *Not* the hospital, remember."

"Right. They should have immediately gotten him to the hospital for care when it became obvious that he was in critical condition. And you cannot tell me that if you, a first responder, saw a man throwing up great gouts of blood like that, you would not know he was in critical condition."

Samuels smiled. "I certainly hope that I would be able to recognize it."

He started to flip through the pages of the preliminary findings. His eyes skimmed over the words and photos. He shook his head. "He was in pretty bad shape. Do you really think anyone could have saved him?"

"Maybe not. Maybe all they could have done was to keep him comfortable. But then at least they could do that and not release him out onto the street. But… I'm not convinced that they did."

"Not convinced that they… took care of him?"

"I am not convinced that they released him. I am wondering if they actually let him die, not realizing how dire his condition was, and then they dumped his body in the alley."

"Why would they do that?"

"I don't know. Maybe they knew that what they had done amounted to more than just negligence. They misdiagnosed him or gave him the wrong treatment. They didn't want anyone to know what they had done, so they cleaned him up and dumped his body."

"You think it *was* the hospital and they wiped him out of their records?"

"I don't think their system allows for that. But I think that whoever it was… for whatever reason, they couldn't call the police or ambulance and explain what had happened. That suggests that it was not just a matter of not being able to save him or get him to the hospital in time."

"What makes you think that his body was dumped after he died?"

"With that amount of blood loss, he would not have been able to walk a block or two down the street. Either he left the clinic under his own power and then bled out, or he bled out there and then was dumped. If he bled out on the street... where is the blood?"

"Ah." Samuels nodded. "No blood on the scene. Are you sure he could not have left under his own power and... just bled internally rather than bleeding out on the sidewalk?"

"No... there was barely any blood left in his GI tract. He threw it up. It should have been on the scene. It *was* on the scene, which is how we know the dump site was not the scene of death."

Samuels leaned back in his chair, making it tilt and creak alarmingly. It was all Kenzie could do to refrain from warning him that he was going to tip himself right over. She gritted her teeth and waited.

"So, somebody, possibly *not* a medical professional, tried to take care of an old drunk while he was sick. He died and they panicked and dumped him. I'm not sure that's a criminal offense."

"They put an IV in. That tells me it was some kind of medical professional. Anyone with that kind of training is obligated to provide the best possible medical care and find him the help he needs if they cannot provide it." Kenzie struggled to keep her voice calm and even. "Whether it is a doctor, nurse, or paramedic, they had a duty to look after him. And if they were not able to get him help in time, to call the police and let them investigate what had happened."

"Okay... well... I'll keep that in mind, Dr. Kirsch. Thank you for bringing this to my attention. It will inform my investigation."

Kenzie had been expecting more. She had expected him to get angry or outraged. To promise to dig into it until he found out the truth. But he was pretty relaxed about it. If he cared what had happened to Lane, he hid it well.

"I will be calling the man who reported finding the body to ask him some questions," she told Samuels.

"I gave you the information I have. Go ahead. I don't think you'll get anything more from him than I did, but you're welcome to try. That's certainly within your purview."

9

When Kenzie got home, she found Zachary in a tizzy. He was moving from one room to another, opening and closing drawers at random. His skin was pale and shone with sweat. He looked at her with panic in his eyes.

"What's wrong?" Kenzie demanded, her heart thumping hard, already trying to figure out what could be triggering such an anxious response from Zachary. He had been feeling pretty good lately. She always let herself get too comfortable, too sure that everything was okay, and then any change came out of nowhere, surprising her and making her feel like her whole life was unpredictable. Anything could happen at any time.

"I can't find it," Zachary said, his breath coming out in short puffs. "I have looked everywhere, and I can't figure out where I left it!"

"Left what? What are you looking for?"

It was clearly something of great value to him. Something expensive? Or some trinket from his past that he had managed to hang on to over the years despite foster homes and fires and everything else he'd been through?

"The stuff! For the gala tonight. The... the thing," he made a motion across his waist, "and the…" a motion to his throat, "the tie! And the…"

Kenzie made a calming motion with her hands, encouraging him to relax. "And the pocket square," she said smoothly. "For the gala."

She had nearly forgotten that the big Kirsch family foundation fundraising gala, which she had been pressured into attending with Zachary, was tonight. She had even seen it on her calendar, noted it, and then gotten wrapped up in her other daily tasks and put it out of her mind.

"You can't find it because it is in my closet. Everything is together so that we would be able to find everything easily. Take a breath. It's not lost."

"I looked everywhere!"

Kenzie removed her jacket and shoes and walked through the house to her bedroom. She removed a couple of dark garment bags from her closet that held her dress and Zachary's tux. Above them on the shelf were a couple of boxes containing her jewelry and Zachary's cummerbund, bow tie, and pocket square. She laid everything out on the bed and opened the bags and boxes.

Zachary let out a huge sigh of relief. "I thought I put it away somewhere safe and I couldn't find it again."

"You probably did, but I gathered everything together a couple of weeks ago to ensure we had everything we needed and wouldn't…"

"Be in a panic when it was time to get ready," Zachary finished.

"Exactly."

"Well…" He ran his fingers through his hair, "What kind of fun would that be?"

Kenzie smiled at him. She took a deep breath and let it out, trying not to betray how fast her heart had been pumping when she had seen Zachary's panic.

"Whew. Well, I am going to go have a sandwich. We won't be eating until late with this gala, and I personally cannot wait that long to eat. And I would be so starving I would eat like a pig when the food finally came. After I eat, I'm going to shower, do my hair, and dress. Are you going to have something to eat?"

"Maybe I should get ready first so I don't get distracted or run out of time."

They both considered this. Kenzie didn't endorse his plan and, in a moment, he waved it off.

"No. I'm not going to put on a tux and then eat a jelly sandwich. I'll end up with red stains all over my shirt and tie. I'll eat first, with you. That's the safest. Then I'll shave, shower, and get dressed."

He looked at her. Kenzie nodded. "Sounds good. We'll keep each other on track. You don't have to do as much to get ready as I do, so you'll probably still have some time to check your email or do some little jobs once you're dressed and ready to go."

"Okay." He nodded his agreement.

Kenzie knew she would probably still have to give him a few reminders to make sure that he was ready to go when she was, but that was just the way things worked. They had different priorities and brains that worked very differently from each other.

As it turned out, Zachary remained focused throughout their preparations, and the only thing she had to remind him to do was to put on socks. She had them ready for him so he didn't have to look for a clean, matching pair. Then he put on his shoes, and they prepared to leave.

"This is going to be fun," Zachary said, his words a little forced. "We're going to have a good time."

Kenzie nodded. "There will be good food, music, dancing, and Lisa will be giving a speech about our featured charities this year. That part might be a bit tedious. There will be a lot of people you don't know wanting to shake your hand, but all you have to do is smile."

"I'm your arm candy," Zachary contributed smugly.

"Exactly."

"I went to events with Bridget, when we were married. Formal stuff with lots of forks…" He swallowed, and she could see this was an area of concern.

"Look, there's nothing to be worried about. If you're not sure what to do, just watch me, or someone else at the table. If you use the wrong fork or spoon, it isn't the end of the world. Seriously. No one will care."

She could see by his dark look that *Bridget* had cared, and he didn't believe her that it would be okay and she didn't care if he made a silly mistake.

"If it makes you feel better, I will make sure I use the wrong cutlery at least once tonight, okay? And you'll see that no one will notice or say a thing."

"If you are going to use the wrong one, and I'm watching you to see which one to use, then I'm going to be copying the wrong thing, and I'm going to get it wrong!"

"You see? We'll be wrong together. If you don't want to get it wrong, then watch someone else. Mom, if she is at our table. But she probably won't be. She'll want to circulate."

"What if I drop something?"

"Just leave it where it falls, unless someone will trip over it. If you need a new one, just ask a server for it. No big deal."

"It's going to be fun," Zachary repeated as they entered the garage to get into Kenzie's car. But he sounded more like he was attending a funeral than a party.

The gala really did go quite well. Kenzie did not catch Zachary using the wrong fork or spoon at any time throughout the evening. But she didn't watch him the whole time, either. Bridget, his ex-wife, had watched him like a hawk, making sure she noted every misstep he made or came close to making and ripped him apart for it.

Kenzie was there to make other connections. To make sure that other people saw her as being active in the family foundation. Showing her support for it, letting them know that the next generation was, in fact, involved. They didn't need to worry that the organization was going to go down the tubes after her parents were gone. And they were not going anywhere for a very long time.

Walter, her father, was not at the fundraiser. He was still under wraps, pretending to be recovering from a stroke. Kenzie was sure he was probably not too disappointed to be missing the gala. Although he had been isolated for a while now, so maybe he actually *would* miss the chance to see everyone.

He could go to next year's. Everything would be back to normal by then. Except it would be the new normal, where he was retired from his work and everyone understood he was not going back to lobbying in the Capitol as he had. *Before.*

Kenzie realized she had gotten distracted from Lisa's speech, and tried to refocus. She smiled and nodded a few times and let her eyes wander around the room to the people at other tables, analyzing who was interested in the speech or in the causes they were supporting, and who just wanted to get out of there. Who would cut a big check. Who would pledge money and then not follow through. She didn't know them as well as Lisa did, but she needed to make an effort. One day, Lisa would no longer be there, and Kenzie would be expected to know it all.

Lisa wrapped up her patter and said that she would take questions. A few people made their way over to the standing microphones to ask their questions.

One of the first questions was about the causes they were supporting.

"The foundation has always been a big supporter of research and treatment of kidney disease and organ transplant. Now it seems like you are defunding those areas and are more concerned about... social issues rather than medical ones. Mental illness, addiction, homelessness. Why have you changed your focus?"

"Since Amanda's death, the foundation has put millions of dollars into kidney disease research and treatment," Lisa acknowledged. "We have, I hope, advanced things significantly. But there are other areas that desperately need funding. Mental health has become an increasingly important part of our lives and needs our attention. We cannot simply ignore the ripple effect mental illness has across many other areas of study. We need to heal minds and spirits, not just bodies."

"What about the charities you have defunded?" the woman asked angrily. "How are they supposed to survive now that you have pulled your funding?"

"We are not the only fish in the sea. There are many other organizations and grants that you can go to. Things do change from year to year. That has always been the case."

She waited for the woman to step away from the mike and, after a few long seconds, she did. There was a murmur through the crowd, and then the next question was posed to Lisa.

Kenzie's mind drifted to Jack Lane. Would the foundation's money have made a difference to him if they had changed their focus a little earlier? Would he have made changes to his life if he had been contacted through the right charity? Could they have gotten him into the right rehab program? Gotten him into housing that would have given him the stability he needed to change his life?

If she could find out where he had been treated and what organizations had worked with him, she might be able to find out something about his past. Whether he had been dealing with mental illness as well as addiction and homelessness. Whether he'd had PTSD or other disabilities.

There were so many other things that she didn't know about him, things that did not show up in an autopsy.

10

Kenzie was thoughtful as she drove back to Roxboro, pondering over the shift in the foundation's focus and the ripple effect it might have on policy in Vermont. And the causes that they had supported for years and were now moving away from. The kidney research and treatment causes would not be happy about losing the foundation's funding. As Lisa had said, there were a lot of other charities and grants out there, but they would have to work hard to replace the generosity of the family foundation. Had they thought that the family's funding would last forever? At some point, it was bound to come to an end. If it wasn't a change in focus, then it might be an economic downturn or the death of one of her parents. There had never been any guarantee that they would keep funding kidney research forever.

Still, the shift away from what had killed Amanda was poignant. Would Amanda have understood the change? Kenzie was pretty sure Amanda would have encouraged Kenzie to pursue funding for the issues that affected Zachary. It wasn't because Zachary needed more funding for treatment, but because there were so many others out there who were afflicted like Zachary but were unable to access the therapy and supports they needed.

People like Rhys, a young black teen they both knew who had

not been given all of the services he should have had to deal with the trauma when his grandfather had been murdered. He was still suffering the effects years later. Yes, he might have still been having trouble dealing with it even with access to all of the therapy he needed, but it would have been less. He would have been further down the road to recovery.

At least, Kenzie assumed he would be.

"Did I do something wrong?" Zachary asked.

Kenzie glanced over at him, surprised. She had been lost in her own thoughts and had not focused on his demeanor. Zachary had been quiet, and she had assumed he was just enjoying the ride and decompressing after all of the social pressure of the gala. He enjoyed highway driving and, even though he was the passenger rather than the driver in this case, she had not twigged to the fact that he was still tense, rather than relaxing with the hypnotic motion of the car.

"What? No. I thought you handled everything really well. I don't think anyone would have guessed that you were concerned with fitting in at the dinner or uncomfortable being there."

"But you did, and I must have done something wrong…"

"You didn't do anything wrong." Kenzie gave him a warm smile and patted his leg to reassure him. "You handled everything wonderfully. Even dealing with Mrs. Carter."

Evie Carter, seated at their table to Zachary's right, had obviously been drunk or abusing some other substance. The eighty-year-old had been giggling, flirty, and clearly attracted to the younger man seated to her left. Kenzie had initially been concerned with how Zachary would react to her constant attention, especially given his history of abuse in foster care. She kept touching Zachary's leg, leaning on him or putting her arm around him to whisper sloppily in his ear.

But Zachary's PTSD had not been obviously triggered by her affections. He had removed her hand multiple times, placing it on the table between them and keeping his hand over it to assure her of his attention, and engaging her in conversation on a wide range of topics. She had rarely seen anyone handle Evie Carter so masterfully. Had Lisa predicted that Zachary would be able to deal with her so well when she had been making the seating arrangements? Kenzie was both irritated with her mother for putting Zachary into such a situation and impressed she had predicted Zachary would be able to handle Mrs. Carter.

"She was harmless," Zachary said with a shake of his head. "Just… a sloppy drunk."

"Well, you handled the challenge very well. I wasn't thrilled about her being seated right next to you."

"She was, uh, persistent."

"She certainly was," Kenzie agreed. She laughed. "I'm surprised you were able to focus on anything else with her there."

"Well, I wasn't, really. I couldn't think of much other than keeping her occupied. Everything else was on autopilot."

Maybe that was why he had not shown much anxiety over the meal that he had been so worried about a few hours earlier, or over meeting the various Vermont bigwigs who had been present at the gala. He had been too distracted by Mrs. Carter.

"Well, I don't know whether that was brilliant thinking on my mother's part or just good luck! But either way, you don't need to worry that you did anything wrong at the event. You did just fine."

He didn't say anything for the next few miles, but kept glancing over at her as if waiting for the other shoe to drop. Waiting for the criticism that was bound to come sooner or later. He scratched the back of his neck, frowning, and stared out the window into the dark night.

"Has she had any help with her problem?" he asked eventually. "Mrs. Carter, I mean. She could afford treatment."

"It isn't always about affordability. There are plenty of people who could afford therapy or a good substance abuse program who don't take the opportunity. I think Mrs. Carter has a bit of dementia as well. She doesn't realize how obvious her behavior is or that she needs to change anything. I don't know whether she had issues before her husband died, and he just hid things and kept her under control, or whether his death triggered something."

"So she doesn't have anyone looking after her now? Does she live alone?" Zachary sounded concerned.

"She has staff. I'm sure they do everything they can to make sure she is looked after. And she has a couple of kids. I don't think either of them lives with her right now, but I know her daughter is pretty involved and often with her at events like this. And she'll have a physician keeping an eye on things, even if she doesn't have a therapist."

"She shouldn't be living alone."

"She isn't alone. There are people around her most of the time."

"No one making sure that she doesn't drink."

Kenzie had to concede that one. She sighed and nodded. "You and I both know how hard that is. If someone is determined to drink, especially someone with her means…"

They had spent a vacation with Tyrrell while he had been secretly drinking, and he had stayed with them between a bad binge and getting him into the right rehab program, and they both knew how hard it had been to keep him away from alcohol. Kenzie could only imagine how hard it would be in a house full of staff, a wine cellar, and a well-stocked wet bar. Even if her children gave the staff instructions to keep her away from any alcohol or pills, she had access to plenty of bribe money to convince one or two of them otherwise.

Zachary nodded. "At least she has a roof over her head."

Kenzie thought back to Jack Lane. At the opposite end of the social scale from Evie Carter, he hadn't had access to the same programs and help, or to a roof over his head. Even if he was one of the "sheltered" homeless, that didn't mean he had the comfort and care he needed.

Where had he gone for medical care? The homeless usually used the emergency room for primary care, but he had apparently not gone there.

So where *had* he gone? And how had they failed him so badly?

11

R oxboro, Vermont was a small town, so there weren't a lot of options for homeless services. Kenzie wanted to talk to the staff face-to-face rather than trying to get information over the phone, so she went to the Roxboro Bluff Creek Shelter in person, aiming for early afternoon when she hoped that it would be staffed but not yet busy with meal prep or intake.

The young lady at the front desk with brilliant pink hair, multiple rings in her left ear, and a zircon stud in her nose was pleasant and professional as she greeted Kenzie.

"Good afternoon," she greeted, her eyes flicking over Kenzie and evaluating her, trying to classify her and determine what she was there for. "How can we help you today?"

"Hi. I am looking for insight on one of your former clients."

"Information on our clients is private and confidential. Sorry."

"I am with the medical examiner's office. There is no confidentially for the deceased. Legislation requires you to cooperate with my investigation. Including information protected by HIPAA."

The woman blinked, considering this.

"I don't know about that," she said uncertainly.

"I wouldn't expect you to. And I don't expect to be asking you any questions. Someone with more seniority would know more about what was or wasn't allowed by law."

"Yeah, of course. That's great. Let me just get someone for you."

She turned her attention to the phone and punched in an extension number.

"Jane? Yeah, there's a woman here from the medical examiner's office. She wants to talk to someone about a client. A *former* client," she corrected.

She listened attentively to the answer, then hung up nodding to Kenzie.

"Jane Woodward will be out in a few minutes to help you. She said to make yourself comfortable, and she'll get to you when she can. Would you like a coffee? Tea? Water?"

Kenzie considered her options. She didn't want to be tired all afternoon, and they had been out late with the gala. She couldn't drink caffeine later in the day, or she would have problems sleeping, so it was really her last chance.

"I guess a coffee. That would be great, actually."

"I'll get it for you." She turned toward the door behind her that probably led to a breakroom. "I'm Emily, by the way."

"Kenzie. Dr. Kenzie Kirsch."

"That's a cool name. I think I've heard 'Kirsch' somewhere before. Do you come from a big family?"

"No. Just me and my parents. You might have heard about one of them. They're both pretty active in Vermont society."

"I'm not exactly a 'society' person," Emily said, wrinkling her nose and laughing before disappearing into the back room. She returned a few minutes later and handed Kenzie her coffee, directing her toward the sugar and creamer on a side table. Kenzie sat down and sipped her coffee, enjoying the chance to relax and take a short breather while she enjoyed the drink, despite the fact it had been sitting on the burner for a bit too long.

An older woman came into the front reception area about ten minutes later and looked around. She discounted Kenzie on her first glance around the room, then apparently decided that Kenzie must be who she wanted.

"From the medical examiner's office?" Jane asked doubtfully.

"Yes," Kenzie stood up. "Dr. Kenzie Kirsch." She held out her hand.

"You don't look much like a doctor," Jane said, shaking her head.

Kenzie fished her credentials out of her purse. She should probably have already had the lanyard around her neck so that there would be no confusion as to the reasons for her inquiries.

Jane looked at the identification card Kenzie presented and nodded her head. "Well, I guess you are who you say you are, anyway. But I don't understand what you are doing here."

"We could talk somewhere more private?"

"Yes, of course." Jane nodded at the receptionist before leading Kenzie out. "Thank you, Emily."

"She seems like a nice girl," Kenzie observed, making small talk.

"She is," Jane agreed. "She's been a real asset for us. Very conscientious."

Jane was a tall, spare woman with her hair pulled back in a severe hairstyle. It was difficult to ascertain her age. Kenzie would put her in her fifties just because of her maturity and how she handled herself, but she could have been an old thirty-something or bordering on seventy.

Jane led her into a small office with a thrift store desk piled high with stacks of paper. There was a steno chair on her side of the desk and a tubular chair that might have been reclaimed from a library on Kenzie's side. Kenzie sat. It was not immediately uncomfortable, but she sensed that she would be regretting it within a few minutes of sitting down. It was probably in Jane's best interest to have an uncomfortable guest chair to ensure that no one stayed to chat for too long.

Jane sat down in her screechy, jiggly chair, and motioned for Kenzie to sit in the guest chair.

"I'm sorry, I hadn't heard of any deaths among our clientele," she informed Kenzie.

"It is quite recent. Are you familiar with a John or Jack Lane?"

"Jack. Sure. He's a well-known character around here." She

shook her head. "What happened to him? I knew he hadn't been doing well lately, but he wouldn't accept any help."

"He had a substance abuse problem?"

"You might say that. He was a raging drunk," Jane said frankly. "A nice old gentleman, but he did not have any control over his addiction."

Kenzie nodded sympathetically. "I guess you see a lot of that here."

"Many people in our service population have substance abuse issues. Most of them are a little more self-aware than Jack, or maybe they just haven't given up on ever being able to overcome addiction. Jack was resigned to the fact that he wasn't ever going to get control of his alcoholism."

"Had he been through any detox programs?"

"Over the years, I am sure he had been involved in a number of them. Not while I've been here, but after being in and out of shelters for so long, I'm sure he's been put through a number of programs to try to encourage him to progress." She shrugged. "After a certain point, there is really no reason to keep forcing them through a program. It has to come from inside. And those who are not independently housed rarely succeed in long-term recovery until they have a secure job and housing situation."

"When was the last time you saw Mr. Lane?"

"*Mr. Lane.* He would have a fit over you calling him that. It was always, 'Just Jack, don't call me after my daddy.'"

"Jack, then. Do you know when you saw him last?"

"Personally? I have no idea." Jane typed a query into her computer and looked through the results. "Looks like he was checked in one day last week. Other than that, he's been sleeping rough."

"Or somewhere else."

"Unless he'd recently made a new friend, he was on the street. There is not another wet shelter he would be able to get to on his own. He didn't have family he would stay with. His friends were the rest of the unhomed."

"A wet shelter?" Kenzie repeated. She pulled a notepad out of her handbag to make some notes. She didn't want to forget anything important.

"A shelter who would take in someone who was drunk or high. Unfortunately, a lot of shelters refuse anyone under the influence. With the percentage of the target population who are addicted… Well, they are not left with a lot of options."

"Where are they supposed to go?"

Jane's shoulders rose and fell. Her face showed no emotion as she answered, "It is supposed to motivate them to clean themselves up and get sober."

"Well, that just seems…" Kenzie was at a loss for words.

Jane nodded. "Ridiculous? Impossible? Ableist? Jack was not the only one who had given up on ever being able to get clean. It was just his lifestyle. He couldn't imagine ever living any other way."

Kenzie nodded. "Well, I'm glad I'm not being naive in thinking that it isn't just a matter of having enough willpower."

Jane snorted. "We won't even go there. So, was that all you needed to know about Jack? When he was last here?"

"And you're sure there is nowhere else he would be, other than out on the street?"

Jane didn't answer right away. Kenzie wasn't sure whether she was thinking through any other possible scenarios or just staying silent for long enough to give the impression that she was.

"I suppose he could have been in the hospital," she offered. "Or in jail. Other than that, I can't think of anywhere else he might have been."

"Had he been in the hospital lately?"

"Not as far as I know, but he was in and out of there regularly. Not overnight, usually. Unless he was just sleeping in the waiting room."

"Do you know about what health problems he was having?"

"He always had stomach problems. He was quite jaundiced last time I saw him. He knew it was the drink, of course. We all knew it was and that he wouldn't last forever." Jane hesitated, then spoke her mind. "I don't understand this line of questioning, to be honest. I'm not sure how there could be any doubt that he died of anything but alcoholism."

Kenzie wanted to point out that even an alcoholic could be mugged, murdered, or hit by a car. But that wasn't what had happened to Jack, and she didn't want to be accused of misleading the director of the shelter.

"There were just a few unanswered questions in the autopsy," she explained. "I'm sure you're right, but I need to tie up the last loose ends. Do you know if he was seeing a doctor? Is there someone the shelter employed or who would have been recommended by your staff?"

"No. I told you. He used the emergency room."

"If you knew he had medical treatment and it *wasn't* in the emergency room...?"

She shook her head. "Really, I don't know. There is a clinic on Fourth Street. They have a Saturday once a month when they serve those who can't pay. But there are so many families who try to get in that day... the oldsters like Jack don't normally compete with them."

"If he went there and was in really bad shape, would they turn him away? Or take him in and treat him?"

"Probably neither one. They would probably call an ambulance and have him taken to the hospital."

"And there aren't any other emergency services or places he could access medical care if he was feeling really sick and didn't want to go to the emergency room?"

Jane shook her head slowly. "There is a mobile clinic that is trying to reach the indigent population. But they don't do much other than stitch up lacerations or prescribe antibiotics, to tell the truth. And they only make the rounds once a week. There isn't a lot available in a town like Roxboro or rural areas. If you want to access all of the programs to reduce harm and serve the homeless population, you need to go to the city. And people like Jack, he wouldn't do that. This was his home."

"Okay. I appreciate that." Kenzie jotted down a couple of memory aids. "Could you tell me who some of his friends were?"

Jane shook her head. "I might have to comply with your requests for information about Jack, but I can't give you information about other people who are still living. They *do* have their rights to privacy and protection from harassment."

"I just want to ask them a few questions about Jack."

Jane shrugged. "My hands are tied."

While Kenzie would have liked to claim otherwise, she didn't think she would get anywhere by arguing the point. She wasn't a lawyer and didn't have a warrant. All she could do was ask for Jane's cooperation on questions that might have some connection with Jack's death.

"Could you talk to his friends about giving me a call? I could leave you with some business cards."

"People will not call you."

"You won't know if you don't tell them…"

Jane shook her head. "I know these people better than you do. They will not call you to be put on the spot about anything Jack might have said to them. Besides, he didn't talk to anyone about his health. He knew there wasn't any point."

12

Kenzie hadn't expected to learn a lot of personal information from the shelter, but she had hoped to get something. As it was, she had learned little except that Jack had not had anyone but the other homeless, and that he got medical care through the emergency room, which she had already guessed. But he had received medical care somewhere else. He had been given an IV. Fluids, at the very least. Somewhere other than at the hospital.

As she left the shelter, people were starting to assemble outside. It was still early in the afternoon, and the working poor who had day jobs would not be able to line up for several more hours yet. She hesitated to approach people cold. She was an authority figure, someone who didn't belong in their world, and she doubted anyone would want to talk to her. But she had a job to do, and sometimes that job included doing uncomfortable things. She went to the nearest cluster of homeless and forced a smile.

"I'm sorry to interrupt you. I'm looking for any friends of Jack Lane. Does anyone here know Jack?"

They looked at her with suspicion and turned away.

"Okay," Kenzie said. "If anyone wants to help, Jane knows how to reach me." She went to the next group of people. "Does anyone know Jack Lane? Is there anyone here who could help me? I'm hoping someone here saw Jack in the last few days…"

"No one is going to talk about Jack," a young-looking woman with short, dark hair told her. She had bright eyes and elfin features, but her skin was scabbed and pockmarked.

"Did you know Jack?"

"*Did* I?"

Kenzie hadn't intended to break the news of Jack's death so abruptly.

"Uh, yes. He died a couple of days ago, unfortunately. I'm sorry."

"Jack?" The woman looked around at the other homeless people around her. "Did you know that Jack died? When did this happen? It's not that long since I saw him."

People who had previously been ignoring Kenzie and her questions started to look around, paying attention to the woman.

Kenzie nodded understandingly. "I'm really sorry," she said, "He died a couple of nights ago."

"How? Why?"

"Well, I'm an assistant medical examiner. That's what I'm trying to find out. I need to find out what happened the last few hours before he died. He was with someone. And someone called in his body to the police within a couple of hours of his death. I'd like to talk to the people who saw him the last few hours."

"Who called it in?"

Kenzie had, by this time, figured out that the information that Samuel had collected from the witness who had called in Jack's body had been false. At first, she had thought that the witness's phone battery had just run down. Which wasn't surprising, because someone who was homeless wouldn't be near an outlet all the time. But she had tried it repeatedly, and there was never any answer. The voicemail hadn't been activated. Wilson Wright did not seem to be a legitimate name; she couldn't find anyone by that name. It would appear that he had given Samuels fake information and split.

"I don't know who called it in," she admitted. "I'm trying to contact him, but the information he gave the police was false."

The woman smirked at that. "And you expected it to be right?"

"Well, I guess not. It would have been nice to talk to him and find out what he knows about what really happened to Jack."

"What do you mean, what really happened?" a man questioned, pushing in close. His odor was nearly overwhelming. Kenzie breathed through her mouth.

"He said that he just found Jack's body. But that isn't where Jack died. So I want to know whether he really did happen upon Jack's body there later, or if he saw it get dumped. Or was the one who dumped it himself."

"Why would he do that? Why would anyone dump Jack's body? You think he was killed?" the woman demanded. She moved closer so that she was in Kenzie's face. "What happened to Jack?"

Kenzie looked at the people who were now crowding in around her. Some of them seemed concerned, others aggressive. She got the definite feeling that at least two of them did not want her there and were willing to do something about it. She held up her hands, trying to calm everyone down.

"Jack was very sick," she said in a soothing voice. "I'm sure that most of you probably knew that. He had been drinking for a lot of years, and it had damaged his body quite severely. I doubt that he had very many good days lately. He was probably in pain all of the time. He probably couldn't eat anything. Or keep very much down."

The people gathered around her looked at each other, nodding or making other signs of confirmation. Meeting each other's eyes. They had all seen how Jack had declined lately. What she was saying did not come as a shock to them.

"He was throwing up blood. Maybe at first, it was only a little bit, and he could ignore it and hide it from everyone else but, eventually, he was so sick that he couldn't hide it anymore."

Trying to discern all of the signals that passed among them, Kenzie homed in on one man who seemed to be the focus of their attention.

"Were you Jack's friend? Are you the one who was with him close to the end?"

He shook his head. "Don't know who you are or what gives you the right to ask everybody any questions," he growled. "You didn't know Jack. You don't know nothing about the way he died. Why don't you go get yourself another job? One where you don't go around harassing innocent people?"

He was older, like Jack. People didn't get really old on the streets, but they looked it. This man was a veteran of the streets. Probably an alcoholic like Jack. Two buddies who shared a few bottles together each night? How many years had they hung out together? How many challenges had they endured together?

"I'm not here to harass anyone," she assured him. "I don't want to cause any trouble or to make anyone feel worse than they already do. I'm just… trying to find out the truth."

"And what do you think is the truth?"

Kenzie took a deep breath. "He had medical treatment before he died. I don't know what kind of medical treatment or by whom. Whoever was treating him was not able to save him. And then they… left the body where it would be found. Were you the one who found Jack there?" He didn't respond to the query. "Or maybe someone else?" She looked around at the rest of the crowd. "I'd really like to find out who was there when Jack was being treated."

"Why does it matter? It ain't like you are going to do anything about it. You're just going to cremate him, put him in a pauper's grave, and go on to the next file. Spend your time on the ones where the upper class kill each other."

There were some growls of agreement from the others.

Kenzie spread her hands apart in query. "I'm here right now, investigating the death of one of your friends. Doesn't that kind of contradict the idea that I only investigate the deaths of rich people?"

The woman who had initially spoken to Kenzie laughed at that. "She's got you there, String."

"Were you with him?" Kenzie persisted. "Before he died? Or the one who called in his body?"

He shook his head, scoffing.

Kenzie wasn't sure she believed him. She was pretty sure he knew more than he was letting on.

"You don't want justice for Jack?"

"What justice is there now? All he gets now is a burial. Maybe a numbered marker. Nobody cares about him."

"I do. I would really like to do right by him. I don't want just to sweep this under the rug. I want to know whether he was treated correctly and why his body was abandoned in that back alley."

String turned his back to Kenzie, shaking his head and making noises as if she were talking gibberish. A few of the others laughed. No one offered to give her any of the information she was looking for.

13

I t was frustrating to be told in the same breath that she wasn't doing anything for Jack and that she was being intrusive in investigating his death. Frustrating to be excluded just because she was in a different class and they didn't want to talk to her.

Kenzie had never ignored or discounted someone's opinion or statement because they were homeless or poor. At least, not that she could recall. Maybe she had done something when she was younger, but not that she could remember. Her parents had raised her with high ethical standards, and one of those was not to treat someone with less money or in another social stratum as if they were somehow insignificant.

She left the shelter and the people who clearly did not want her there infringing on their world and went next to the medical clinic Jane had referred to. There was a strong possibility that Jack had been treated there. There couldn't be a lot of places where he would have been given an IV. It had not been the hospital or the paramedics. She suspected that Jane was right and it was not the mobile clinic van, which could do little more than patch people up with a few stitches and antibiotics.

The waiting room in the clinic was full, and the phone was

ringing off the hook. Two receptionists were answering calls in tandem while trying to deal with anyone who came in the door looking for an appointment. Babies and children were crying, mothers talked in tired and irritated voices on their cell phones, and a man in the corner with a chronic cough or tic that was loud and sudden made Kenzie jump every single time he barked out another.

Kenzie approached the counter, peering through the plastic shield at the two staff members manning the phones and appointments. One of them held her finger up at Kenzie in a "wait one minute" gesture, and when she finished the call she was on, turned to Kenzie.

"Can I help you?"

She didn't ask if Kenzie wanted an appointment, and Kenzie wondered if that was because she recognized that Kenzie wasn't her usual clientele. "I would like to talk to someone about a former patient of yours. Mr. Jack Lane. I am with the medical examiner's office." She held her ID up and pressed it against the shield so that it would be as clear as possible.

The woman looked at her partner, who was not paying any attention to the conversation, and then back to Kenzie.

"You realize that we cannot divulge private medical records," she pointed out. "We cannot even confirm or deny whether this person was ever a patient."

"Actually, you can when it is a medical examiner's investigation. You are required by law to comply. I need to gather as much medical information about Mr. Lane as possible to make a ruling on his cause and manner of death."

The woman in the pink smock looked like she had never heard such a thing before. She shook her head. "You'll have to talk to one of the partners to get permission. I can't let you see anything."

"Yes, I understand that. Is one of them in today? Or can you reach them by phone?"

"Dr. Slater is in. He's with a patient right now and has several more lined up." She looked irritated. "It's going to back everything up if you interrupt him." She looked out at the waiting room full of patients.

"I'm sorry. It really is important."

"You have to do this *now*?"

Kenzie really didn't, but she knew that if she left, they would not call her back. She would have to come back again and again stand in front of them, begging to see the doctor. And to be fair, a man *was* dead, and if it was because of malpractice, then she really should find out before somebody else was killed. He had a waiting room full of people to treat. What if one of them was killed or injured because Kenzie had let it go, giving them extra time to hide what had happened and avoid her questions?

"It shouldn't take very long," Kenzie said. "He can tell you to release the records to me, I can find out what happened the last time he treated Mr. Lane, and that will be all that is required. It shouldn't take more than a minute or two."

"I'll let him know when he is finished with the patient he is with now."

"Thank you."

Kenzie looked into the waiting room but really didn't want to sit down with all of the sick people, breathing their air.

"You can sit down," the receptionist told her.

"I'll just wait here."

"I'm sure you would be more comfortable sitting down."

"I've sat too much today. I'd rather stand."

It was another half hour before she was able to get in to see Dr. Slater. Kenzie was sure he had probably seen several patients during that time, not just finished up with the one he had been in with when Kenzie arrived. But had instead cleared all of the examination rooms where patients had been stacked up waiting for him. Eventually, Kenzie was escorted to a small office where the doctor, a short, dark-haired man, was waiting for her.

He looked at her over the top of rectangular-shaped glasses, then at the door, and back at her.

"Miss Kenzie, is it?"

"Dr. Kirsch."

"Ah, of course. A medical doctor."

"Pathologist," Kenzie agreed. "I am the Assistant Medical Examiner. I need to get information on Jack Lane and his recent complaints and treatments. John is actually his given name, but he went by Jack."

"And you need this because…"

"Because he has died, and I am investigating his death."

"Is that… usual?"

"Yes, of course it is. I investigate all deaths that did not take place under a physician's care."

"But you don't usually come here, looking for that patient's records."

"I usually call for them, if I know he was treated here recently."

He looked as if he doubted that fact.

"What seems to be the problem?" he asked. "Most of what we do here is treat colds and the flu. Some vaccinations, antibiotics, well baby checks. Patients who are deathly ill go to the hospital."

"We already checked with the hospital and they said that Jack had not been treated there."

"Then he was not treated."

"But he was. He had a fresh IV jab."

Slater looked surprised by that initially, then shrugged. "A drug user, perhaps."

"He didn't have tracks. He had one single puncture mark. No signs of intravenous drug use. He was an alcoholic, not a drug user."

"Then he died of alcoholism."

"Maybe. I am still investigating the circumstances of his death. We don't know for sure what killed him until we get some more tests back. And even then, we need to get all the outside information possible to sort out what happened."

14

After a certain amount of cajoling, Dr. Slater brought Jack's records up on his computer screen and looked over them. He shook his head.

"We haven't treated Mr. Lane for several months. The last time that he was treated, he needed a head laceration stitched up. He said he had tripped and hit his head when he fell. Not unusual for an alcoholic. Or he might have been targeted by someone out to beat up a bum. As much as you think our society might have progressed, that kind of thing still happens."

He shook his head and leaned back in his seat, looking at Kenzie.

"There isn't much on the record to say whether we thought it was a fall or a beating. I don't see much mentioned besides the facial lac, so we'll assume it was a single blow. He tripped or passed out, hit his head when he fell, and he came here to have it treated rather than going to the hospital emergency room, where he would likely have had to wait for six hours to be seen. And then they might just release him with a couple of sterile strips on it."

Kenzie nodded. "Can I get a copy of his full medical file with you?"

He hesitated at first, then shrugged. "Of course. Talk to one of the girls out front, and they'll see to it. We're happy to help the medical examiner's office in whatever way we can. I'm sorry to hear of Mr. Lane's death," he expressed sympathy for the homeless man's demise for the first time, "It is a tragedy, no matter what kind of life he chose to lead. If there's anything else I can do to help…"

"I need to find out where he was treated. There can't be many places in Roxboro where he would have been given an IV."

"I agree. But I can assure you that it wasn't here. There is nothing on his record to indicate that we ever gave him an IV or that he was treated in the last month. The only thing I can suggest is that he died of alcoholism, one way or another. He lived a high-risk lifestyle and he knew that it would kill him sooner or later."

While Kenzie knew that was true, it still angered Kenzie to hear Slater brush off his death so matter-of-factly. He knew nothing about Lane, how he lived, or the people who cared about him. He didn't know anything about how Lane died, but was willing to brush it off as an alcoholic death without knowing anything about it. She kept her temper under wraps.

"Thank you for taking a look at the record." That was all that Slater was required to do, and he had confirmed that they had not treated Lane before his death, which was all Kenzie needed to know. There was no point in getting in a snit over attitudes. There would be plenty of other people with opinions that were as bad or worse. She couldn't fight them all.

Hopefully, the work that the Kirsch family foundation was doing could have a positive change in the community. That was all she could hope for.

Dr. Slater said a firm goodbye and ushered Kenzie out of his office to the front. He leaned closer to the plastic shield to make his voice more easily heard by the nurse receptionist closest to him without making it audible to the rest of the waiting room.

"Please give Dr. Kirsch copies of whatever records of Mr. Lane's she needs."

The woman, whose name tag said "Angie," nodded. "Yes, doctor."

He gave her a quick, cold nod and returned to the hallway.

Kenzie saw him grab a chart from the wall outside one of the exam rooms, then enter without knocking as he looked down at the clipboard.

"What do you need?" Angie asked Kenzie, looking tired and worn.

Kenzie had told Slater she would need everything, but she reconsidered. Did she really need anything that had happened to Lane a year before? Two years? However long he had been living in the neighborhood and going to that clinic? There was no point in going back that far. What had killed him had been much more proximate.

"Records of any visits over the past year," she decided.

She should be able to copy or print that much information while Kenzie waited. If she asked for everything they had, it might take days before they bothered to send it to her.

"Okay. It will take me a few minutes to get that going."

"Thanks."

Kenzie again did not choose to sit down with the patients as she waited. She stood there waiting, so Angie could not ignore her or put her off.

"You don't know where else Mr. Lane might have been treated, do you?" she asked.

"At the hospital, I guess."

"Anywhere other than here and the hospital? What are the alternatives?"

Angie rolled her eyes. "There are other private practices. But most of them won't take some homeless guy. They choose their clients carefully. He could go into Burlington or something."

"How would he get there?"

"I don't know. A friend with a car. The bus."

Kenzie nodded. "Maybe."

But she couldn't see Lane going all the way to Burlington for medical care before the hospital.

"Where else?"

The woman shook her head. "It's a small town, doctor. There aren't many options for those who can't pay."

The indigent were still supposed to be able to access medical care, and Lane had been able to receive it at the clinic or hospital, but there were a lot of other places that would have just turned him away.

Angie was watching her.

"There is only so much that we can do." She gave a slight tip of her head toward the waiting room full of people. Clearly, there was more demand than the clinic could fulfill. They were supposed to close in an hour, and Kenzie figured there were probably four more hours' worth of people waiting. Most of those who remained would be turned away.

"I see that."

"We would do more if we could, but we have limited resources. There aren't enough doctors or hours in the day. We all have families to take care of. There is... a gap in care, especially for people like Mr. Lane."

"And you don't know where he would go if he couldn't come here. If he couldn't go or didn't want to go to the hospital, and it was late at night... where else is there...?"

Angie blinked and looked like she had just thought of something, but she pressed her lips together and didn't tell Kenzie what it was.

"There isn't any other place to go at night," she said crisply.

A couple of the waiting room patients were watching them, apparently listening in on the conversation. When Kenzie looked at them, they didn't immediately look away.

"Now, if you'll excuse me, I need to get this done," Angie said, turning away from Kenzie.

Kenzie shrugged and waited for Angie to print out the requested records.

The printer was slow, and Jack's records were not at the front of the queue, so it took some time before they were printed. Angie went through them and collated them to ensure she had everything she needed before passing them on to Kenzie.

"That's it. Sorry we couldn't be of more help."

"I appreciate it. I know there's only so much you can do."

"Yeah." Angie nodded dismissively and returned to her work, calling the next patient forward.

Kenzie squared the pages, tapping them against the counter, then left the clinic. She was glad to get out into the fresh air. There were so many sick people in the clinic waiting room that it would be a miracle if she didn't pick up some virus from breathing the same air and touching the same surfaces. She probably hadn't mitigated her risks very much by refusing to sit down to wait. She had maintained a few feet of distance, but that was probably not enough.

"Hey!"

Kenzie turned to look at the man who called out to her. Probably not someone she wanted to stop and talk to. The man was in his mid-thirties, Hispanic, his face stained and missing at least one tooth. Homeless, perhaps. Or just the working poor. Kenzie wondered whether he was going to ask her for a handout. She was clearly a different class from most of the people in the clinic, other than the doctor and staff.

"Yes?"

"You're looking for a doctor? At night when everything is closed?"

Kenzie was about to say she wasn't, then caught herself. "Yes. Do you know where I could go? It doesn't seem like there are any options at night other than the hospital."

He nodded sagely. "Sometimes, if you are lucky, you might find the Night Doctor."

15

Kenzie cocked her head and studied the man. "The Night Doctor? Who is the Night Doctor?"

"He doesn't have a name. Just the Night Doctor."

"And... where is he? Where would I find him if I needed him?"

"He's not around every night. And you can't predict where he will be. He goes around to different places where his patients are likely to be."

"Patients who are looking for someone to treat them at night."

The scruffy man nodded his agreement. "Or sometimes not looking. Sometimes, he just comes to you. Because he knows that you need him."

"I see... sounds like a ghost or something. Are you sure he's real?" Kenzie teased.

"Oh, he's real, honey. Just as real as you and me. More real than these folks," he hooked a thumb back toward the interior of the clinic. "Are they here every time you need them?" He shook his head in answer in case she didn't know the right answer. "They are only here for a few hours of the day. Try to cram as many people in as they can. Not like the Night Doctor, looking for those who need him."

"So, what, he just walks around looking for people to treat?"

The man nodded. "Yes. Walks around. Drives around. Checks out all of the spots he thinks there might be people who need him. He takes care of the throwaways. All of the people who can't get care at a place like this. People who deserve better."

Kenzie drew closer, very interested in what he was saying. His smell was pungent, so she didn't get too close, but she wanted to hear what else he had to say.

"What will he do? What kind of medicine?"

"Anything. Whatever you need done, he can do that." He shrugged. "Maybe not surgery. He says that you need an operating room and anesthetic and an assistant for that. He can't do it by himself. Or out here." He gestured, indicating the open air around him.

"No. You need a sterile environment," Kenzie agreed.

"That's what he says."

"So… if you needed an IV, could he do something like that?"

He wrinkled his nose. "Why would you need an IV?" He looked her over. "You don't need an IV."

"No, I don't. I am looking for someone for a friend, not myself. If I had a friend who was really sick and needed an IV, maybe because he was dehydrated or needed some kind of medication, could the Night Doctor do that?"

"Yeah, sure. He could do that. What's wrong with your friend?"

"He's been very sick," Kenzie invented. "He can't go out. Can't make it to the clinic, and I can't usually take him anywhere during the day when the clinic is open. I asked them if there was someone who would make house calls, and they said they didn't know of anyone who would come to you. They say I just have to call an ambulance and have him taken to the hospital, but he doesn't want to go there again."

The man nodded. He sidled closer to her, reaching his hand out in greeting. Kenzie suppressed her instinct to pull away from him and shook hands. His hand was hard and dry, calloused from years of manual labor.

"Anthony," he introduced himself. "I am Anthony."

"Kenzie. Do you know how I can get in touch with this Night Doctor? Find him to treat my friend?"

"You need to be somewhere our people hang out," he explained. "Near the shelter. On the embankment. Under the overpass. Those are places he goes. Sometimes, if he hears that someone needs him, he will go to them. Find them in a bar or back alley." Anthony looked around. "Where is your friend?"

"A few blocks from here. I don't know if I can get him to move to one of those places. He doesn't get around very well, especially now."

Anthony nodded understandingly. "You will have to come out. Let people know you are looking for him. He is not here every night, or I don't know where he is. Maybe he goes places I don't hear of."

"Is he a real doctor? You don't know his name?"

"He is a doctor," Anthony assured her. "He knows how to do everything. He is very good."

"But you don't know his name?"

He shook his head. "He doesn't tell his name. He's like... the Lone Ranger."

Kenzie stifled a laugh at this. A Lone Ranger Night Doctor?

"And you don't know what kind of doctor he is?"

"He is a good one," Anthony said with a shrug. "He can do everything."

Kenzie highly doubted that. Surgery was out. There were probably other procedures that were too dangerous or specialized for him to do. And maybe he did make mistakes, if he was the one who had treated Jack Lane. Something had not gone according to plan with him. Maybe it was not his fault, but he should have known how sick Lane was and taken him to the hospital or called the ambulance before it was too late.

"So if I come back later, over near the shelter or somewhere else people hang out after dark, then I might find him?"

Anthony nodded his agreement. "If you bring your friend there, we will help you to find the Night Doctor."

16

Kenzie stopped by the office to drop off the printed reports from the clinic before going home. Dr. Cook was still there, and she lingered to talk to him.

"I know that you're not from Roxboro," she said, "But have you ever run across someone who goes by 'the Night Doctor'?"

Dr. Cook frowned, his brow creased deeply. "The Night Doctor. Where did you hear this? Sounds like some old horror movie. Or a Mexican wrestler."

Kenzie laughed. "It does sound very dramatic. But that is the only way he was referred to. The guy I talked to didn't know his name, specialty, or anything about him. Other than apparently he goes around to homeless encampments and treats people, performing various procedures that they need done."

Cook shook his head. "Sounds like a myth. People probably wish that there *was* such a thing. Make up stories to make themselves feel better. Give each other some hope."

"You've been doing this longer than I have. You haven't run into this guy before? Here or in any other city? If he has been treating people for a while, we might have worked on the body of someone who was a past patient."

"I don't remember ever hearing a rumor like that. We usually know who has been treating them, if anyone. We don't usually end up with bodies where medical procedures were done by an unknown party."

"No," Kenzie agreed. "But sometimes, we don't know who their doctor or regular clinic was. The procedures have been routine, and we didn't think they had anything to do with the death. You don't remember anything like that?"

"Not specifically." He shrugged. "I don't think this is going to lead anywhere."

"Okay." Kenzie was a little puzzled about why he wasn't more interested in the rumor of a Night Doctor who was performing possibly unauthorized medical procedures on the homeless in the middle of the night. Even if it didn't lead anywhere, it was an intriguing idea. Something that she thought Dr. Cook would be interested in.

But maybe he had other things on his mind, or he was just really focused on resolving Jack Lane's case and did not want to be distracted by a theory he considered unlikely.

"Well, I might do a little looking around, see if I can find anything out about this guy," Kenzie told him. "Maybe a bit of internet sleuthing, talk to a few of the homeless and see whether they have had any contact with him or even heard anything like this before."

"Your guy was probably schizophrenic. Delusional. It all sounds pretty bizarre."

"Maybe… but he seemed pretty grounded."

"I wouldn't waste any time on it if it was me."

But Kenzie wasn't Dr. Cook.

The text tone sounded on Kenzie's phone. The one assigned to Zachary. She needed to get things wrapped up and get home. Zachary would be wondering where she was and what she was doing. He wanted to spend some time with her. And he would want her focus on him, not on some mythical person.

She filed the reports for the Lane case and locked everything up. Too late to work on any more today. She was finished. She needed to put it behind her until she returned on Monday. Then she could look at it with fresh eyes. She needed the break to regain some perspective.

Kenzie picked up her phone and, when she was finished locking everything up, she looked at the screen. It was a text from Zachary, as she had discerned from the tone. She swiped and unlocked it to read the message.

Can you meet for supper at Old Joes?

That was a surprise. She couldn't remember his bringing it up earlier and, usually, he gave her lots of warning if he wanted to go out to eat. And more than that, she always went home, and they left from there. Zachary already being at Old Joe's and wanting her to meet him there was unexpected and she wondered what it meant.

Maybe he had been out on surveillance and had ended up close to the restaurant and decided he wanted a steak. Or perhaps he had met there with a client and now thought it would be nice to start his evening with Kenzie there, in a semi-romantic setting.

Whatever his reasons, she certainly didn't mind the prospect of being wined and dined. She stopped to think about whether it was an anniversary. Maybe of their first date or another special occasion. But she couldn't think of anything that fit. She tapped out a message back to him.

Sure just leaving office now

He texted her back almost immediately. *See u soon*

Kenzie hummed to herself as she drove. It was a nice way to end the day. And tomorrow was Sunday. She would not be going to work and, in a departure from their usual schedule, she wouldn't be going to Burlington to see her parents or south to see Lorne Peterson, an old foster father of Zachary's, and Patrick Parker, Lorne's partner. It had been Kenzie's weekend to see her parents, and they had seen Lisa at the gala, so she had fulfilled her daughterly duties and could just have a rest day on Sunday.

A romantic dinner and a rest day. It didn't get much better than that.

It was early evening, so Old Joe's wasn't too busy yet. There were plenty of parking spaces to choose from. Kenzie stepped in through the doors at Old Joe's and into the welcoming, hearty smell of steak and potatoes. She looked to her right to the table that Zachary usually picked if it was free, and saw him sitting there.

He was wearing a collared shirt, not a t-shirt or hoodie. Dressing up, but not too formal. Something nice for their time together. Zachary was not looking at the door. He was talking to someone, but she couldn't tell who from that angle. The waitress, probably. Letting her know that his date would be joining him soon. Maybe ordering her a drink so that it would be ready when she arrived.

Kenzie waved off the hostess who was stepping forward to offer to seat her. "I see him. It's fine."

The woman let Kenzie proceed on her own, and she walked over to the booth.

She was surprised to see that another woman was sitting across the table from Zachary. She blinked, stared at the woman, didn't recognize her, and looked back at Zachary.

"Oh, here's Kenzie," Zachary said. "I'm glad you could make it. I was afraid that you might have been too busy with this new case."

"No, no. I've spent most of the day on it when I should have been home. I was just finishing up when you texted. But... you didn't mention that we would have company."

She looked again at the other woman. There was no sign that it was a romantic relationship or ever had been. The woman was older than Zachary. She had on several layers of clothing and, after spending the day talking to a number of homeless people, Kenzie thought she recognized the look. The Black woman was neat and clean, with her hair arranged in tight cornrows that ended in colored beads. She had on no visible makeup. Looking discreetly around the woman, Kenzie saw a large backpack at her feet and a stuffed shoulder bag on the bench seat beside her. The multiple layers of clothing and accompanying luggage were the only things about her that said "homeless." Otherwise, her appearance was small-town professional, and Kenzie would not have pegged her as a homeless person.

"Kenzie, this is Maria Sanchez. Um… it's sort of a long story. Why don't you sit down, and we'll start from the beginning?"

Zachary patted the bench next to him and slid over a few inches to give Kenzie more space.

"Um, okay," Kenzie agreed, smiling and nodding, and trying to look as relaxed about the situation as possible. "Sounds interesting."

Zachary had ordered Kenzie a glass of red wine, the glass positioned at her place setting once she slid in next to Zachary. Kenzie took an appreciative sip.

Maria watched Kenzie drink but, like Zachary, she had only a glass of water. Or something that looked like water. Kenzie settled in, relaxing and resting her hand for a moment on Zachary's thigh. Being affectionate and, at the same time, trying to get a read on him. Tense? Relaxed? Unsure of what he was doing or confident in himself? How did he feel about this meeting?

He seemed to be fairly relaxed, so Kenzie also tried to release her tense muscles. No need to start the unexpected interview all wound up. Whatever this was all about, she had her boyfriend, a glass of wine, and a good meal and free day to look forward to.

"Maria was at the gala on Friday," Zachary said. "Yesterday, I mean. It seems like it was longer ago than that."

"At the gala," Kenzie repeated. She remembered that there had been several guests at the event. People who were representative of the change the foundation wanted to effect. People who had overcome addiction. People living in halfway houses or other forms of transitional housing. People with mental illness who had previously been on the skids but had been able, with community outreach, to turn their lives around and make better lives for themselves. Maria must have been one of those special guests. Each one a success in their segment, celebrated for what they had done. "Well, it's nice to meet you, Maria. I'm sorry we didn't have a chance to speak face-to-face last night."

"I couldn't get up my courage to talk to you last night," Maria confessed. "I wanted to, but... I needed to get an introduction."

Kenzie nodded, frowning. "An introduction... through Zachary?" she nodded to him.

"Well, yes. But first I had to get an introduction to Zachary."

"You didn't need an introduction to me," Zachary told Maria in a teasing voice. "I'm not a big bad private investigator. I wouldn't have turned you down."

"But it's better... if you know someone. You didn't know me from Adam. Or Eve, I guess," she gave a nervous laugh. "So I had to talk to Ella."

"Ella was a woman who helped me out when I was investigating the cold case into Robbie Elder's disappearance," Zachary explained to Kenzie.

Kenzie nodded. "Okay..." She remembered Zachary searching for Tyrrell's old friend, a boy who had disappeared when they had been teens.

"Zachary was introduced to Ella by Ivy," Maria contributed.

Kenzie scratched her head. "Uh-huh."

"I knew Ivy when I was a teenager," Zachary said. "She was on the street while I was in and out of different group homes, and then when I aged out."

Zachary had basically been dumped on the street once he had turned eighteen. Kenzie knew there had probably been extension programs and assistance offered but, by that time, Zachary was so embittered by the system that he would not have accepted anything offered if it came with additional supervision or with rules and expected behaviors. He had been done with government care, done with everything they had put him through. He'd found his own way without their transitional supports.

"Ivy helped me out then," Zachary told her. "She knew her way around, kind of mentored me. Now, she's running the community center and all kinds of outreach programs. She knows everything that goes on in the neighborhood. Or if she doesn't know, she knows who does."

"And Ella knew Maria. And Maria wanted to meet you," Kenzie pointed to Zachary.

Maria nodded. "I'd heard about Zachary from Ella and Ivy before."

"That's how you knew him at the gala."

Maria nodded. "And I could see he was sitting with you. They introduced you at the beginning, and it's *you* I wanted to talk to."

"Got it," Kenzie said with a laugh. "You wanted to talk to me because of the foundation? I don't make any of the policy decisions or the choices of what programs get funded…"

"No." Maria fidgeted with the buttons on her coat cuffs. "I wanted to talk to the medical examiner."

"Is this about a case that I am working on?" she asked, "Or is this like… you want a second opinion on a report given by another medical examiner?"

Zachary sometimes came to her with reports issued by other medical examiners when he had a client who believed that the wrong finding had been made and that if she read through it, she might find the evidence they needed to solve the case.

"A current case," Maria said softly.

"A case I am working on?" Kenzie did not think Maria was from Roxboro, but from Clintock, where Zachary had grown up. Then what was her interest in a case that Kenzie was investigating?

"Jack Lane," Maria said, even more quietly. Kenzie wasn't even sure she had heard correctly. Maria was interested in the investigation into Jack Lane's case? She must have gotten it wrong.

"Jack Lane?" Kenzie repeated, more loudly than she had intended.

Maria nodded. She darted a glance in Zachary's direction as if hoping for his support. Zachary didn't say anything, but gave Maria an encouraging look.

"I can't tell you anything about the Jack Lane case," Kenzie told her. "The investigation is ongoing. I haven't even released my preliminary findings yet."

"I know. But I didn't think you knew everything about what happened."

"And you do? How could you know when you don't even live in the same city?"

"Homeless grapevine," Maria said with a shrug and a tentative smile. "You would be amazed at how quickly word gets out. About something like that... or about someone asking questions."

"It's my job to ask questions. I can't very well proceed without asking some very detailed questions in this case. There are... some outstanding issues that need to be explained."

"Yes," Maria agreed. "There are some questions that no one wants to answer. But... it's your job to answer them. And I don't want Jack to be buried without... without those questions being answered."

17

"Okay." Kenzie laid down the menu she had been fiddling with. "Cards on the table time. What do you know about the Night Doctor?"

Zachary looked surprised by this. Whatever he had been expecting, Maria had not told him anything about the doctor.

Taking Kenzie's motion with the menu as a signal she was ready to order, a waitress approached and asked them about their orders. They all dealt with the interruption. As impatient as Kenzie was to find out the details of the Night Doctor, she was also starving. The waitress departed and Kenzie looked at Maria.

"Please. Tell me what you know about the Night Doctor."

"Nobody knows very much about him," Maria said cautiously. "He does not tell anyone his name. He doesn't follow a specific schedule or work out of a certain location. So he could be anywhere at any time."

"How do people get treated, then, if they need help? Can someone send for him? Is there any way?"

"No. There is no way. He comes and goes. You can put the word out that you are looking for him and, if you are lucky, then someone will know where he is that day or will be able to get a message to him. Like I said, we have a pretty good gossip network.

Word spreads quickly and, if we are working together, sometimes we can find him or get a message to him."

"But he doesn't have an office. And no one knows his name or his phone number."

"No."

"That sounds like a very irresponsible way to work."

"He's very good, though," Maria said sincerely. "he is a miracle worker. He can get supplies and do procedures that we can't get otherwise. You don't know how it is, living like we do, trying to stay healthy, to get specialized treatments."

"I've been learning about it today," Kenzie said. "I'm sure I don't know even a hundredth of it yet, but I am learning a lot that I didn't know before."

Maria looked reassured by this. "You make it sound like he is doing something wrong, but he is not. He's going out... to the people who need him the most. He's providing a service no one else does. Street medicine."

The mobile clinic van and several other providers were also trying to provide street medicine. Doctors and legislators knew that it was needed, but there were many constraints.

How did you service a population without fixed addresses? How did you keep medical histories for people who bounced from one doctor, shelter, or clinic to another? What about people who had medicines that needed to be refrigerated? That needed to be administered by a doctor or intravenously? What do you do when people are afraid to go into a hospital for fear that they would never come out?

Some of them had outstanding felony warrants or were afraid of having to spend even a little time in county jail. There were parents with little children who had nowhere safe to leave them while they were treated. Or who knew they would lose their children if their case worker found out they were living on the street. Every contact with a professional meant danger.

Kenzie didn't know how the Night Doctor could treat anyone effectively. He was running some kind of unregulated program. Where did he get his supplies? How did he write prescriptions?

Who paid for his expenses, the transportation from one place to another between Roxboro and other nearby towns? And what if he made a mistake? What kind of accountability did he have? What regulatory body was supervising him? Without those checks and balances, how could anyone be sure he was doing the good he claimed to be?

"I know there is a need for street medicine… it is the only way to serve some people. But I don't know how he could have a viable practice this way."

"He does what he needs to. And people… help him when they can."

"What do you mean, help him? Does he have other people working for him? Do they pay him? If he's not practicing under his own name, then how does he get the funding? Or supplies? How does he give people prescriptions?"

Maria licked her lips. "I don't know how it all works," she mumbled. "I don't think that it is all… it doesn't operate the same way as it does in the hospital or the clinic."

"Is he stealing supplies? Prescription pads? Or prescription drugs?"

"I don't know. I don't think *he* is."

"But you think someone else might be stealing them for him."

"I don't know how it works," Maria repeated. "I never asked anyone. Why would I? He operates however he operates. I was never part of his organization, I never stole anything for him. If other people are, they never told me about it."

"I'm not accusing you," Kenzie said. "I'm sorry if it came across that way. I'm just wondering who this guy is and how he is able to operate. If he is operating outside of the established channels, then you don't know what his qualifications are and if he has really been trained to do the things that he is doing. You don't know if he is using drugs that are stolen, expired, or counterfeit."

"He's not doing anything wrong," Maria insisted. "He's saving lives. People who don't have anywhere else to go."

"Jack could have gone to the hospital. And he probably should have."

"Not everyone can go to the hospital."

Kenzie shook her head. "Why not? Jack used the emergency room as his primary care. So why didn't he go to them that last day?"

"They don't listen to you," Maria snapped. "Do you think they want to treat homeless people? They just want to get rid of them. They say that there's nothing wrong. Or that they should stop drinking. Or eat better or find somewhere to sleep where there aren't any fleas or bedbugs. All we need to do is to get into a program, and then everything will be fine."

"But they still have to treat him. They wouldn't have just turned him away. Or dumped him in an alley."

Maria's eyes widened, then filled with tears. "Oh, poor Jack."

Kenzie tried to put her hand over Maria's to comfort her.

"I'm sorry. I don't want it to sound like I don't care, because I *do*. That's why I'm asking questions and trying to find out what happened. I do care, and I don't want the same thing to happen to someone else."

"Jack was my friend," Maria said in a strong voice, "he wasn't just… a piece of trash to be discarded."

"No," Kenzie agreed. "Nobody should have done what they did." She patted Maria's hand soothingly. "Did you know him well? Did you see him even though you lived in different towns?"

"Not a lot," Maria admitted. "But we were still friends. And it didn't matter if things did change and I got off the streets, I would still have been friends with him."

"How did you contact each other?"

"We have ways." Maria's answer was curt. She turned her head to look out the window next to her. She gave a long, searching look, and Kenzie thought she might be waiting for someone. Maybe whoever had brought her to Roxboro to talk to Zachary and Kenzie was coming back to pick her up.

Kenzie looked at Zachary. She wasn't getting very far with Maria, but maybe Zachary would have better luck. He was closer to this community than Kenzie. He had been one of them. Maria had sought him out.

"Did you hear anything about how Jack died?" Zachary asked. "Or about what happened to him before that? Was it the Night Doctor who was treating him?"

"He's a good doctor," she said sullenly.

"He's helped a lot of people," Zachary stated.

"Yes, he's helped a lot of people," she echoed.

"You don't want anything to happen to him. You're worried that if you talk about him, something will happen that will make him stop treating people. And that would not be a good thing. A lot of people depend on him and his services."

She was nodding in agreement with all of his statements.

Kenzie wanted to assure Maria that she didn't want to do anything to stop the Night Doctor and that nothing negative would happen as a result of her investigation. But she was afraid that wasn't true, and that Maria would sense her ambivalence.

"It's important that people like Jack get the treatment they need," Kenzie said instead. "The very best they can. Jack was very sick, and I don't know how much anyone could have done for him, but he deserved to have the best treatment possible. Whatever that was."

Maria nodded her agreement.

"You said that you know I don't have all of the answers, and there are things that I need to know in order to make a proper ruling on Jack's case. You came to me." she reminded Maria.

18

Maria nodded slowly. She looked out the window again. Watching for someone to come and get her? Or worried that someone might have followed her or might see her there?

"I'm glad you came to me," Kenzie encouraged her. "I would really like to know who treated Jack and what procedures he followed. I would like to know more about what went wrong. Why they made the decisions they did. It's a lot to ask, I know."

Maria nodded.

"Were you there?" Kenzie coaxed.

Maria didn't answer the question directly. "He was bleeding. He'd been coughing up blood for a few days, but it was getting worse. He was throwing up... so much. They said he needed a donation. A trans..."

"Transfusion," Kenzie contributed. "A blood transfusion to try to replace the blood he was losing."

Maria nodded. That squared with the presence of an IV. They had needed to get blood back into Jack if they were going to keep him alive. From the appearance of his organs, he had lost a tremendous amount of blood. "It must have been very hard to watch that.

Did the doctor think that he would be able to save Jack? If he could get enough blood into him?"

"There were... There was so much blood. But he was getting better. He was getting stronger."

Kenzie raised her brows. "When they gave him blood? He was starting to look better?" Kenzie tried to envision it, to remember everything she had learned in her medical training that would help her to get the details from Maria. "His skin started to get pinker. He was more alert."

Maria's nods got more vigorous. "Yes. He was better. He was waking up, talking. Everyone thought it was working; he was beginning to get better."

But they hadn't been able to keep up with the blood loss. Jack had massive bleeds through his upper GI tract. He needed surgery. Someone needed to open him up and clamp off those bleeders. Possibly to remove the most damaged part of the intestines. Not to allow him anything by mouth, giving his stomach a chance to heal. He would need to be detoxed immediately because every drink he took was killing him. The detox itself was dangerous and would have to be doctor-supervised.

All things considered, it was unlikely they would have been able to save him even if they'd had the surgical facilities to make the attempt.

If Jack *had* gone to the hospital, would they even have tried? Or would they understand that there was no point in putting Jack through all of that and just provide palliative care, trying to make him comfortable until the end?

"Then what happened?"

Maria shook her head. "Something... went wrong. I don't know what. He got a fever. His back hurt, and he wanted the IV out. He said it hurt, but they said he had to keep it in so he could get the blood. If he didn't get the blood, he was going to die. But..."

"But it didn't matter; he died anyway," Kenzie finished for her.

Maria looked out the window. "They couldn't have followed me here. I was careful."

Zachary looked sharply at Maria, and then he, too, looked out the window, his eyes scanning the parking lot.

"Who?" he asked. "Did you see someone?"

Maria pressed her lips together, looking out the window and then looking around the inside of the restaurant as if someone might have followed her inside.

"Who followed you?" Zachary asked insistently. "Do we need to be worried about something?"

"They're always watching me." Maria twisted around, looking in every direction for the unseen observers. "Ever since I first saw him."

"Saw who? Jack?"

Maria shook her head. She was growing more agitated. Kenzie tried to think of something that might help calm her down.

"I don't think anyone followed you. I haven't seen anyone looking in your direction."

"You wouldn't see them. People like you don't know what to look for."

"*I* know what to look for," Zachary told her. "Tell me what you noticed. Is there a certain person or vehicle…?"

"They are everywhere. They change cars. They change how they look. But they are still out there. Don't discount them just because you don't see them."

"I have worked surveillance for years. If you tell me something about the people following you, I will see what I can find. Help to protect you."

Kenzie tried to catch Zachary's eye. It was obvious to her that this was not a security issue, but paranoia. Maria struggled with mental health issues. That was probably why she was on the street in the first place. She was seeing watchers and was paranoid about being followed, but it wasn't because there was any truth to it.

"The Night Doctor," Maria said. "People have been watching me. Ever since the first time I saw him, they've been following me."

Zachary's brow furrowed. "Why?"

Maria looked around again before facing Zachary and meeting his eyes. Kenzie sensed that Maria was forcing herself to look straight at Zachary and not look around for the watchers, not wanting to attract attention to herself.

"They want to shut him down. They don't want him to be able to keep operating, so they send people out to watch his patients. To see what happens to them. To…" Despite her efforts to look inconspicuous, Maria's glance darted around the restaurant again, "To see whether there are any *accidents*. Maybe… to make sure there *are* accidents."

"To discredit the Night Doctor?" Zachary asked.

Maria nodded. "Yes."

The waitress came over with their food, all smiles and chirpy comments and questions, ensuring they had everything they needed to make their meal a wonderful experience. It took a few minutes to get rid of her graciously. But Kenzie welcomed the interruption and thought it might be just the distraction that Maria needed to take her mind off anyone who might have followed her there and a conspiracy against the Night Doctor.

Rather than continuing to discuss the anonymous doctor, they dug into their meals, discussing how delicious it was. Maria huddled over her food, giving it her undivided attention, but Kenzie could see that Zachary's attention was distracted. He looked around the room, glanced out the window, and excused himself to use the restroom. Kenzie assumed he was checking the back hallways and door, looking for anyone or anything that seemed out of place.

She hated to think that he was buying into Maria's paranoia. Zachary really didn't need another thing triggering his own obsessive and paranoid behavior. She anticipated an uptick in his door-locking and burglar-alarm-checking rituals.

As a private investigator, it was good for him to be extra careful, and his security precautions had saved them from harm in the past, so she couldn't complain about them. But she did not relish the constant checking and hypervigilance.

Zachary returned to the table, smiling and casual, and resumed his meal. Maria looked at him once or twice, but seemed to have moved on from her paranoid episode for the moment.

Kenzie waited until the meal was finished before making any further comment on her case.

"I appreciate you coming to me and letting me know more about the Night Doctor," Kenzie told Maria. "If you could let me know if you see him or hear where he is, I'd really appreciate it." Kenzie wrote her cell phone number on her business card and slid it across the table to Maria. "I'm not trying to shut him down; I just want to hear what happened when he treated Jack. Then I'll be able to close my file."

"He's a good doctor, and we *need* him."

"I understand. And do you have a safe place to stay? Are you at a shelter in Clintock?"

Maria stared at her. "I'm in a transitional house funded by *your* family's foundation."

"Oh. Of course. I don't know how I forgot. Sorry for asking such a silly question."

Maria shrugged and shook her head. "I'm sure you have a lot on your mind."

"I do… thank you for understanding. Can we give you a ride somewhere?" It was dark outside and Kenzie didn't like the idea of Maria wandering around alone, especially if she had another episode of paranoia. No matter how well she was doing in the program she was in, she clearly was still challenged by mental illness. Kenzie knew that it wasn't something that could be "cured" with a few pills. They could help to reduce her symptoms. Like with Zachary, it would be a matter of balancing the symptoms that the medications relieved against the side effects they caused, and whether taking meds on a fixed schedule was something she could manage.

"I don't need a ride. I have my bike," Maria snapped. "I take care of myself."

Kenzie made some agreeable noises, a little hurt by Maria's response to her offer to help. She hadn't meant to infantilize Maria because of her mental illness or housing situation. She just wanted to offer a hand if Maria needed it. It was hard to tell where the line was for some people. Everyone was different.

They walked out with Maria, but she turned a corner and was out of sight. Kenzie knew better than to follow her to make sure that she found her bike and that it was adequate for getting around. Instead, she took Zachary's arm and walked with him to her car.

"Did you drive?" She looked around the parking lot for his vehicle.

"No, walked. Figured it would be good exercise, and then we could go home together."

"Perfect. Let's get home and unwind."

19

M aybe it was too much to expect to be able to go home and unwind.

It had been a long day for Kenzie, and her mind was whirling with everything she had discovered. She needed to know more about the Night Doctor. She needed to talk to someone who had actually been there when Jack had died and knew something about what had happened. Maria's description, though compelling, did not include anything that made Kenzie believe that she had been there in person. Maria had likely heard what had happened through the homeless grapevine, maybe from someone who had been there, or maybe a story that had been repeated several times. But there wasn't anything in her narrative that assured Kenzie she had been there.

And it was clear that Zachary was keyed up by the meeting. Maria's paranoia was enough to have set him off. But Kenzie suspected there was even more to it than that. Maria was a connection to Zachary's past and, one way or another, Zachary's past was always trying to swallow him up.

Now he was thinking about Maria and her connection with Ella and Ivy Shane. Ivy Shane had been a big part of Zachary's life during that transitional period between aging out of foster care and being able to stand on his own two feet. She had been a few years older than he was, beautiful, and part of a group of friends, while Zachary had been an outsider, alone, not as ready to start his new life as he and Family Services had hoped. He had envied everything about her.

Zachary tried to sit down and visit with Kenzie, suggested a couple of activities to pass the evening together, and got up every few minutes to look out the windows and check the burglar alarm. The first few times, Kenzie ignored it, hoping that if she didn't say anything, Zachary's anxiety would subside and he would be able to relax with her. But eventually, she had to say something.

"You know Maria was being paranoid, right?" she asked. "No one is following her all over the state. It was just her paranoia."

"You don't know that."

"I know paranoia when I see it."

"I know she was paranoid... but you don't know that no one was following her. She's paranoid, but that doesn't mean she's wrong."

"You think someone is following a homeless woman all over Clintock and Roxboro because she might break the news of the Night Doctor and what he's doing?"

"Or to make sure that things happen to the people he treats, so that it looks like he is treating them incorrectly," Zachary reminded her.

Kenzie shook her head. "That's just paranoia. There's no way that's happening."

"You haven't even looked into what's happened to his past patients. How can you know that?"

"Because it doesn't make sense. It isn't logical or likely."

Zachary looked out the window again and shrugged. "Neither are the things that have happened in some of your other cases. But people... push the boundaries. They dig themselves too deep and then try to cover it up. Or they're afraid of being exposed, so they strike out against anyone who they are worried might know something or be about to find something out. Don't say it could never happen, because you and I have both seen it happen."

"In a few isolated cases, yes, but…"

"This could be another one. You don't know that."

Kenzie raised her hands in surrender. "Okay. Fine. There could be a conspiracy out there. There could be something nefarious about this Night Doctor. He could be out to kill people, or people could be out to discredit him by killing his patients. But I really don't think so."

"Maybe not. Probably not." Zachary peered out the window. "But I'm not willing to say definitely not."

20

Sunday was more relaxed. Kenzie got some cleaning done, read a book, and spent half the day in her jammies.

Monday morning dawned crisp and clear, a beautiful Vermont spring day. Kenzie needed to get to the office to take care of the emails and reports that had come in over the weekend, but then she wanted to get out to talk to a few more people.

"Listen, do you have much to do this afternoon?" she asked Zachary as they prepared breakfast.

"This and that. Why?"

"I'm wondering if you would consider joining me while I interview a few more people about the Night Doctor and see what I can find out. I think... since it will mostly be street people, that might be more in your wheelhouse than mine. They might be more comfortable talking to you, like Maria."

Maybe Kenzie should be concerned that he would get more paranoid about the Night Doctor if he continued to be involved in the discussions, but she thought it would go the opposite direction. Most of the people they talked with would not be paranoid. They would know that there was nothing to worry about and be eager to talk about what they had seen and heard. The myth of the Night Doctor would be dispersed, replaced with the hard facts.

Zachary's eyes were alive with interest. "You want to go out together? Interviewing homeless about this rogue doctor?"

Kenzie nodded. "Remember, we don't know yet whether he is rogue. He could be a perfectly legitimate doctor donating services in an unconventional way. Like Maria said, street medicine fills a gap in services, helping to provide homeless people with the care they need in their own... communities." She had been about to say "in their own homes" but caught herself in time.

"But that isn't what you think."

"I... am reserving judgment. I am obviously prejudiced by what happened to Jack Lane. But I don't have any proof that he is the one who worked on Jack or that the doctor who worked on Jack did anything wrong. He was on the brink of death after years of alcohol abuse. When the crisis hit, he should have been treated in the emergency room. But if he refused to go there, or could not be moved, or no ambulances were available... someone might have had to do what they could for him in a different setting."

"But you think it was the Night Doctor and that he did something wrong."

Kenzie shrugged. She didn't like to say one way or the other. She was trying to remain objective. But Zachary was right; she already had her suspicions, which might or might not be correct. "That seems like the likeliest scenario at the moment," she admitted.

Zachary nodded his agreement. "Well, I'd be happy to come along and help. I don't know how much help I'll be with medical stuff, but I can talk to people and help sift through the stories."

Zachary had never been homeless in Roxboro, or, at least, not out on the street. However, his PI work made him far more familiar with the more impoverished areas and where the homeless tended to congregate than Kenzie's work at the medical examiner's office. She had only recently started to go out on scene of death calls that might take her to these parts of town, having previously only worked out of the medical examiner's office in the basement of the police services building. Not a lot of homeless people hung out with the police.

So Kenzie let Zachary take the lead on where to go for their interviews. They also took Zachary's nondescript white compact rather than Kenzie's beautiful red convertible for obvious reasons.

Zachary normally had two or three days' growth of beard. With some faded and worn blue jeans, he easily passed as homeless. If he was on surveillance, it helped him to blend into his surroundings because people did not want to meet a homeless guy's eyes and would not remember him later. If they did remember him, it would just be the vague memory of some homeless guy, faceless and nameless. Because he had cleaned himself up and shaved for dinner at the restaurant the night before, he only had a twenty-four-hour growth, but he grew whiskers quickly, and it was enough to make him look unsavory when combined with some ratty clothes.

Kenzie was impatient as Zachary started his inquiries. She was used to a direct approach. Walk up to the people she hoped to get some answers from and ask them straight out. But Zachary wouldn't let her do that. She would just scare everyone off. Instead, she and Zachary stood some distance down the block from their target group, wandering at a slow pace from one garbage can to the next. Kenzie stood out like a sore thumb. Zachary had advised her to put on the grubby clothes she would normally do her housecleaning in, and to pull a knit cap over her wild, curly hair, even though it was a warm spring day. She felt naked without her usual makeup, especially the bright red lipstick she loved. Zachary told her she looked fine, but she looked so different from usual that she was sure everyone must be staring at her.

It took some time before they reached the group of people standing around talking in the middle of the afternoon. And when they did, Zachary gave no sign that he intended to stop and talk to them, but continued to walk by, looking for anything promising in the garbage cans. When Kenzie stopped, he grabbed her arm and encouraged her to keep moving. But they didn't get far. One of the men in the group called out to them.

"Hey, buddy."

Zachary hesitated, then turned toward them. He looked over the members of the small band and raised his brows. "Me? Yeah?"

"Don't think I've seen you here before. You new?"

Zachary took his time answering. At first, he looked like he would just keep walking. Then he touched Kenzie again, pulling her closer so she was cuddled against him. He looked around again as if there might be trouble, then finally looked back at the man who had addressed him.

"Been around for a while. Came from Clintock."

There were looks exchanged between the members of the group, but none of them stepped forward to say that they were from Clintock and didn't remember ever seeing him there before.

"Clintock, sure," the man said in a mild, soothing voice. "So you're a Vermonter."

Zachary nodded. And offered nothing more. He was wary, not rushing in to make friends with these guys.

"You guys got a place to stay? Gonna be around for a while?" the man asked.

"We don't need anything." Zachary put his hand over Kenzie's, resting on his arm, and shook his head as if she had asked him something. "We're good," he assured the strangers. "Just getting the lay of the land."

"We can help. Not trying to horn in or anything. Just willing to help out fellow humans. It's easier if you know where everything is, who you should talk to, some of the ins and outs. Save yourself a lot of time and effort. Help keep you and your girl safe."

"We're fine. Only—" Zachary broke off and shook his head. "We're good."

"You've got a place to sleep? Still gets cold at night; I guess you know that from Clintock. And you know the soup kitchen? Where you can get breakfast?"

"We don't do breakfast. Especially now that—" Zachary started to smile, letting out a short laugh, and then shut it down. "No, we're good." He rubbed Kenzie's lower back, gazing into her eyes.

Kenzie didn't know how he could convey so much in a few

words and gestures. But the small group of men and women was clearly eating up his unspoken story. A man and woman alone, with no one to help them, Kenzie possibly pregnant and seeking some sort of help that he wasn't willing to voice to these strangers. How he thought keeping quiet and not making any attachments was the safest course of action.

One of the women sidled closer, trying to connect with Kenzie. She smiled as if she knew all about Kenzie and wanted to be her new best friend.

"Things can be tough out here," she offered. "We try to help each other out. No one makes it on their own, you know. We all need each other." She smiled a smile as warm as a sun-drenched daisy.

You can trust us.

No one said it aloud, but it was what they were all trying to convey.

And Kenzie, having had no experience on the street, had no idea whether they were trustworthy. She had no idea what she would do if she were really on the skids, trying to figure out her path. Would she trust them? Would she think them too pushy? And if she trusted them, would they give her all of the things their smiles promised, or would they wait for the right moment to take advantage of the new couple after they'd had a chance to evaluate their strengths and weaknesses and what they might have that was of value on the street?

"What do you need?" the man who had called them over pressed. "We're happy to help you out."

Kenzie looked at Zachary questioningly. He shrugged, gazing back at her, then finally turned to the man.

"Just, like… it's nothing. Just maybe some antibiotics."

None of them looked surprised. Zachary had played his part like a pro.

"Emergency room at the hospital," the leader suggested.

"Sit there for six hours waiting? With sick people? We want to get better, not worse."

"There's a clinic—" the woman pointed in the direction of the clinic Kenzie had been to on Saturday to get Jack's medical records. Kenzie started to shake her head, hoping they would come up with something different.

"Never mind," Zachary cut them both off. "We don't need any of that kind of help."

The man's mouth opened to protest.

"We're fine," Zachary insisted. "I can find something. A friend. Someone we can trust."

"If you need medical care, you have to be willing to go to a doctor. There aren't a lot who will take on new patients in our... situation. That's why you have to rely on the hospitals and clinics. They won't turn you away."

"We need something *private*," Zachary said stoically.

"They can't even tell anyone they're treating you. It's the law."

"Doesn't stop loose lips. Too many people in those places. Too many ways word could get back to..." Zachary looked at Kenzie and stopped.

She gave a slight nod.

The man and his little group looked at each other, considering the question and what to do about it. They murmured to each other, their voices too low for Zachary and Kenzie to hear them. But she thought she heard the word 'doctor' and wondered if they were discussing the Night Doctor. Was that all it took? A homeless person only had so many options for medical care.

Private practices did not want to take them on. If they wouldn't go to the hospital or clinic, then what was left? A friend who was a nurse? A vet tech? The Night Doctor?

21

"We know a guy," the leader of the group said eventually. He looked around as if making sure that no one was eavesdropping on them. He motioned for Zachary and Kenzie to get closer, within the confines of the group.

After looking at Zachary, Kenzie moved toward them, and he followed, sticking close to her side.

"I'm Darius. Look, there's a doctor," the man offered in a confidential tone. "He helps us out sometimes. Antibiotics, stitches, setting broken bones. He does all that kind of thing."

Kenzie nodded. "Some kind of medical student?"

He looked surprised that she had spoken, but didn't comment on the fact or insist on only talking to Zachary.

"A real doctor. Not just a student or some foreign guy. Real, board-certified doctor."

"He can do anything," the smiling woman trying to befriend Kenzie told her. "Not just antibiotics. He can diagnose and everything. He can't do surgery, 'cause he doesn't have an operating room, you know, but other stuff... he's really good."

"This is Helen," Darius introduced, gesturing toward her.

"Why doesn't he have a practice like anyone else? Or work at the hospital?" Kenzie demanded.

"He wants to help the people who really need it. To take care of people who would fall through the cracks otherwise. I've seen him help people. He really cares what happens to us," Helen explained.

Kenzie looked at the others in the group, inviting them into the conversation. "You all know him? You've all used him?"

They didn't all answer, but Kenzie thought she could discern affirmation in some eyes but a negative response in others. Pretty much split down the middle.

"I dunno," Kenzie displayed her reluctance. "Where does he work? How much does he charge?"

"It's all free," the leader told them. He jerked his head, flipping long hair out of his eyes. "He doesn't charge anything. He helps anyone who needs it. It's like... street medicine. Like a mobile clinic, only..."

"Where is he? He works out of a van?"

"No," Darius explained. "He's got a car—well, a van, yeah—but he doesn't have a bed inside or anything like that. He doesn't treat people inside there; he's just got his equipment and stuff, and it's his wheels. He goes where people are, and treats them there. Like an old doctor doing house calls, right? Except... we got no houses."

"I don't want to meet him in some back alley."

"It's safe. It isn't like that. He'll treat you where you are. If you've got a shelter or a tent, or a house, whatever. If you don't got nowhere, he'll find something. A hotel room or an empty house. Somewhere clean and safe."

Kenzie doubted that all of the treatment sites were completely hygienic. But then, the worst infections were the antibiotic-resistant strains people contracted at the hospital.

She looked at Zachary, then back at Darius.

"How do you get ahold of him? If I want to see him, how can I? I can't just... wait for him to come around somewhere."

"We can put the word out. There are certain people who are...

in the know. We'll get word to him. Get together others who need to see him, because he wouldn't want to come for just one person, just one antibiotic prescription."

"And then he'd come? If there were enough people for him to see?"

Darius and the others nodded. Kenzie pondered this. If that were true, that he tried to only come when there were enough people to make it worth his while, then others might have seen what had happened to Jack. Other people might have been around when it happened.

Unless he had known that Jack's condition was serious enough, it had demanded his immediate attendance, regardless of whether anyone else needed him.

Who were the people who knew how to get him? Who knew his phone number?

"Is he really any good?" she asked doubtfully. "There must be... a reason he doesn't have his own office."

They exchanged looks. Darius and Helen frowned and scratched their heads.

"Doctors can't cure everything," Helen pointed out. "Sometimes it doesn't work out, but that's true of any doctor."

"Or there are side effects," another girl contributed, looking away and not meeting Kenzie's gaze. She was a redhead, quite young, but with old eyes. "Stuff that... you didn't know would be a problem. A doctor can't know all of that stuff. People have side effects, right?"

Kenzie nodded slowly, but something in the girl's eyes made her wonder if she was just talking about side effects or if something else was going on. "What kind of side effects?"

"I don't know... maybe allergic reactions or something... like a brain thing. Like a brain fog or not being able to remember what happened."

"What happened? Like at his office? At the appointment, I mean?" Kenzie pressed.

"Yeah. Like when you're at the dentist and they give you the gas, then you can't remember what happened after, right?"

"I thought he didn't do anesthesia."

They all looked at her.

"You said he didn't do surgery because he doesn't have an operating theater," Kenzie pointed out. "So why would he be giving anyone anesthetics?"

They looked at each other and didn't have an answer to that.

22

"I would be really suspicious—" Kenzie started, then realized that she was falling out of the role that Zachary had set up for her. She was not the medical examiner. She was not a medical professional. She was a woman in a vulnerable position, seeking help from people she didn't know, having to rely on them for what they knew about the mysterious doctor. "I mean... I don't want to go to this doctor and not know what happened to me. I just want antibiotics, not some... weird encounter with the guy."

"If he's just giving you antibiotics, he doesn't need to give you anything else," Helen assured her, with a quelling glance at the redhead. "Maybe examine you, but he doesn't need to give you anything to... help you relax, or anything."

Kenzie pulled on Zachary's arm. "Do you think this guy is kosher? This doesn't sound right."

"Things are done differently out here. You need to be willing to do things differently. To work with people who are... maybe they don't fit into the normal system. Maybe they are... eccentric or do things differently. You're not looking for someone who does things the same way. Right?"

"I just want..." Kenzie held her arms over her stomach, as if feeling cold. "I want someone who will give me what I need without..." She looked at Darius and the others.

"Without leaving a trail," Zachary suggested. "We don't want anyone who is going to tell people where to find us, tell them our business. Medical care is supposed to be private, but then you have doctors reporting to social services or the cops, and that shouldn't be allowed, right?"

The others were nodding. They understood what it was to fear authorities, to know that, no matter how bad things got, they could always be made worse by some bureaucrat who thought he knew better and thought it was his place to control other people's lives. The counselor who decided someone was a danger to himself or others. The social worker who thought a child was in danger when everything was perfectly fine. The doctor who knew better than the patient what she needed, or started asking questions about legal matters that were a person's private business and not anyone else's.

"The Night Doctor isn't like that," Darius assured them. "He wouldn't tell anyone anything. He doesn't need to know your real name or where you come from."

Which meant that he wouldn't be able to access a patient's medical history, with previous treatments and diagnoses and what adverse reactions he might have had in the past. Only the little he managed to get out of them when they met.

"Can we talk to *you?*" Kenzie nodded to the redheaded girl who had made the comment about brain fog and forgetting what had happened at an appointment. "Just you by yourself?"

The redhead looked at the rest of the group, asking questions with her eyes and body language. Kenzie didn't move and didn't look at Zachary, not wanting to give herself away. He was better equipped to understand what was being communicated and give her whatever reassurance she needed.

"I don't know you," the girl said, shaking her head. "You guys just show up here today, looking for help. I've never met you before."

Zachary nodded and started to turn away from the group.

Maybe reminding them that they were the ones who had called Zachary and Kenzie over and initiated the discussion, pushing to find out what they wanted. It hadn't been their idea.

Kenzie experienced a moment of panic. She didn't want to separate from the group when she felt like they were just starting to get answers. But she had to trust that Zachary knew what he was doing and was more experienced in getting answers from people and dealing with distrustful street people than she was. She allowed him to steer her away from them, to return to the course they had been following along the street before they were stopped. They had taken just a few steps when they heard someone following. Kenzie looked back to see the redhead, who wasn't ready to let them just walk away.

Zachary kept Kenzie walking when she would have stopped to resume the conversation. They put a few more steps between them and the group.

"There's a place up here," the redhead murmured. "We can get coffee."

She moved in front of them and led them a block further to a street vendor at the edge of a park selling baking and fancy designer coffees to the wealthier businesspeople who could afford to throw away money for such things. He looked up at their approach and nodded. When they reached him, he pulled a few cups from the lower shelf in his cart and handed them over. No money changed hands, and the young woman led them away into the park.

"I'm Venice," she told them. She sniffed at the coffee and took a sip. "Sometimes people make an order and then don't want it or say something is wrong with it. They changed their mind or forgot to say to use soy milk or whatever." She shrugged. "Moth doesn't like to have to just dump them out. So he hangs on to them until they get cold, in case someone else wants them."

"Moth?" Kenzie repeated.

"I forget his name, like Mothershead or something like that. He's a good guy. You never know what you'll get, but they're always good." She sipped her coffee, then wiped a bit of foam from her lip. "Mmm."

Kenzie tried her coffee, which was still hot, but cool enough to drink, and she tasted notes of vanilla and cinnamon. It *was* pretty good, even if it wasn't something she would have ordered. Zachary's expression was comically tentative as he brought his up to his lips as if he were afraid someone had spat into it or might have slipped him poison. He tipped up the cup and nodded.

"Mmm," he agreed, "it *is* good."

Kenzie suspected he hadn't even tasted it. He was just playing a part. They were all getting to know each other, sharing an interesting experience, having a drink together, bonding over it. Something that would get them closer to the answers they were looking for.

"So," Kenzie reintroduced the subject a few minutes later as they walked through the park and sipped the rejected coffees. "This guy, this Night Doctor…"

Venice nodded. "Everybody says how good he is," she said. "And how lucky we are that he comes around, that he's willing to do stuff for us. Make 'house calls' like an old-fashioned doctor." She laughed. "Only without the house."

Kenzie chuckled over this as well, waiting for more. "But he's not as good as they say he is?"

"I think he's good. He's really smart and he helps a lot of people. Does more good than the mobile clinic," she rolled her eyes, "or the missions that come with blankets and medical supplies sometimes."

Zachary nodded encouragingly. "Sometimes people have to take things into their own hands. Break away from the bureaucracy, cut through all the red tape, and just give people what they need."

"Yeah. Exactly. He doesn't sit around waiting to see what they'll let him do. He's there, getting his hands dirty, doing what needs to be done."

"I hope his hands aren't really dirty," Kenzie muttered.

"No." Venice gave another nervous laugh. "Of course not. He's always very good. Scrubs up, changes gloves, stuff like that. I don't think…" she trailed off.

They kept walking, kept sipping their cups of coffee. Eventually, she spoke again.

"But no one wants to talk about the other stuff. Not to outsiders, especially. I hear things sometimes, and I think... he's not quite as lily-white as they say he is. I think maybe he's doing it for other reasons."

23

"What kind of things?" Zachary asked.

Venice glanced at him and scratched the back of her neck. "I think sometimes he makes mistakes. Maybe he has a problem. Like, a drug problem or something."

Kenzie swallowed. That would explain his operating outside of the law. Not having a private practice of his own with a clinic to work out of and staff and all of the things that went along with that. She didn't say anything, letting Venice think about it and feel her way along.

"Sometimes, things don't turn out so well, and people have to go to the hospital or they get worse."

"That happens to regular doctors, too," Zachary pointed out.

"Yeah. Sure, I know that. But it isn't just that. There's also... people who disappear."

Kenzie stopped abruptly. Zachary was walking close enough to her that he collided with her side and grabbed her to stabilize both of them, apologizing. Venice took another step or two before realizing that they had stopped and turned to see what had happened to them.

"People who disappear?" Kenzie demanded.

"I mean, not people who just needed antibiotics," Venice

assured her. "Most of the doctoring he does, stitches and antibiotics and all of that stuff, it's perfectly fine. But I had a friend, a guy I knew when I first got to Roxboro. He had a disease, something to do with his blood, and I knew he had been to see the Night Doctor. And then… he was just gone. No one knew where. I asked around, and they said he must have just taken off, left town for something else."

"But you don't think so," Zachary suggested. He stood with the cup of coffee in his hand, seemingly forgotten.

"I never heard anything else about him, and there's lots of talk between street people, lots of gossip. Even if someone goes to another city, you still hear back now and then."

"That's pretty scary."

"Sometimes it happens. Things happen to people. You know how it is on the street. People disappear and you never know what happened to them. But then there was another girl who went to the Night Doctor to have her baby. Or he came to her, I mean, because she was having trouble with it. And… I wanted to know what had happened. No one said whether she was okay or if the baby was okay. I wanted to know, but no one could say."

"There wasn't anyone else with her?" Kenzie asked. "A friend or doula or something?"

"I don't know. Any time I asked about it, people just said to let it go, not to talk about something that was going to get people in trouble."

"Get who in trouble? The Night Doctor?"

"I don't know who else would be in trouble. And he could only be in trouble if something had gone wrong, right? But I never knew what had happened. No one would tell me."

"What do you think happened?"

"The baby must have died or something. But I don't know what happened to Trisha either. So… what happened? Did she and the baby both die? Did he take them somewhere else where they were safe? Or did he have the baby taken away? Or did she give it up for adoption? But I never saw her again and I don't know where she went."

"She just disappeared. Like the guy."

"Yeah." Venice took a drink, staring off into space. "So you can see why I wonder about him. I think he does some stuff really well, but he might screw up too. And maybe people are covering it up because they don't want him to stop coming. They still want him to keep helping out. So they don't say anything about this other stuff. Hush it up."

"And you had a bad experience with him too. This brain fog or amnesia about what happened when he treated you."

"I don't know if it was a bad experience. I was okay. But I couldn't remember what had happened for, like, a day, and I've never had that going to a regular doctor."

"Did he give you something? What did you go to him for?"

"I hurt myself. Uh… broke my arm. He said he would look at it and might be able to set it if it wasn't busted up too badly. It didn't have a bone sticking through the skin or anything like that."

"And then what happened? Did he have an X-ray machine? Did he set it?"

"He set it. I… don't know what kind of equipment he had, whether there was an x-ray machine. I don't remember any of that."

"He must have given you something."

"A painkiller. And then… I don't remember anything that happened after that clearly. Not until the next day, when it was all done, and I was back on the street. I don't remember what happened in between."

"Did you have anyone with you? Who else was there that he treated that day?"

Venice looked at Kenzie through narrowed eyes, clearly suspicious of the questions.

"Darius said that he likes to have several people to treat at once. You get them all together so that he can be efficient and treat them all at the same time," Kenzie reminded her. "So… were you the only one he treated that day? Or were there others who might remember what happened?"

"There were others," Venice said warily, "But they don't want to talk about it. Don't you think I have asked about it? I didn't want to find out that the guy had messed with me or something, but I still wanted to know."

"And they wouldn't tell you?" Zachary asked.

"They answered. They said it was nothing. I went in, he set it, and nothing weird happened. I just couldn't remember for some reason. Maybe I was in shock from the break."

"Were you?" Kenzie asked.

"No! I remember him—I remember it getting broken. And walking over there so he could look at it. And I remember sitting down with the other folks to wait for my turn. And then… that's it. The next day, everything was back to normal…"

"And they didn't think that you had been behaving strangely? Before you started to come out of the fog?"

"They thought it was just from the painkillers. I was doped up so that he could work on it. I went with the others. They kept an eye on me and let me sleep off the painkillers." Venice shrugged. "It was nothing. Right?"

"Maybe," Kenzie said. Roofies? Ketamine? Maybe she had just been doped up on morphine or codeine. Even fentanyl. It wasn't unheard of for someone to not even remember what they had done while on a strong painkiller. They had told her that the Night Doctor didn't have a surgery, and didn't work with an anesthetist. She couldn't imagine that he would have set her arm without doing an X-ray first, but he couldn't have taken an X-ray machine everywhere he went. Had he taken Venice somewhere else for an x-ray and nobody wanted to fill her in on the details? "How has it been?"

The woman looked at her blankly.

"Your arm that he set. Did it heal properly?"

"Yeah. It was good." Venice held out her right arm, coffee held in her left, and displayed it, rotating it and bending it to show that she had full range of motion. Kenzie could not see any imperfections, nor were there any surgical scars. Just a simple break, non-surgical. Maybe he had set it without an x-ray, assuming that it was not displaced, or feeling the bone while Venice was under the influence of strong painkillers to ensure that everything was correctly aligned. It could have happened the way her friends had told her. Or not.

"Do you know other people who don't remember what he did? Are you the only one?"

"There are others… but nobody seems to care about it. No one wants answers. They just want to keep everything quiet."

"So that he keeps coming."

"Yeah." Venice finished drinking her coffee and threw the cup into the closest garbage can. Zachary walked over and deposited his after it, not throwing it. Kenzie suspected it was still full. She had another sip of her coffee, but it was getting too cold to drink.

"I'm not saying he's a bad guy or a bad doctor. He's always treated me just fine. I haven't had any bad reactions—other than that brain fog—no infections or allergic reactions or anything. So I say he's a good guy. He does what he says he will. I just don't know about the secrets. I don't like secrets."

"Do you know his name? Even a clue. Someone who calls him by a nickname, or someone mentioned a first or last name in passing…"

"No."

"Does he have any staff? A nurse or assistant that he brings with him?"

"No. Sometimes he needs an extra hand, and he'll recruit another patient. Like to help hold someone's arm still so that they don't keep jerking away from the needle."

"Or to keep an eye on you until you weren't feeling foggy anymore."

She nodded.

"Who calls him? Someone has a number for him."

"I don't know."

"Darius?"

"No, I don't think so."

24

They were both quiet after separating from Venice. Kenzie pondered the news of the Night Doctor, sifting through her thoughts and impressions about him.

The homeless that he served clearly needed someone on their side. There were many services they could not access for one reason or another. Limited hours during which they could access a doctor, overflowing waiting rooms, lack of money or insurance, no fixed address, and all of the other difficulties that came with homelessness.

But people disappearing? The possible use of memory-altering drugs? What was the Night Doctor up to?

"What do you think?" she asked Zachary finally.

"Do I think he's the savior of the homeless in Roxboro? Or a sinister villain?"

"Either one. Or what percentage of each? I can't see him clearly. Is he a good guy, trying to help the marginalized?"

"Sure. But is he perfect?" Zachary shook his head. "Operating without any oversight... that's the problem, isn't it? And if he is an addict, or making mistakes, or making people disappear..."

"Why would they disappear? Or if he made them disappear,

then why not Jack Lane? Why dump him where he would be found instead of getting rid of him?"

Zachary considered. "Maybe the ones who disappeared weren't killed or trafficked. Maybe they were moved to somewhere good. Maybe he found places for them to help them get back on the road to recovery."

"Then why the secrecy? Why not make it known that's what he was doing? Make people see he is trying to help in every way he can?"

Zachary considered. "Maybe the demand would be too great. He'd have people trying to get him to help them, too, to find them places. And he couldn't find everyone places."

Kenzie didn't think that was the case. It was a nice idea and might allow her to put the worry aside for a while, but it was a fairy tale. Something intended to make her feel better even though it wasn't true.

"If this guy is even partially what Venice suspects he is… we'd better find him. And put a stop to it before he puts someone else in the ground," she said after a while.

"You think that he screwed up when he treated Jack? That he should have done something different?"

"I think he should have gotten him to the hospital where a team could have taken care of him, but that doesn't mean he did anything wrong. I think he provided all the support he could, but it probably just happened too fast for him to even evaluate, and it was too late to save Jack."

Kenzie spent a restless night trying to decide what to do. She had a lot of avenues to pursue, everywhere from writing up her preliminary report and setting the file aside until she got the lab tests back and could finalize it, to going out and doing more investigating or even sounding alarm bells to warn other agencies about the possible danger in the homeless community.

She decided to approach Detective Samuels and give him the

information she had in the hopes that he would be able to advance the ball down the field. He had the training and the resources for such an investigation.

"Dr. Kirsch." Detective Samuels sat behind his desk and leaned back with a long shriek from the springs in his chair. He indicated a mug of coffee he had set out for her beside a stack of files on his desk. "Yours. How can I help you today?"

"I wanted to give you a heads-up on the Lane case. There have been some… developments."

"Okay. Enlighten me. You found something else since we last talked? Did you talk to the man who called in the body?"

"No. It was a fake number."

He shrugged with one shoulder. "Not surprising. Even if he gave us a real number, he probably would have dumped the phone once he thought about it."

She was irritated that he hadn't followed it up himself and was so casual about it. But for him, dealing with people who did not want to be called back was perfectly normal. It was the usual state of affairs.

"So that's it, you aren't going to try to find him?"

"Is there a need to find him?"

"He might know more of what happened to Jack than he told you at the scene."

"And you think he would want to tell me this additional information? Or to tell you?"

"Sometimes people can be persuaded to tell what they know."

"Sometimes," Samuels allowed. He stretched and returned his chair to an upright position. "Is that everything?"

"No. I have been talking to the shelter, the clinic, and some of the homeless people in the area."

"Have you? Find anything useful?"

"There is a man who has been treating the homeless, who goes by the name of the Night Doctor."

"That's dramatic."

Kenzie agreed. She couldn't very well argue that. The doctor had a flair for the dramatic. He liked to view himself as a romantic figure. The anonymous patron. A light in the darkness. Service in the sewers. Control over life and death. A psychologist would probably have a field day digging into his personality.

"Some of the stuff he is doing is very routine and probably beneficial, and some of it would not even require a medical license. But there are rumors of problems with some of the procedures he has performed, and if he doesn't have a valid medical license, they would be illegal for him to perform. And, of course, prescribing drugs requires a license."

"Do you have any leads on his identity? A name, maybe? Description? License plate of his vehicle?"

"No. I think he is pretty careful to remain anonymous. No one I met talked about him by name. Someone knows how to get ahold of him when he is needed, to set up a time and place to treat people, but they wouldn't tell me who it is. The homeless are a pretty closed community. They don't trust new faces."

"I could have told you that."

Kenzie rolled her eyes. "I knew that too. I was still hoping we could get more information from them... but no luck yet. Just... rumors and whispers. I'd like to meet the guy. Or at least see a picture of him. I want to know if he is really a doctor or not."

"My guess would be yes, but there have been known to be people who masquerade very successfully as doctors, even surgeons, when they never spent a day in medical school."

Kenzie shuddered at the thought. There was so much to learn as a doctor. She couldn't imagine doing it without the proper training.

"Well, let me know if you get any closer to identifying him. Any identifying information at all would be appreciated. And, of course, if you can tie him definitively to Mr. Lane's death..."

"We did find a witness who said that the Night Doctor was the one who treated Lane before he died. That he gave Lane a blood transfusion, but he died shortly after."

"You said he lost a lot of blood, so that sounds like a logical treatment. And it explains the IV."

"Yes. But I'm not convinced that the person we talked to was actually an eyewitness. She might have just repeated what someone else told her."

"Either way, it does sound like this Night Doctor was trying to treat Lane. Maybe he was just too late."

Kenzie nodded her agreement. "Jack was in pretty bad shape. I don't know if anyone could have done anything to save him. Other than rewinding five or ten years."

Kenzie returned to the medical examiner's office after her meeting with Samuels. She had hoped that he would have made some progress on the case, and was disappointed that he did not seem too interested in pursuing the case. It was a refrain she had heard repeated too many times—that the police were not interested in following up on the deaths of the indigent. That beautiful white, wealthy victims ended up in the media and others were swept under the rug.

Kenzie was determined that every one of their "guests" would be treated the same way, with the same respect and the same effort put into finding out what had killed them, allowing law enforcement to bring the responsible party to justice, in the case of homicides. She wouldn't just look the other way.

"I'm missing a couple of preliminary reports from you, Kenzie."

Kenzie had been staring balefully at all of the emails that had piled up in her inbox and hadn't even seen or heard Dr. Cook's approach. She startled, nearly knocking over her water bottle. It was a good thing it had a spill-proof lid.

"Sorry," Dr. Cook apologized, smiling.

"I don't know where I was. Yes, I'll get those to you by end of business today."

"We can't afford to spend all our time and attention on one case. We need to keep all of them moving forward."

He had, of course, noticed Kenzie's extra time and attention being focused on the Lane file. Even though that effort had not resulted in much progress.

"I know. It's just that this one has a few intriguing points that I think if we can clear up, we will have a better picture of what killed him."

"Alcohol killed him. That is clear. His body was so ravaged by alcohol, no one could have preserved his life. Another day, a few hours, even minutes... I doubt anyone could have squeezed out any more time. He had come to the end of the line."

Kenzie sighed. "You're right, of course. If it wasn't one thing, it was another. All of his systems were failing."

"Yes. We're not looking at murder here. I agree that it was unfortunate he was dumped unceremoniously in a back alley as he was. We expect people to show greater respect than that, especially doctors. But that doesn't change the fact that nothing could have been done for him. It is our job to determine cause of death; the police are the ones responsible for any charges for things like improper handling of a body."

"I'll get those other reports written up."

"Great. If I can approve them, we can get them out the door. We don't like things to get piled up in here, do we?"

Zachary would have had some kind of wisecrack at that, but Kenzie couldn't think of anything in the moment.

25

Kenzie's phone started to vibrate. Even though she was supposed to be spending couple's time with Zachary, Kenzie reached for it and flipped it over so she could see the face and the caller ID. Just in case it was something important. She shouldn't have to cover a callout, unless Dr. Cook had already been called to another scene. Or it could be Dr. Cook himself with something she needed to look after as soon as she got to the office, or an update from Detective Samuels.

Unlikely, maybe, but still possible.

The white lettering across the screen declared UNKNOWN CALLER.

Kenzie reached over to dismiss it, but it stopped by itself. Maybe a wrong number.

She watched the phone screen for a minute to see if a voicemail message popped up, but it remained blank. She turned her attention back to Zachary, who was waiting for her to answer the trivia question on the card he held. She had no recollection of what he had asked.

"Crank call?" Zachary asked.

Kenzie shrugged. "I get a lot of 'unknown callers,' but I'm not on duty. I don't need to answer them. Unless they leave a message. An important message."

"You're getting a lot of them?" he asked, brow furrowed.

"Not *a lot*," Kenzie amended. She didn't need to give him something else to worry about. "I get unknown callers because a lot of the police and other official numbers don't show who is calling. So, it doesn't necessarily mean it's a spam call when it's directed to the medical examiner's office. And, of course, the detectives and law enforcement officers I deal with have my cell number. So I get a good number of unknown callers, but they aren't spam calls."

"Have you had more the last few days?"

Kenzie shook her head and tried to determine whether she had received any more than usual.

The thing about the calls she got from law enforcement was that they left messages or talked to her. Spam calls were another story. Sometimes they were robocalls, with an automated voice warning her of the dire things that would happen if she didn't respond. Others were a few clicks and a hangup. They were not as likely to leave voicemail messages.

And there had been an increase in those spam calls lately. But they often came in bunches, where she would get a lot for a few days and then nothing for a few weeks.

"Maybe," she admitted with a shrug. "But it certainly isn't anything that I worry about. No more than I do about spam emails. They just get trashed."

"But it *could* be something."

"What?"

"It could be someone trying to track your movements. Even if they haven't managed to get a tracker onto your phone to spit out its location, they could be tracking your pick-up habits. When you're at the office, you pick them up, and when you're at home, you don't. They can call to see which you're at. If you do answer it, they can analyze the background noise. If they have a StingRay or dirtbox, they can find all the phones broadcasting in a certain area and trace them."

Kenzie raised her brows. "Why would anyone be trying to track my movements?"

"I don't know. But you have to consider these things. The technology is there. It's not even hard for criminals to get their hands on. If you know where to look, you can download the instructions to build your own."

"No one is trying to track me," Kenzie assured him. "It's just a spambot."

"You share your location with me."

"Yes."

"Do you share it with anyone else?"

The question had never come up before. They had each agreed to share their location with the other to reduce misunderstanding and stress if they couldn't reach each other. And to discourage Zachary from parking in front of his ex-wife's house. But the question of whether anyone else could access the same information had never come up.

"Well... Walter. We share with each other since... you know."

Since she had been snatched off the street. And since he had gone missing. They each felt better knowing where the other was.

"What about you?" Kenzie returned. "Who have you shared yours with?"

His cheeks reddened. He had probably not intended her to turn the question back on him.

"Uh. Tyrrell and I share with each other. And I share with Dr. Boyle."

There was a period at the end of his sentence, and yet something unfinished still hung in the air between them. Kenzie cocked her head.

"And who else? Bridget?"

"No. Not anymore."

"And are you still tracking hers?"

"She never shared her location with me through one of those apps."

"But you had other ways to track her. You put a tracker on her car."

"Once," he admitted uncomfortably.

"And you know her routine. Where she is likely to be on any particular day or time."

"I used to. Her routines are different now. With Gordon and the twins, it's completely different."

"And you know what her routine is now?"

"No. Sometimes. Sometimes I see her car. But I don't have a tracker on her."

"And have you ever used one of those... StingRays?"

"I've... yes, I've used the technology. But it's not strictly legal."

"To track Bridget?"

His face turned a deeper red. "No. Not for personal use. Only for cases. And only if there was no other way to track or surveil a suspect."

Kenzie looked at him for a moment, trying to decide if he was telling her the truth. Eventually, she nodded. He seemed sincere. And he had told the truth before when faced with questions about stalking Bridget, electronically or otherwise.

Zachary looked out the window into the darkness illuminated at intervals with streetlights.

"What was the question?" Kenzie asked.

He turned back to her, frowning. "What question?"

"The game." She indicated the card still in his hand.

"Oh... yeah." He looked down at it. Then his eyes flitted back to the window again. "Are you expecting a delivery?"

"No." Kenzie refrained from pointing out that not every delivery truck that stopped on their street was destined for her house. Again.

Zachary stood up to get a better vantage point and watched the street. "He's coming here."

"Well, maybe *you* ordered something."

He was far more likely to forget about something he had ordered online than she was. Though Kenzie could admit to one or two orders slipping her mind, especially if they had long delivery windows.

Zachary took another step toward the window, shaking his head.

"He's not in uniform. The van doesn't have a logo on it." Zachary picked up a pair of binoculars from his laptop bag and focused on the van parked a door down. The driver of the car didn't go to the neighbor's house, though. He was coming up the sidewalk to Kenzie's house, as Zachary had said.

Kenzie tamped down the anxiety she felt at a stranger coming to the house at night without warning. *Had* he been the one to call her phone, checking to see if she was home? She walked toward the front door and brought up the feed from the outdoor camera on her phone.

"Do you want me to call the police?" Zachary asked. "The security company?"

The man looked toward the front door camera, smiling, and looked down at the object in his hand. His phone? A package?

Suddenly, she knew his face.

26

Kenzie hurried to the door and threw it open before he reached the doorstep. He was startled, but his face broke into a happy grin when he saw Kenzie standing there.

"Simon!" Kenzie exclaimed. She gave him a quick, enthusiastic hug, "It's been forever! How are you?"

"I'm doing well."

Kenzie ushered him into the house.

"And how is Kenzie?" Simon inquired, "Or should I say, the eminent Dr. Kirsch?"

Kenzie laughed. "Working from a basement? I don't think eminent is the right word."

"You make it sound like a dungeon. The position of assistant medical examiner is not exactly Igor."

Zachary was standing worriedly in the doorway of the living room as they came down the hall and entered. Kenzie smiled to show that there was nothing to be concerned about and ushered Simon into the room.

"Zachary, this is Dr. Eric Simon. I interned with him."

"Oh." Zachary nodded. He didn't relax as much as Kenzie had hoped with the revelation of their visitor's identity. "It's nice to meet you, Dr. Simon. Kenzie, I think I'll just…" He reached for his closed laptop, jerking his head toward the bedroom. Clearing out so he wouldn't be in the way while she talked to her old friend.

"No, no. Stick around. I'd like you to get to know each other."

Zachary hesitated, then sat down, watching Simon with some suspicion. Kenzie ignored his attitude. Zachary was on high alert because he had been talking about someone following or stalking Kenzie, and then someone had pulled up to the house. He now associated Simon with stalking, even if consciously he accepted him as a family friend. It wasn't that easy to shake away the anxiety.

Kenzie sat on the couch next to Zachary, allowing a buffer zone between them, and motioned for Simon to take the easy chair.

"So, what have you been doing?" she asked Simon. "I haven't heard anything."

He told her about his family and job, confirming that both were doing well. He was an established doctor and made a comfortable living.

"So, what brings you by?" Kenzie asked eventually.

There was no point in pretending that he had just stopped by to see her because he missed her or was wondering what she had done with her life. He already knew that she was the assistant medical examiner. Roxboro was a small town, and Vermont was a small state; news like that spread quickly to all corners of the medical community. He had come with a purpose, and Kenzie wanted to get that out in the open from the start.

"I do some work with the mobile clinic," Simon explained. He shifted in his seat and looked at the van parked outside the house. "We serve several towns in the area, going from one to another to provide much-needed medical care to members of the community. Especially the indigent."

"Sure. I've heard of it. In fact… I've heard of it a few times in the last few days. More than I ever did before."

"Yeah. I guess our paths have crossed. I heard about your recent patient, Jack Lane."

"Did you know him?"

"I had run into him on occasion. He didn't usually want any

attention, even though it was obvious he was living a very rough life and was not in good shape. But you cannot make people accept medical care, however much you would like to."

"No. Treating people against their will is... a kind of violation."

"Yes. It is something we do in very few circumstances, with a very limited scope. Psychiatric patients, children of parents who don't believe in modern medicine, unconscious patients."

"And dead ones," Kenzie finished.

"Well, I guess that's true. You don't exactly get consent, do you?"

Kenzie grinned. "No," she laughed. "Not exactly."

They all chuckled. Kenzie thought about drinks. She should have offered Simon a drink right away, but she hadn't suggested something as soon as he came in, and it felt a little awkward to bring it up now. She didn't want to appear to be avoiding the topic of discussion.

"So, being familiar with the homeless population through your work with the mobile clinic, you thought maybe we could talk about Jack Lane? I can't discuss my findings."

"No, I wouldn't expect you to. And I assume that Jack died of one of many of his health issues in relation to alcoholism."

Kenzie shrugged. He could assume whatever he liked. "And maybe you know something about who treated him or what happened in the minutes before his death?"

Simon leaned forward, putting his elbows on his knees. "I wish that I could tell you something definitive. A treatment that I participated in or saw with my own eyes. But that is not the case, so all I can bring you is rumor and speculation."

"That's pretty much all we are getting from the homeless community."

"I'm not surprised. This guy works in the dark."

"This guy?" Kenzie repeated, meeting Simon's eyes.

"The so-called 'Night Doctor.' I know you must have heard of him during your inquiries."

"Yes. He came up. Do you know who he is?"

Simon hesitated. He ran his fingers through his hair. "There are some things that made me suspect someone… but I don't have any proof. No direct evidence, just… things that seemed to point in the direction of a particular person."

Kenzie leaned in eagerly. "Yes?"

Simon was still uncertain. He didn't want to jump right into this. "I don't want to be accused of carrying a grudge or being out to get this guy. We do… have a past. We have not seen eye-to-eye on a number of things, especially in how to administer the mobile clinic. And I… was morally bound to step forward and take a stand on his continuing to practice in light of certain… circumstances."

"Because he was making mistakes?" Kenzie guessed. "Maybe had a substance abuse problem?"

Simon shifted in his seat. "Like I say, I don't want to be accused of throwing accusations around. I don't harbor any ill will against the guy. I'm not trying to take away the last vestiges of his dignity…"

27

Kenzie nodded, impatient for Simon to get on with it and tell her who he suspected.

"I believe the man you are looking for is Dr. Evan Hartfield," Simon said slowly. "His license was revoked a year ago. And I suspect he has now popped up as the 'Night Doctor' despite the fact that he is no longer licensed to practice."

"We wondered whether it was something like that." Kenzie put her hand over Zachary's.

Simon looked curiously at Zachary. "We?"

"Zachary is a private investigator. He has been giving me a hand trying to track down this Night Doctor."

"A private investigator? How interesting! I don't think I have ever met a real-life private investigator."

"He's been an interesting addition to my life," Kenzie said with a smile. "We are making some inroads with the homeless community, but it is difficult to break into. Slow work, building up trust. We know that some people in the community know how to get in touch with the Night Doctor, but I haven't been able to identify who those people are. People say they will pass messages along, but you don't know who they are being passed on to. There are layers of protection..."

"Well, maybe with a name, you'll be able to uncover what has been going on and find out whether he is acting as the Night Doctor."

Kenzie glanced at Zachary. He would be able to get a lot with a name. "What can you tell me about him? About Dr. Evan Hartfield, that is."

"Dr. Evan Hartfield." Simon sat back in his seat. "I don't suppose I could get a glass of water, could I? I'm very dry."

"Of course!" Kenzie shifted to get up, but Zachary beat her, springing up and striding toward the kitchen before she finished shifting her weight.

"I got it."

Kenzie expected Simon to begin immediately, but he waited until Zachary returned with the water and sipped it before starting.

"Evan Hartfield was a smart and very promising student," he said. "I would have predicted great things for him. He had great hands and a brilliant mind. He was a skilled surgeon, and I thought he would have a great career, and we would be hearing a lot about him."

"But something happened," Kenzie suggested.

"You might think there was a single catalyst, but there was not. If I had to point to one thing, maybe it would be the student culture... as far as we have come in our modern methods of training and study, in knowing how the brain works and all of the wonderful technology we have for teaching, research, and study, there is still a 'party culture' from the time young people enter their secondary studies."

Kenzie could well remember it. She had entered medical school later in life than most of her fellow students, and the alcohol and illicit drug trade had been pervasive. Hazing, keg parties, drugs to stay awake and focus, drugs to relax and let loose. Kenzie had already been through her rebellious period, and drugs had never been part of that. She was used to having a glass of wine at the various events she went to at Lisa's request. There had been nights when the party had continued after whatever dinner, gala, or fundraiser Kenzie had attended, but she did not like being hung over the next morning. She had gone back to school as a mature, focused student and had not been interested in wild parties.

"You thought that drugs or alcohol were affecting Hartfield's performance?"

"At first, everything seemed to be fine. I was pleased to have him intern at my practice. He had done very well in school and his hospital rotations. He memorized copious amounts of material easily. He was even-tempered and performed well under pressure. Until he didn't."

"What did that look like?"

Simon sipped his water. "Mistakes came out of left field. Stuff that he knew and had done a hundred times before, he would suddenly miss a step or introduce a new problem. Cut the hepatic artery." Simon closed his eyes and shuddered. "He had no idea what he had done; suddenly there was blood everywhere. He shouldn't have been anywhere near that artery." He shook his head. "Removing the wrong organ. Not realizing a patient was septic. Prescribing the completely wrong medication, as if he was a first-day medical student mixing up two similar-sounding names. A couple of times, the pharmacists caught it and prevented disaster."

"Could it have been something else?" Zachary asked, his eyes bright. "ADHD or dyslexia?"

Simon looked at him. "ADHD is not unheard of in doctors," he said slowly. "In some ways, it can be an asset. But dyslexia? So much reading is required. Not just studying, but reviewing charts, communicating with the other doctors on a case..." He frowned. "I don't think a student with dyslexia could get through the medical program. Unless it was very mild."

"Memorizing is one of the strategies dyslexics use. And there are a lot of text-to-speech options available now. More mature now than they were eight or ten years ago but, even back then, you could buy a text scanner that looked like a highlighter and would read the information to you. But charts and prescriptions would be more difficult, easier to mess up."

Simon pondered, steepling his fingers and staring off into the distance. "Well, that is something I never considered, I have to admit. And there was a definite substance problem. I saw evidence of that more than once. Maybe the two together made him that much more erratic. Dangerous. Using an intern like that, who would make a serious mistake or judgment call out of left field with no warning, and put patients' lives in serious jeopardy… I couldn't allow him to stay in the practice."

"So you bounced him?"

Simon nodded. "Yes. I washed him out. Told the school he was not able to handle the rigors of a practice like mine and that he needed addiction intervention. I was surprised when later, they graduated him and he got his license. They'd had to do a lot of work to get him to the point where they thought he had been rehabilitated and was able to practice safely."

"I don't think I'd be happy to find out that my doctor had a history like that!" Kenzie said, "Do you think they were wrong?"

Simon cleared his throat. "I think subsequent events prove that."

"How could they do that? How could they approve him after all you went through with him?" Zachary questioned.

"Medical schools are concerned with training students to become better doctors, not in vilifying them for making mistakes. A mistake in procedure is seen as a failure of training or as a natural part of the learning process. Once he has completed his training, that will not happen."

Kenzie shook her head. "We have to be much more rigorous in medicine. Protect the patients."

"And allowing someone with substance abuse problems to get through the program seems a little… shortsighted," Zachary added.

"He was rehabilitated," Simon repeated, spreading his hands apart. "What are you supposed to do about that? If he was in recovery, and alcohol and drugs were no longer a problem, you can't hold it against him. It's wiped out. No longer a problem."

"Except that not everyone in recovery is able to stay sober. People slip up all the time. Or sometimes it's more than a slip-up." Kenzie thought about Tyrrell's recurrent binges. What if he had been a doctor? What if he was hitting the bottle again without anyone realizing it? When he had started drinking again, they had both asked him about it, and he had reassured them that he was not. But he had been, and had gone off on a huge binge within a few weeks.

Zachary nodded his agreement.

Simon sighed. "Well, I was told that—rather, I heard through the grapevine that he had gone through some retraining and addiction rehabilitation, and he was able to complete the program. He took an extra year to certify, and I'm sure that must have been an embarrassment to him, but he stuck with it and achieved his goal. So I thought, 'Good for him,' and was impressed that he had stuck it out through all those challenges. I thought it would make him a stronger, more compassionate doctor."

There was silence as he sipped his water, and they considered his story. Kenzie had not yet heard anything to connect Hartfield to the Night Doctor. Was Simon just jumping to conclusions? What else did he know?

28

"So what happened after that?" Zachary asked. "You ended up working with him at the mobile clinic?"

"Yes," Simon sighed. "Now that he's a grown-up doctor in his own right and has a few years under his belt, he ended up volunteering for the mobile clinic, which is one of my babies."

"Simon always had projects," Kenzie told Zachary. "He was always trying out some new thing. Different ways of practicing medicine, new models, reaching out to different populations. Teens, immigrants..."

"Homeless or indigent," Simon agreed with a nod and a slight smile. "We need to ensure that everyone has access to medical care. Everyone, not just those who can afford good care or those who have houses or refrigerators. We need to find ways to overcome those obstacles. So, one of my ventures was the mobile clinic."

"How did Dr. Hartfield manage to get accepted to work there when it was your project and you knew his history?" Kenzie asked. She shook her head. She couldn't imagine his being willing to take Dr. Hartfield on again when he had made such serious errors in the beginning.

"I was not involved in interviewing or accepting volunteers. I left the administrative stuff to my partner, Lilian Grace. So it was a shock to me when I signed on one day and saw my old intern was on with me."

Kenzie imagined that moment and shook her head, smiling a bit.

"How did you handle it?"

Simon gave her a stern look. "I assumed that the school had done its job and that he was a competent doctor who no longer had a substance abuse problem."

"And how was he about working with you, after you had fired him?"

"There was definitely some tension there." Simon gave a rueful laugh. "It was not easy for us to accept each other and just get down to work. But we were there to serve the people, to act as healers for a population that has been marginalized and ignored for a long time. We were both quite passionate about it. So, for the first little while, things went well. We put our differences aside and focused on the people and their needs." He took a sip of water. "And I asked Lilian not to schedule us together unless there was no other choice," he said with a wry smile.

Zachary chuckled. "Good call."

He nodded. "But I started hearing things from the other doctors who worked with the mobile clinic. That Dr. Hartfield had done this or that. Made a mistake that had to be corrected. Or a patient came back with a complaint about how he had handled their case or an adverse reaction or iatrogenic complication."

Zachary's eyes slid over to Kenzie for clarification.

"*Iatrogenic* means something caused by the doctor," she explained. "If he leaves the sponge inside during surgery, prescribes the wrong medication, or infects a laboring mother by not washing his hands. Any kind of injury or disease caused by the doctor himself."

"Ah. Okay."

"So you started to hear things that suggested that Hartfield hadn't been rehabilitated after all," Kenzie summarized.

Simon nodded. "He was a bright student, I freely admit that. A brilliant mind. He could have been a fabulous surgeon. But he made too many mistakes. It wasn't just bad luck or coincidence. He was making some serious errors. The mobile clinic doesn't do a lot of serious procedures. We do wound care, simple orthopedics, prescriptions and renewals, birth control, and consulting on various conditions. We do not do surgical procedures or anything invasive."

He sighed and shook his head. He had another sip of water and drummed his fingers on the outside of the glass.

"You wouldn't think that there would be much opportunity for harm in such a situation, but if you mix up clonidine and clonazepam, it could result in a very serious situation. If you forget to find out a patient's allergens before writing a prescription or advising them to take an over-the-counter product, you could kill them. An infection from an improperly cleaned wound could result in the loss of an eye, limb, or life. A mistake in reading a patient's BGL before administering insulin could result in coma or death."

Kenzie had a suspicion that these were not just random examples. Thinking of Dr. Evan Hartfield treating patients now with no supervision nauseated her.

"So you had him kicked off of the volunteer rotation for the mobile clinic?"

"Yes. But I knew that wasn't enough. He was still practicing medicine and, in his day job, he could do exponentially more damage. I couldn't let him just continue to practice when I knew the kind of harm he was capable of inflicting."

Kenzie nodded in agreement.

"So, after doing the 'right thing' when he was my intern and reporting him... I had to do it again. This time to the medical board." He sighed. "It was not something that I undertook lightly. I felt like I had reported him once before; I had done my job. If the school and medical board thought he was qualified to practice, I had done everything I was required to by reporting him the first time."

"But if you didn't report him, then you were party to the harm he caused."

"I didn't want to be personally liable for what he did. Or for the mobile clinic to be liable for what happened under its auspices. I wanted to grow the program, to get more vans, operate in more communities. I didn't want it getting shut down because of one of Dr. Hartfield's screw-ups."

"Right. Yeah. So you had to fire him as a volunteer and go to the medical board."

"I did. It wasn't pretty. I asked them to keep my name confidential, but these things have a way of getting out. Or maybe Hartfield just knew it was me because it had happened before. Either way... there was lots of noise about how he was going to ruin me and ruin the mobile clinic program. He said he would go to the papers but, of course, he didn't because he would have been outing himself. The story would have ended up being about him making serious mistakes."

They all nodded, reflecting on the situation and where they were now. How to move forward now that they had this tidbit of information.

"What was he like?" Kenzie asked. "I mean... as a doctor, as an employee... did he come across as competent? He must have, or your manager wouldn't have hired him in the first place."

"He's very friendly, very personable. Good bedside manner. Comes across as very competent and confident. I don't imagine any patient would have any second thoughts about letting him perform a medical procedure. Why would they?"

"And how was he to you and the other staff? You said that it was awkward... did the others notice? Did you have to explain what was going on?"

"You know, you would have thought he was my boss, the way he acted. As far as he was concerned, the mobile clinic was his baby. He knew how it should be run. He was... Surgeons are noted for being arrogant. We have to have confidence in ourselves and know that we are doing the right thing, or we would be too tentative to do it. You can't be concerned about what you are doing when you cut into someone. You have to *know* that you are doing the right thing and that you are going to heal them. Or at least give them a chance."

"And sometimes that arrogance shows up in other parts of their life." Kenzie suppressed a smile at this. Surgeons *were* well known for their egos. They saved lives. And they knew they were the only ones who could do it.

"Unfortunately, it does," Simon agreed. "Put three surgeons in the same room to debate an idea, and they will have three different opinions, and none of them will back down or consider any other viewpoint. Dr. Hartfield's vision of the mobile clinic was very different from mine. It didn't matter that I was in charge and he was merely a volunteer. He obviously knew what he was doing much better than I did, and he was the one who should be making the decisions about the clinic's direction."

"And he thought you wanted him out of the way because of that," Zachary suggested. "That you didn't like him having a different opinion and wanted him gone because of it."

Simon raised his brows. "That is very insightful," he admitted. "I don't think he ever considered the possibility that his work was subpar and that the reason I wanted him out was to preserve lives. And to keep the clinic from being sued. He really did think that it was over an old grudge."

29

Kenzie got herself a drink of water from the kitchen and refreshed Simon's. Zachary had a cup of coffee, but it was too late in the day for Kenzie to have caffeine. She settled herself again and turned her attention to the next question, which the discussion with Simon had not yet answered.

"What is it that makes you think that Dr. Hartfield is the Night Doctor?"

Simon cocked his head and nodded, admitting that it was a fair question. So far, all he had done was give her Evan Hartfield's background, and Kenzie couldn't see anything in it that connected up with the man who was now providing medical services to the homeless in Roxboro. Other than the fact that he had been doing the same with the mobile clinic, and had been kicked off of that team and the medical register.

"Well, the timing is one part of it," Simon told them. "The Night Doctor showed up shortly after we released Evan from his duties with the mobile clinic. I heard about his arrival on the scene within days. And I could see he was doing things the way Evan— Dr. Hartfield had been saying that the mobile clinic should do things. I never saw him. He's been quite careful not to show up in the same place as the mobile clinic. As if he knew where and how it was being scheduled. Of course, that *might* just have been observation; it doesn't mean he had prior knowledge."

"Do you have a complex schedule?" Zachary asked.

"No. It is pretty much the same each month."

"And is it posted online so your patients know when you will be there?"

"Yes." Simon shrugged. "Okay, it would be pretty easy for the Night Doctor to avoid us whether it is Dr. Hartfield or not."

Simon ran his thumb back and forth across the arm of the armchair, staring down at it intently. "I have treated a few people after the Night Doctor or heard about what he has done from other patients. It seems like he is making similar mistakes to what Dr. Hartfield made both while he was at the mobile clinic and when he was an intern." He looked up from the chair to Kenzie, meeting her eyes. "I don't want you to think that I am accusing Dr. Hartfield or that I have any proof that he and the Night Doctor are one and the same. I haven't seen or encountered him in person. I have only heard second- and third-hand rumors. But... I figured you having one more lead wouldn't hurt. I don't know how much information you have already. Maybe I'm not telling you anything new."

"We didn't have any tips as to who it might be," Kenzie admitted. "We've been trying to get a name or maybe a phone number for him. But the guy might as well be named the Phantom. We've been grasping at wisps of smoke."

"Well, I hope this is the break you need. When I heard that Jack had been seen by the Night Doctor the very night that he died, I knew I needed to get you what information I could."

"I appreciate it. I wasn't sure where to go next."

"I know it is still under investigation, and you haven't gotten back all of your lab reports yet... but is there anything you can tell me about the cause of death? Did Evan make another mistake? Was it something he did?"

"I don't think so," Kenzie reassured him. "Of course, he should have taken Mr. Lane directly to the emergency room or called an ambulance, but I don't have any evidence that he did anything to cause his death. And the kind of shape he was in… I don't think anyone could have saved him."

"Really?" Simon's voice went up in tone.

Kenzie nodded. "Really. There are several different causes of death right now. Hard to figure out which of them got him first. If you had treated him previously, you probably know what kind of shape he was in."

"Are you, as the medical examiner, asking me for his medical history?" Simon asked.

Kenzie nodded. "Yeah," she said in a firm tone, smiling at him. "Tell me what you know."

"He'd been a hard drinker for a lot of years. He was jaundiced, which indicated liver damage. He complained about black, tarry stools, which indicates internal bleeding. Obviously, the bleeding was not severe at that point, or he would not have lasted more than a few hours."

Kenzie nodded. "Yes, both of those conditions showed up on autopsy."

"And if there were other organ failures, we are probably looking at kidneys, spleen, maybe an aortic rupture or something equally devastating."

Kenzie nodded again. "As I say, I don't think there was much that could have been done, even if the treating doctor had gotten Mr. Lane into an operating room. With how fragile his health was, surgery would probably have failed and he would have just suffered a few more days in pain."

"Well," Simon blew his breath out slowly. "Thank goodness for small mercies. I'm glad Evan didn't kill him. If I were only confident that he wouldn't kill anyone else…"

There was a grim silence as they all contemplated this.

"There's nothing else you can do," Kenzie told Simon. "You've already reported him to the medical board. I guess the only thing left is reporting him to the police. From what I've seen, they aren't too eager to do anything about it."

"Whyever not? He could cause severe harm. Right now, we're just talking about an old alcoholic who would have died in weeks anyway, no matter how he was treated. But he could kill a child. A mother of five. Someone who fled here from a war-torn country who has spent years looking for safety." Simon was emphatic, his voice loud.

"Because right now, they see him as a mysterious but benevolent figure. They don't know who it is, so they don't know if he is licensed. They don't have any evidence he has harmed anyone, and they really aren't looking to rein in some wildcard just because he is secretly treating homeless people."

"Will they do something about it if you tell them who it is and that he is not licensed and might kill someone?"

"I'm doing my best. But you should file a complaint. You're the one with firsthand information."

"But only about his history, not what is going on right now. If I go to them and say I've reported this guy twice and now I want to do it again, they're going to think that I'm just some crank with a grudge against him."

Kenzie rubbed her forehead. "I know, but... someone needs to do it. You're the one who knows his history. Here, let me give you the information for Detective Samuels, he's the one working on Jack Lane's death. I'll give him a heads-up that you're going to call and that he should take it seriously, okay?"

Simon nodded. "Okay. I appreciate that."

30

fter saying goodbye to Simon, Kenzie didn't know whether she was exhausted or keyed up. She felt like she was on the verge of collapse, yet Simon's story ran through her mind continuously. Her brain seemed determined to study it from every angle and analyze every word and shade of meaning, and she didn't think she could sleep for hours.

"Well, what do you think of that?" She asked, sinking back into the couch after seeing Simon out. She settled into the warm spot she had previously occupied and tried to relax her muscles. Zachary watched Simon get into the van and eventually drive away.

"Did you re-arm the burglar alarm?"

"Yes."

"Are you sure?"

Kenzie nodded and met his eyes. "I'm sure," she told him firmly.

Zachary looked out to the street again, head swiveling back and forth.

"Why are you so worried?" Kenzie asked. "I know Simon. He came to share crucial information with me. I'm grateful to him for that. It can't be easy for the poor guy; he keeps having to report

Hartfield, but the guy keeps popping up again; it doesn't seem to matter what Simon does."

"That's his story," Zachary agreed.

Kenzie studied Zachary's face. He was worried, which shouldn't come as a surprise after the last few days. Ever since the meeting with Maria, he had been on the lookout for anyone who might be watching or stalking them. Simon was a magnet for his anxiety.

"What makes you think it might *not* be true?" she asked him.

"It's an unverified story. It could just be what he wants us to believe until... whatever he has planned happens. This might just be a story to keep us looking in the wrong direction."

"*Whatever he has planned?* Like what?"

"I don't know. Maybe something to do with the case. Maybe they want us to relax our vigilance. Maybe something to do with Maria or the homeless population. Why would someone be following her? We don't really know yet. Except that she isn't afraid to reach out to an outsider. Criminal enterprises don't like people who talk and ask for help."

"No one is out to get Maria. She is paranoid. You know what it's like to see danger where there isn't any. She *thinks* someone is following her, but that doesn't make it true."

"She's the one who told you about the Night Doctor. Now you know everything she said is true. She was right about that; what makes you think she isn't right about the rest?"

"Because it was clearly paranoia. You saw the way she was talking and acting."

"She was right about the Night Doctor."

"Yes. She was right about him. And now we have more information from Simon. A possible ID. But you're acting like that is a bad thing instead of a good one."

"You don't know that it is true. You only have his word for it."

Kenzie shook her head. "I know Simon. He wouldn't be lying to me."

"What about the phone calls?"

"What phone calls?" It took Kenzie a few seconds to remember the discussion with Zachary before Simon's arrival. "That was nothing. I get hang-ups and blocked calls all the time. So do you."

"It could have been Simon. Checking to see whether you were home or not."

"He was already in the neighborhood. Why would he come all the way here before checking? And why wouldn't he just call to ask me if I was home? I don't think it was someone trying to track me, and I don't think Simon was trying to track me or verify my location."

"But you don't know that. And you don't know that anything he said tonight was true."

"Well, I should be able to verify some of it," Kenzie said, grabbing her computer.

She opened the clamshell and navigated to her browser window. It only took a few seconds to find the licensed doctors database, where she searched Evan Hartfield's name and found dates for both his license issuance and revocation.

"So that much is true," she informed Zachary.

"But that doesn't tell you anything about him."

"No. But would Simon come here to tell me stories like that about someone? He would know it would come out if he lied to me. Would he ask me to go to the police about it if it was just lies? The repercussions against him would be... I don't know—he could get charged with interfering with an investigation. Libel. It might make the medical board look again at the facts he swore to before when he reported Dr. Hartfield. Why would he want to face all of that? What exactly would he accomplish by telling me a story like that?"

"I don't know. But we can't always see what is right in front of us. Sometimes it takes someone with distance. Some perspective."

31

Kenzie knew that her perspective would be better in the morning. It was always difficult to gauge things at night when she was tired and she didn't know if she might be overreacting because of her fatigue. Things always seemed much bigger and more worrisome late at night when she needed to sleep. She told herself that she would be able to judge better whether she was right about Simon being a concerned citizen just trying to help her out and to make sure that the Night Doctor didn't cause any more harm in the future, or whether he had a grudge against Dr. Hartfield or another reason to lie or exaggerate and implicate him.

Simon had been one of her mentors in medical school. She had interned with him—which had, happily, gone much better than Evan Hartfield's internship—and they touched base occasionally when their paths crossed or one of them wanted to use the other as a sounding board.

She was sure she could say that Dr. Simon wouldn't lie to her about Evan Hartfield. But he wouldn't have any reason to, anyway. The only thing that either of them wanted to do was to protect the public. Especially those who were more vulnerable.

Kenzie had a restless night, tossing and turning and muttering at herself to just relax, stop thinking about anything, and go to sleep. It didn't work, and she arose in the morning feeling like she hadn't gotten a wink of sleep. She felt more tired getting up in the morning than she had been going to bed.

She didn't get into the shower right away, but pulled on her housecoat and went to make some fresh coffee and talk to Zachary.

He had not spent much time in bed the night before. Kenzie knew that her tossing and turning had probably kept him awake. He was not an easy sleeper and only got a few hours every night. He had slipped away from the bed at two or three in the morning, not saying anything to her. If he was lucky, he had fallen asleep on the couch for a couple of hours, away from Kenzie's restless kicking.

Kenzie walked into the living room yawning, caught by surprise by a huge, throat-opening yawn, her mouth wide open and showing Zachary a fine view of her tonsils until she managed to cover the yawn and then force her jaw closed again. A shudder went through her body like the yawn had awakened something deep inside her.

Zachary was grinning when Kenzie closed her mouth and opened her eyes. "Still a little tired?" he guessed.

"Oh, my goodness. I don't think I've ever opened my mouth that wide in my life." Tears squeezed out the corners of Kenzie's eyes, and she wiped them away. "That must have been terrifying," she joked.

"Like looking into the jaws of death," he agreed with a laugh. "Did you get *any* sleep?"

"A few hours, I guess. Not very restful, though. How about you?" She smothered another yawn, forcing her jaw to stay closed this time and breathing the yawn out through her nose.

"I'm not sure how long," Zachary said with a shrug. "I'm okay this morning. You need some coffee? A pot or two?"

"Yes." Kenzie turned toward the kitchen.

"What's in there is pretty fresh. I figured you would be up before long. Grab your travel mug and you can drink it in the shower. I'll get another pot on while you're in there."

"I'll be wired by the time I get to work."

"Hopefully," he agreed.

Kenzie chuckled to herself and did what Zachary had suggested, taking the mug with her so she could nurse the coffee while she showered, dressed, and prepared herself for the day. By the time she was presentable, she was not feeling too bad. Her lack of sleep was not obvious in the image in the mirror. The circles under her eyes were carefully concealed, and she'd had enough caffeine that she was no longer dragging and yawning. She could hear Zachary in the kitchen as she finished getting ready and, when she walked in, he already had out her plate and marmalade and was taking her toast out of the toaster to butter it.

"How are you doing now?" he asked as Kenzie sat down.

"Not bad, actually. I think I'll manage until early afternoon, at least. Then I will have to find something active to do, or I'll fall asleep at my desk."

"Maybe there will be a body to dissect."

"I live in hope."

Zachary chuckled. He watched Kenzie get settled and got a yogurt out of the fridge for himself. He was probably too anxious to deal with the misophonia caused by the noise of the granola bar wrapper, his other go-to choice for breakfast. Maybe later, after she was gone and there was no other activity in the house, he would be able to deal with the pain and anxiety caused by the noise, which was like fingernails on the blackboard to him, only amplified.

"So," he said casually, "Have you already talked to Dr. Cook about the Night Doctor?"

"Briefly," Kenzie assured him. "Obviously, we didn't know who it was at that point, but he thought it was interesting."

"Does he know Dr. Simon?"

"Uh… I have no idea. They have probably run into each other at some point. Vermont is a small place, and the medical community is even smaller. You do tend to run into the same people over and over again. Like Simon did with Dr. Hartfield."

Kenzie took a couple more bites of toast, then raised her brows at him. "Why?"

"He and Hartfield know each other."

Kenzie looked at Zachary, trying to figure out what he was saying. "Who? Simon and Cook?"

"Hartfield and Cook."

Kenzie blinked. "Well... like I said, it is a small community. They could have met. How do you know they know each other?"

"Found a couple of news articles. Did you know that Cook defended Hartfield when he was accused of being a danger to the homeless population he was serving through the mobile clinic?"

"Well, no, obviously I didn't. If I didn't know they knew each other, I didn't know that Cook defended him. What did he say?"

"That the only reason Hartfield was being accused of anything was an old grudge. That he was a good doctor and hadn't done anything wrong. People sometimes have adverse reactions. Medical procedures sometimes go wrong. No doctor is infallible."

"Well... Dr. Cook is entitled to his opinion."

Kenzie was already trying to figure out how to handle this information. How could she go in to work now and tell Dr Cook that they might have identified the Night Doctor, and it was his old friend Evan Hartfield? And worse, that he might have been somehow responsible for Jack Lane's death.

She was still thinking about it, trying to figure it all out, when she arrived at the medical examiner's office. She went about her morning tasks without any thought, working through the familiar procedures by rote. She phoned Detective Samuels and left a message on his voicemail with Hartfield's name. If he wanted to look into the ex-doctor, he could. He had much better resources than Kenzie and would undoubtedly be able to come up with something. She left him Simon's name as well, letting him know that he might get a visit or call from the doctor.

Eventually, she knew she had no choice but to go see Dr. Cook and advise him of the information she had received. It would have to go into her report, so he would see it anyway. Better if she did not surprise him with it or try to bury it in her report in an obscure footnote. She was glad that Zachary had given her advance warning that Cook and Hartfield were friends. This way, she was prepared for him to react negatively to it and would not be taken off guard.

She tapped on his open door as she entered his office. Cook looked up at her.

"Kenzie, I was just going to bring these two preliminary reports out to you. They look just fine. Go ahead and issue them; send copies to the appropriate parties." he twirled his finger to indicate the circulation. "Then those can be put to bed until we get any lab reports back."

Kenzie took them from him. "Great. I'll get them out. I, uh, got some more information on the Jack Lane file. On the Night Doctor...?"

"Uh-huh?" He looked down to flip through the pages of a report, then looked up again. "What did you find?"

"It has been suggested that it might be a former doctor, Evan Hartfield."

Dr. Cook raised his brows. He searched Kenzie's face. "Well, that's a name from the past. Who gave you that information? Is it reliable?"

"Dr. Simon. I interned under him. Apparently, Dr. Hartfield did too. Different years, of course. Dr. Simon had... some issues with Hartfield."

"I'll say he did. Tried to ruin his career. And eventually did, I suppose. It was a nasty business."

"That's too bad. I guess you heard Dr. Hartfield's side of it?"

"He was a good doctor, Kenzie. Really smart. Great bedside manner. Patients liked him. Other doctors were sometimes jealous of how well he was liked. He was just one of those doctors with a magnetic personality, the kind that patients are drawn to."

Like Dr. Cook himself. Kenzie had been surprised at his choice of pathology, where he wouldn't be treating live patients. With his Hollywood good looks and charming smile, she was sure the patients he had treated as he had been training had loved him too. But he had chosen not to deal with them. But then, so had Kenzie. She was pretty. Not Hollywood pretty, maybe, but she knew she was attractive. She related well to people. Her parents could have introduced her to plenty of different contacts, and she could have gotten a good job at the hospital or in private practice. But she had not gone into medicine to treat patients. She had been focused on pathology from the start.

"And you don't think he had anything wrong," she said. "You think it was just a personal vendetta for some reason."

Cook shrugged. "I don't know all of his reasons. I'm not inside his head and haven't talked to him about it. But I know Hartfield, and he's a good doctor who really cares about people and outreach to the poor, especially the homeless. Would you want to shut down someone like that?"

"No. But I guess it would depend on what was going on. If he was doing harm, I would have to say something, even if I didn't want to."

"And what evidence do you have that he *was* doing harm?"

"We don't know what happened in Jack Lane's case. But he did treat him without a license."

"If he did, then he gave a dying man an IV. Is that a crime?"

"No. Well, I don't know all the ins and outs of charging someone with practicing medicine without a license. I imagine the authorities would need more than just giving a patient blood. I don't know what level of involvement it would actually take."

"Nurses and paramedics can give IVs."

"Do you know how to get ahold of him? We should talk to him about what happened. If you are his friend, maybe you could set it up."

"Do you have proof that he did anything improper or caused any harm? Do you have some physical evidence that I don't know about?"

"I have a witness who suggested that it might be him."

"Might be. Based on evidence?"

"Nothing physical. Only circumstantial."

"Then I suggest we leave it alone. See if any other physical evidence comes in. See what the police find. At this point, there is nothing to suggest that anyone did anything that resulted in Mr.

Lane's death. Nothing but what he did to himself. Let's not start a witch hunt. Especially a witch hunt for a man who is dedicated to helping others who have fallen through the cracks and has already been unfairly vilified and harassed."

Kenzie looked for some counterargument, but couldn't find any.

"I would consider it a personal favor," Dr. Cook told her, gazing at her with his dreamy blue eyes. "I'm not going to order you not to do something that is required by your position. But in this case, I think you have plenty of discretion. You have done the autopsy and are waiting for lab results back. You have interviewed witnesses, and no one can point to any wrongdoing being committed."

"There are rumors around the Night Doctor. That he has made mistakes and that he might be a danger to the community."

"The people who know him and have firsthand experience are the ones who are responsible to report any wrongdoing. You are not required to investigate or report on rumors. And you have already attempted to get clarification without any success. I think you have done all that you can. You've told the detective on the case already, haven't you?"

Kenzie nodded. "Yes. He has been updated on everything."

"Then leave it to him to investigate and take any appropriate action."

Kenzie nodded slowly. As much as she wanted Dr. Cook to be outraged at the possibility that his friend was possibly engaged in something illegal, she had to admit that she had done everything that her job or the law required of her.

She could set the Jack Lane file aside until she had all of the tests back. She had done all she could.

32

It was an uneventful day, which was probably a good thing. Kenzie turned her attention to the routine cases she needed to take care of, catching up on her emails and reports, making sure that all forensic samples were appropriately cataloged and sent out for testing. Keeping track of evidence and making sure that all of the files kept progressing until everything had been properly processed. It was tedious, but one of those things that could not be forgotten or put to the side.

She was home in good time, and she and Zachary had a pleasant, quiet dinner together. But as much as she tried to ignore it, Kenzie could see that something was bothering Zachary. He didn't bring up any concerns even when she prodded him for information about his day and how everything had gone.

But the next day was couple's therapy, and she could bring it up and see whether Zachary was willing to discuss whatever it was with Dr. Boyle, his therapist. In the meantime, she would have to accept that he didn't want to bring it up.

She was stretched out on the bed with a book unwinding after dinner, ignoring the fact that she had chores and other responsibilities to attend to. Some days were just not meant for vacuuming and dusting.

"Kenzie?"

She heard Zachary call her from the living room, but pretended she didn't. She didn't want to get up, and it was probably just some random question that had popped into his head, which there was an even chance he would forget in the time it took her to walk from the bedroom to the living room. If she pretended not to hear him, he would forget he had called her and just go on with other things. She would be sure to spend some time with him later, after she'd had some alone time.

"Kenzie!" Zachary was coming down the hall toward the bedroom to make sure she had heard. Maybe someone was coming to the door, or he had a question about the next weekend they were planning to spend with Lorne and Pat.

She looked up as he came through the doorway. His expression was worried, a pronounced frown line on his brow.

"What is it?" Kenzie asked.

"On the TV. You should come see this."

Kenzie grabbed her phone and checked the screen. If there had been a natural disaster or a bad traffic accident, she hadn't been called out to the scene yet. But that could be because it was still too dangerous. A shooting or chemical spill that hadn't yet been cleared.

"What is it?"

"It's about the—you should come see."

Kenzie followed him to the living room, irritated that he couldn't just tell her what it was about. If it was a new pizza joint that offered delivery, she was going to be really upset.

Kenzie positioned herself in front of the TV and looked at the news story that was running. A yellow-on-red ticker declared "Investigation into local charity," and a woman stood under a streetlight on the dark street, the microphone clutched close to her face as she told the viewing audience in dramatic tones that she was looking into the untimely death of a homeless man.

"The gruesome death of a man who had been treated by the mobile clinic is under investigation by the police and the medical examiner's office. Sources say that he had been seen only days before his death by the outreach program spearheaded by Dr. Eric Simon, and indeed may have been seen by Dr. Simon himself."

She widened her eyes at the camera and clutched her coat against her throat as if an icy wind had just raced through the street.

"In another twist, I am told that the investigation by Assistant Medical Examiner Dr. Kenzie Kirsch may be tainted by the fact that her family foundation is one of the sponsors of the mobile clinic."

Zachary looked at Kenzie to see what her reaction was to this report. She swallowed and shook her head, unable to respond.

"Dr. Kirsch, once a student of Dr. Simon, would be unlikely to be an unbiased investigator into anything touching on Simon's brainchild, the mobile clinic."

Kenzie sat down on the couch, her knees weak. A "graphic content" warning flashed at the top of the screen.

"Suspicions were raised by friends of Jack Lane, a homeless man who died after being treated by the mobile clinic. Witnesses say that he was vomiting large quantities of blood and died horrifically in a pool of his own bloody vomit."

Kenzie swore aloud. Zachary sat down beside her and rested his hand on her back. "Where did they get this?"

"I don't know. They got *someone* to talk."

"The circumstances of Mr. Lane's death lead to questions about the efficacy of the mobile clinic, a volunteer-led program that takes patients away from the hospital and legitimate emergency clinics. The mobile clinic does not have the equipment required for emergency situations. They have no sterile surgery, no X-ray machines, and very few medications or supplies on hand. As the mobile clinic travels from town to town, there is no continuity of care, no monitoring of adverse effects or medication schedules. It is a hit-and-run approach designed to treat as many people as possible in a short period of time. They are only equipped to treat minor illnesses and injuries, not serious conditions like Mr. Lane suffered, which should have been treated at the hospital."

"They make it sound like the mobile clinic is trying to provide substandard services," Kenzie said, shaking her head. "Like they're trying to take people away from the hospital instead of treating people who can't or won't get treated there! Simon is implicated in Lane's death because he tried to help him? He must have done something wrong because Lane died? They have no idea what they're talking about."

"I know."

"And I can't even talk to them!" Kenzie seethed, pounding the arm of the couch in frustration. "I can't talk to the media about an ongoing investigation. They must know that!"

The reporter went on:

"Should Dr. Kirsch have declared a conflict of interest in this case, knowing that her family foundation funds the mobile clinic? The Kirsch family foundation has been known to be changing their focus from kidney disease research and other physical diseases that have long been their central interest, to projects related to mental illness and addiction, the homeless, and human trafficking. This new focus is believed to have been at the behest of Dr. Kirsch herself, heir of Walter Kirsch's and Lisa Cole Kirsch's considerable fortunes. Is this the result we can expect? A departure from hard science to half-developed ventures like the mobile clinic, which has been the subject of considerable controversy ever since its launch?"

Kenzie rubbed her eyes and the ridge of her brow, swearing to herself. Her phone started to ring. Texts were coming in at the same time as emails and phone calls, notification after notification flashing across the screen. It would appear that everyone who had seen the report was now reaching out to her.

She didn't know how many would be words of support and how many would be questions of how much of what the reporter had said was true. Surely anyone who knew her would understand that she wasn't involved in some nefarious plot to kill off all of the homeless people who desperately needed care.

She had already felt some backlash from some of the organizations the foundation had cut the funding to. In some cases, the foundation had dropped the donation amount significantly; in others, they had cut off altogether. Kenzie always felt guilty in these situations, but they had to spend the money where they thought it would do the most good, and they had funded kidney research for years. Other causes were desperately in need of the most basic funding.

Kenzie had not called for the new focus on mental health and addiction, but Walter and Lisa had seen how important it was to Kenzie and Zachary. Mental health and addiction issues affected so many people; it was time for those programs to get more attention and for the money to go where it would make the most difference.

Kenzie just stared at her phone for a minute as it buzzed, dinged, and chirped, banners scrolling across the top one after another. She held down the power button until it shut down. She looked at Zachary.

He shook his head. "I'm so sorry!"

"You didn't have anything to do with this, did you?" A knot of dread grew in her stomach. If he had been asking questions or had tipped off the media, and this had been the result…

"No!" Color rushed to Zachary's face. "No, I would never do anything that would hurt you. I just mean I'm sorry it happened to you. You must feel like you got punched in the gut."

"Pretty much," Kenzie nodded and held her arms over said gut. She wasn't sure if she wanted to throw up or to have a big drink. She had anxiety pills and sleeping aids from Dr. Boyle that she had refused to take except when she had been at her very worst. If she took those with a nice glass of wine, she could just crawl into bed, pull the covers over her head, and shut out the world for eight to ten hours. Maybe by that time, things would have settled down.

Of course, they were not supposed to be taken with alcohol, so she would have to forego the glass of wine.

"What do you want to do?" Zachary asked. He muted the TV but did not turn it off. The woman kept standing there talking into her big microphone, her eyes wide with the shock and horror of the story, even though it was nearly a week old.

"I don't know. I don't want to look at Bambi there anymore."

He turned the TV to another channel. Kenzie would have just turned it off, but maybe he was right to look for something else that might interest them and distract them from what had just happened.

Kenzie didn't want to think about it, but she immediately started calculating the impact that news report would have on her life.

She might lose her job.

They had told her before that she needed to be careful that nothing that the foundation did impacted any part of her job as a medical examiner. She needed to be aware of possible conflicts of interest and manage them proactively, giving her boss and her boss's bosses a heads-up so that they could handle things before they hit the news.

This was a major foul-up.

She had been vaguely aware that the foundation gave some money to the mobile clinic, as it did to a number of other charities for mental health, homelessness, and other similar and crossover issues. But she hadn't known until the night before about Simon and the Night Doctor being associated with the mobile clinic, or that the mobile clinic had treated Jack Lane in the days before his death.

It wasn't surprising, but she had not anticipated all of those facts coming together and making it look like she might be involved in something she had nothing to do with.

There was no conflict with the foundation helping the homeless. There was no plot between Kenzie and Simon. Simon hadn't done anything to harm Mr. Lane. He had not been the person who had caused Mr. Lane's death.

How had the Night Doctor and his name not been mentioned in the news report? The reporter seemed to know everything else that related to the case. But nothing about Evan Hartfield.

Now *that* was interesting, wasn't it?

33

K enzie left her phone turned off for the rest of the night. Technically, she wasn't allowed to do that. She needed to be available for callouts if Dr. Cook was not available.

But a callout wasn't an emergency. Roxboro was a small town, and a cop could come to her door if something urgent came up. Or they could look at her personnel record to find her emergency contact and get ahold of Zachary on his phone.

She did not want to talk to anyone. She was unavailable for comment, no matter what the question, until things blew over.

She did not sleep well. But since her phone was turned off, once she fell asleep, she stayed asleep and did not wake up until mid-morning. Looking at the clock, her heart started thumping in panic and anger. Panic because she was so late getting into the office and anger because Zachary had known what time it was and hadn't woken her up. She knew he was awake and knew what time it was, because Zachary never slept that late, even if he hadn't slept in twenty-four hours.

Zachary could clearly see Kenzie's blazing eyes and heavy, barely controlled breaths when she entered the kitchen, where he was refilling his mug of coffee.

"Whoa." He held both his hands up as if she might haul off and punch him. She had never done anything violent around him and didn't think she deserved that reaction. But she knew how he had grown up. He had been in abusive situations for years, so of course his first reaction was that she was going to hit him.

He lowered his hands. "It's okay," he told her. "Everything is okay. I talked to Dr. Cook. You're taking a mental health day. He said he didn't want you to come in. He'd rather stay under the radar for a few days until things settle down. We have our couple's session with Dr. B this afternoon, and if you want to talk through any of this stuff, we can."

"What made you think it was okay to talk to Dr. Cook about me?" Kenzie demanded, barely able to keep her voice in an even, controlled tone.

"Because… you barely slept and were finally asleep. And you need sleep more than anything. I was going to ask Dr. Cook if he wanted me to make sure you were up and into the office as usual, but he didn't even let me ask. He told me right out that you were to take a mental health day today."

"He thinks I'm a nut case. He doesn't think I can handle this."

"No. He doesn't want you in the spotlight. He said things are quiet at the office right now and you can afford to take a few days. If anything important comes up and he needs help, he will call. He has my number, so if he can't get you on yours, he'll call mine."

"I can't believe you didn't wake me up. You should have let me make the decision myself."

"If I woke you up, you wouldn't have been able to go back to sleep even if you wanted to. I was trying to help. You and Heather help me with my ADHD and anxiety. You worry about my sleep. Why can't I worry about yours?"

"Because me working at the medical examiner's office isn't the same as you working for yourself. I have to look good in front of my boss. That isn't something you have to worry about."

"I have to look good in front of my clients."

"It's not the same."

"Would you like coffee?"

He didn't wait for her to answer; he just poured her a cup anyway and handed it to her. Kenzie was still mad and would have liked to throw it back in his face or at least dump it into the sink, but the fact was, she needed it and knew that her anger was out of proportion to what he had done. She had woken up in fight-or-flight mode, and was spitting mad.

Kenzie forced herself to sip the coffee slowly so as not to burn herself. Zachary watched her anxiously, his eyes darting back and forth as he watched for danger and tried to figure out the best way to deal with her.

"Thank you for the coffee," Kenzie said in a controlled voice.

"You're welcome."

"And thank you for the sleep. And for dealing with Dr. Cook. Though I should have done that myself."

"I didn't mind being your secretary for one day."

"If I don't have any obligations, maybe I'll start with a soak in the tub. See if I can calm myself down."

Zachary nodded his approval. "Do you want breakfast before or after your bath?"

"After. And I want waffles."

Zachary's eyes widened. Kenzie always had toast and marmalade for breakfast. Although that had become a much more strict routine since he had moved in. Before that, she had toast and marmalade some mornings, but not all. Zachary had assumed that since it was her usual breakfast, it was what she wanted to eat every day.

"Waffles?" he repeated.

Kenzie could see that he was thinking of homemade waffles cooked in the waffle iron, which would be quite an undertaking for someone who didn't cook.

"Frozen waffles. In the freezer. You stick them in the toaster."

"Oh," Zachary sighed loudly in relief. "I can probably manage that."

"Syrup instead of marmalade. And some strawberries would be nice. Also from the freezer."

He saluted. "Waffles, syrup, and strawberries. Check."

She should have known that the peace and quiet wouldn't last. She didn't get reporters at the door, which she was grateful for. They respected her privacy and simply left polite messages on her voicemail. The call that came through for her on Zachary's phone was not from Dr. Cook, but from her mother. Kenzie had been lucky to avoid her up until then. She would have predicted that Lisa would call her as soon as the news story had aired. She probably had, and it hadn't occurred to her until the next morning that Kenzie wasn't going to turn her phone back on and she should try Zachary's number instead.

"Are you okay, Mackenzie?" she asked, her voice louder and higher than usual. "I imagine you are being harassed by reporters and people asking for money or outraged that a man died."

"I haven't been answering any calls," Kenzie said, "so I don't know who has been calling or what they wanted to say to me. It's much better this way."

"I agree. That was very wise. But you're okay? I have been very worried."

"I probably should have called you last night, but I really wasn't in any shape to talk to anyone. Not even Zachary. I was just a mess."

"I can certainly understand that." Lisa's voice took on a confidential tone. "I have found it very difficult myself. And I have been dealing with this kind of thing for a lot more years than you have."

"Are *you* okay, Mom? Have you been talking to anyone?"

It must be just as hard for her to defend the choices the foundation had made, even if the changes had been necessary and well-thought-out. Even though Lisa had experience with this, that didn't mean it was easy or that she enjoyed it.

"An emergency meeting of the board of the foundation was called this morning," Lisa said with a sigh. The board consisted of a number of very competent people, only three of whom were Kirsch family members. Walter, Lisa, and Kenzie herself. Obviously, Kenzie had not gotten the notice or made it to the meeting. "I had to account for the changes that have been made, even though they were all discussed at the board level before they were implemented. And I had to explain the mobile clinic in particular and to assure them that it was a necessary service and was helpful, not detrimental, to those who use it. They are hoping that when you are cleared to do so, you will be able to tell them about Mr. Lane's death, and whether we need to talk to our insurers about liability in his death."

"No," Kenzie assured her. "Mr. Lane refused to go to the hospital. No one could have made him go. He was a long-term, heavy alcoholic, and no one could have saved him. And… there is more I will tell you when I can, when I have the evidence in place. I can promise you that Dr. Simon and the mobile clinic had nothing to do with his death."

"That is good to hear. I was sure that was the case, but it is good to hear it confirmed. When you are able to speak officially on the matter, I look forward to seeing your full report."

"So you're okay?" Kenzie asked. "That must have been tough, being called on the carpet like that."

"Yes, of course it was difficult. These things are. And many people are not happy with the new direction our funding is going. But even more are calling to thank us and say how much the funding is needed in these areas."

"And Dad's okay?"

"He is fine. I can get him if you want to speak to him. But he is putting."

"Putting?"

"Golf. It's like meditation. I don't like to interrupt it."

"Oh," Kenzie laughed. "Okay. That's fine. I just wanted to make sure he was okay with this. It is his family name, after all."

"He has a much thicker skin about these things than you or I. And… you're okay? You're not at work today."

"No. Decided to take a few days off until this blows over."

Or it had been decided for her.

"That's an excellent idea, dear. I'm sure it will only be a few days, and then you will be able to get back to the routine."

34

It seemed like the morning was gone before Kenzie had had a chance to do anything to take advantage of the day off. She had spent longer on the phone with her mother than she had expected and, between the call, her long soak in the bath, and a late, lazy breakfast of waffles, the morning was gone, and time was marching on toward their couple's therapy appointment with Dr. Boyle.

"Do you want to cancel it?" Zachary asked. "I understand if you don't think you're up to it this week. It hasn't been the easiest day."

"Actually… it's probably a good idea for me to go today. I've spent the morning de-stressing, so I should be able to talk this afternoon about anything that is bothering me. Though I think… it's already all out in the open."

"That will happen when they announce it on the news!" Zachary contributed with a wry smile. "I think you're handling it really well. But maybe I'm not catching your signals."

Kenzie shrugged. "I don't think I'm hiding anything about how I feel. I had a good talk with Mom this morning… and that helped. I haven't actually done anything wrong."

"All you're doing is your job," he agreed. "And I think you're pretty darn good at that."

"Well, thank you for that." Kenzie shook her head. "Keep the appointment. It's too late to cancel it anyway."

"I could still go and do individual therapy if you didn't want to do couple's today."

"True, but I'm okay with it."

Kenzie hoped to bring up Zachary's latest issues rather than her own. He was so jumpy and paranoid that she was on edge any time they were in the same room together. And should they be ambushed by a reporter, she worried what would happen.

It wasn't like Zachary was the hard-hitting, gun-toting PI of TV. She never had to worry about violence from him. But she didn't want him to have a meltdown on camera because he was so wound up with anxiety.

It wasn't long before they headed out like usual to Dr. Boyle's office for couple's therapy. Or not like usual, because usually they arrived separately, Zachary from home, waiting on pins and needles, afraid Kenzie wasn't going to show, and Kenzie from work, her mind filled with all of the job stuff and not quite ready for processing relationship issues. Instead, they arrived together, Kenzie focused, and Zachary... still jumpy and paranoid, but at least not worried that Kenzie would forget about the appointment and not show up.

After a brief wait in the waiting room, they were ushered into Dr. B's office, where she was already sitting at her desk looking over her notes from their last session.

"Thanks for coming. I wasn't sure whether everything would work out, based on... what's been in the news."

Kenzie made a motion to wave this away. "That's just work stuff. It isn't anything to worry about. I took a mental health day today, and it is bound to blow over in a day or two."

The therapist jotted a note on the notepad in front of her. "I'm glad to hear that. So... you haven't found it to be too stressful?"

"It was pretty overwhelming last night, but I've had a chance to process it and, if I just wait it out, I'm sure everything will be fine."

"It won't affect your work?"

"I didn't do anything improper," Kenzie said firmly. "Yes, my family's foundation gives money to the mobile clinic and a lot of other causes in Vermont. The mobile clinic didn't do anything wrong in treating Mr. Lane. There is no indication yet that he died of anything but natural causes. It's just... a tempest in a teacup. A bunch of unrelated facts strung together to make it look like a conspiracy or something... when it isn't. It will all fall apart when the facts are tested."

"And it doesn't bother you that people might think you were involved in something illegal or unethical?"

Kenzie set her jaw and shook her head. "People who know me will know that I wouldn't do that. And people who don't know me... what do I care about that? They'll soon forget about it and go on to the next thing."

"Well, I'm glad it hasn't affected your work. That would be very disappointing. So this isn't something that we need to discuss?"

Kenzie shook her head firmly. She looked at Zachary. "I don't feel that it is. Are you ready to go on to other things?"

Zachary held her gaze for a moment and nodded. "I think she's handling it really well. So far."

Kenzie eyed him for the "so far," but let it go. She looked back at Dr. B.

"Yeah, so I think we are okay to address other things."

"When I heard the news, I was also concerned about how you must feel after dealing with this death. I realized that this is your job and you see dead bodies all the time, but this sounded like a particularly bloody and gruesome death scene, and... well, I was concerned about how you might be feeling after that. We don't often talk about how police officers, doctors, and other service providers are affected by the trauma that they deal with in their jobs. Society is just coming around to the fact that first responders often have PTSD from dealing with the horrific things that they have to face on a day-to-day basis."

"I don't have PTSD," Kenzie assured her.

"Why don't you tell me about the case you are dealing with? If

Zachary doesn't mind me focusing on that for a few minutes and it isn't triggering for him."

Zachary shook his head. "We've already talked about it. I enjoy talking forensics with Kenzie, so we've already been over it."

"It sounds like it was a particularly bad scene," Dr. Boyle directed her attention back to Kenzie, meeting her gaze with a frank, sympathetic expression.

"Actually, they got it wrong. I wasn't called to the scene of death. I was called to the dump site. There were no pools of blood. That was something I noted about the scene when I did the autopsy. There should have been a lot of blood, but there wasn't."

"Oh," Dr. Boyle looked taken aback by this. "Well, that is good. Better for you, anyway."

"That means," Zachary said slowly, "whoever talked to that reporter was present when Jack Lane died. Doesn't it? There isn't any other way they would have found out that he was vomiting blood."

"Not unless it came from the medical examiner's office. We have had some information leaks in the past, so I suppose it is possible. But... my first guess would be that it was a witness. We know that *somebody* is talking because this isn't the first time we've heard a first-person description of Mr. Lane's death."

"Then you know who it is."

Kenzie looked at Zachary to see what he thought about it. "I don't think Maria would have talked to a reporter, do you?" She addressed Dr. B. "She's paranoid. She came to us because she had a connection to Zachary. I don't think she would have otherwise."

"A reporter might have been able to make a connection with her. That is something they do."

Kenzie nodded slowly. "You're right... but I think it must have come from someone other than Maria."

"So there was more than one witness."

"From what we understand of the way this guy works, this so-called Night Doctor, he gets together a group of people who need treatment. And then does them all at once. So there probably were a number of people who were gathered together and saw it, or some portion of it..."

"The Night Doctor?" Dr. Boyle repeated.

"Yeah, they kind of left that out of the news report completely, didn't they? Acted like it was the mobile clinic that was responsible for Lane's death. But the mobile clinic wasn't the last one to treat him. The person who was treating him when he died was Evan— was a disgraced doctor who they call the Night Doctor. We think he is a doctor who was kicked out of the mobile clinic because of his mistakes. So that's why he wants to make it look like the clinic is guilty of something."

"That makes sense. And you think he made a mistake in this man's treatment and that his death was the result of medical malpractice."

Kenzie shook her head. "The lab results are not all back yet, but I don't think there was anything anyone could have done to save him. But the Night Doctor doesn't know what I think, because I haven't talked to him."

"Well, that is fascinating. It sounds like a very different story from what was reported."

Kenzie nodded. "Exactly."

"And you are finding it easier to deal with because you know they didn't really have a clue as to what you had discovered and the events that took place."

"I guess so, yeah. At first, I wanted to explain everything and get them to report my side of the story. But, of course, they're not interested in the truth. Just in sensationalism. And that will pass. People will forget all about it when the next thing comes up."

"That's very wise. A good way to frame it."

35

Kenzie smoothed her fingers along her pants. Without looking at Zachary, she voiced her own concern. "I'm actually doing okay. But I am worried about Zachary."

Zachary shook his head. "I'm fine," he said immediately.

Kenzie and Dr. B both smiled and shook their heads.

"Fine?" Dr. Boyle repeated.

They had agreed in previous sessions not to say that they were fine—or anything else that brushed off any concerns and pretended that everything was fine—when they were not. They would either attempt to describe their feelings and what was bothering them, or explain that they were not ready to talk about it yet.

Zachary blew out his breath. He looked around the doctor's office, starting and stopping a few times before finding what he wanted to say.

"Kenzie thinks that I am being paranoid, but I am not. I am just being careful. Because there are real dangers. If there are really dangers, then it's not paranoia. Just good judgment. Being concerned about something that is a real threat."

"Okay," Dr. Boyle nodded. "Why don't you tell me about that, then? What is it you are worried about?"

"Like Kenzie said, there is this Night Doctor. Operating an

unlicensed medical practice. Maybe he didn't actually kill this guy, or maybe he did. But if he keeps it up, he *will* kill someone." Zachary leaned forward. "And Maria—the person who saw Lane die—she said that they have been following her."

"But what are the chances they actually are?" Kenzie demanded. "I saw her. She was being paranoid. Not calm and reasoned."

"You wouldn't be calm and reasoned if someone was following you, either," Zachary pointed out.

Kenzie rolled her eyes. "Zachary, I'm telling you, she was paranoid. No one is following her, hoping she'll have an accident they can blame on the Night Doctor."

"We don't know the reason, but if she says she was being followed, I am not going to discount it. How would you feel if I ignored something you were worried about?"

"That's different. I'm your partner, and I don't have a history of paranoia."

"You don't know that Maria has a history of paranoia."

"Well…" Kenzie was taken aback. "She is homeless, which means odds are, she's fighting some kind of mental illness. Schizophrenia is very high in the homeless population."

"But you don't know *her* history. Just what we heard when she spoke at the gala."

Kenzie was embarrassed to admit that she couldn't remember anything Maria had said about her challenges on the street when she had spoken at the gala. She cleared her throat and scratched the back of her neck. "I, uh, don't remember much of what she said at the gala. Did she include anything about her medical history?"

Zachary considered. "She has asthma, which is why she lost her last job. She couldn't keep up anymore and barely had any energy because she wasn't breathing properly. And she had arthritis. Hard to get up in the morning. Some days, she couldn't get out of bed at all. Lost her job, her apartment. The shelters gave her trouble because she took too long to get moving in the morning. You have to get up early in those places."

Kenzie found it hard to believe that someone wouldn't be able to go to a homeless shelter just because they had trouble getting mobile in the morning. But she knew that they tended to have many rules to keep everyone in line. If they didn't, it would be chaos.

But Zachary had not mentioned anything to do with mental health or addiction. Maria had not been drinking at the meal she had shared with them. Nor did she smell like alcohol or have a flask that was obvious. Most of the homeless drunks Kenzie had occasion to meet had carried quite an odor.

"She didn't say anything about depression? Any other mental health challenges?"

"No."

But that didn't mean anything. Mental health challenges were very common among the homeless. But people kept those details to themselves. Maria would not necessarily have disclosed any mental illness.

"Well... all I can say is that what I saw wasn't normal. It wasn't just a woman who was nervous someone might be following her. She was over the top. Paranoid."

Zachary folded his arms. "You're not a psychiatrist."

"No. I know that."

"You can't tell just by looking at someone that they are paranoid rather than anxious about a real threat. You only saw Maria for an hour or two."

"But this isn't really a discussion about whether or not Maria was paranoid," Dr. B broke in. "The question is about your mental health, Zachary. Kenzie is worried about *your* level of anxiety and the belief that you are being followed."

"I don't know for sure," Zachary admitted. "I'm just being careful. Keeping my eyes open."

"Do you have more specific concerns, Kenzie?" Dr. Boyle asked. "A particular behavior or incident that has you concerned?"

Kenzie tried to sort it out in her mind. "He's hypervigilant. He is anxious all the time, watching out the window for anyone who might be targeting us. It doesn't matter where we are or what we're doing. He's always watching—expecting to be attacked."

The therapist turned her attention to Zachary, looking serious.

"It sounds like this is affecting your quality of life. And affecting Kenzie's."

"I need to keep us safe."

"You have a security system at home. You can't trust that to keep you safe?"

"It helps, but no system is invulnerable. We've had other attacks even with the system in place. It helps, and the security company is really quick to respond if something happens, but it doesn't replace being vigilant."

"Do you think maybe you are being too vigilant? Should we increase your antianxiety pills a little and see if that helps?"

Zachary shook his head immediately. "I don't want to change anything in this cocktail. It's working better than anything else in years."

"We don't have to swap anything else; just see if increasing the dosage helps."

"No. Too much of an antianxiety med can have a paradoxical reaction. I could end up being more anxious instead of less. It should be kept at the lowest level possible."

Dr. B gave a little shrug, conceding that Zachary was correct and that he was the best judge of whether he needed an increase right now or not. They had pushed him in the past. Kenzie had been sure he was seeing danger where there wasn't any. Until it turned out that someone had planted a bomb in his car or delivered one to the house. Now, using an explosive sniffer before opening any packages they received seemed normal and reasonable rather than paranoid.

"How are you sleeping, Zachary?" the therapist asked.

"About the same as usual."

Dr. Boyle studied Zachary's face and then looked at Kenzie. "What do you think? About the same? Has there been any significant change in sleep?"

"No, I don't think so."

"And the depression?" She persisted, looking back at Zachary.

"Good," he assured her.

Which didn't mean that he didn't have any depression, but

merely that it was at a functional level and he wasn't being bothered by intrusive or suicidal thoughts.

Again, Dr. Boyle gave Kenzie the opportunity to express a dissenting opinion, but she didn't. She just shrugged.

"I wasn't concerned about depression or sleep, just paranoia. Anxiety. The hypervigilance that is eating him up and setting me on edge."

"Can you tolerate it for a while longer and see if it settles down on its own? It may be that it will fade naturally when nothing happens."

Kenzie sighed. "Fine. Just don't expect me to buy into it," she told Zachary. "I'm not going to placate you. I'm going to push back if I think you're being too paranoid."

Zachary surprised her by smiling instead of getting angry about her stubbornness. "Good. I don't like to be humored."

Kenzie nodded. "I won't, then. I'm going to be upfront about it."

36

The weather was perfect, and Kenzie didn't want to waste it by going home and staring at computer screens for the rest of the day. They usually had ice cream after couple's therapy, a positive reinforcer they looked forward to. It was a fun tradition, and even better on such a beautiful, clear spring day than on a cold, dark one. They stopped at the Fro-Zone to pick out their favorite flavors, and then went for a slow walk around the park with their cones, watching the mothers pushing young children in strollers, the teens skipping school, and the occasional businessperson or couple. Not everyone worked bankers' hours and were closeted in their dreary offices.

Not that Kenzie usually thought of her office as dreary. She enjoyed working at the medical examiner's office; the morgue and the bodies did not get her down. But it was a nice change to be out in the sunshine and fresh air for once.

Zachary grasped Kenzie's arm suddenly, pulling her abruptly off the path and onto the mown grass, sheltering partially hidden behind a tree. Kenzie looked at him in shock and opened her mouth to remind him that she wouldn't let him act paranoid without pushing back about it. He adjusted her gaze, directing her with his eyes and a nod toward a figure walking toward them. A black woman with cornrows wheeling a bike.

Kenzie recognized the woman an instant later. They had, after all, just been talking about her.

"Maria?"

It was a minute before she reached them. She looked around as if they were surrounded by watchers, even though no one else was showing the least bit of attention to Maria or to Zachary and Kenzie. They were just people at the park, walking with their ice cream cones or bike. Enjoying the fresh air and bright green growth of Vermont.

"How did she find us?" Kenzie asked Zachary.

He just looked at her and raised his brows. He was the one who had been watching for people to follow them. Kenzie had said that he was being paranoid.

"Dr. Kirsch," Maria greeted them a little breathlessly. "I'm so glad I found you. When you weren't at the medical examiner's office or at home…"

"How did you know I wasn't either of those places? And how did you find me here?"

Maria swallowed. Her smile was strained, but determined. "I just… had a feeling that you would be here."

Kenzie studied her. How? Zachary would have a raft of theories, she was sure. Starting with the one he had proposed a couple of days before, that someone was tracking Kenzie's cell phone location. What had Zachary called it? A sand trap?

"You came all this way by bike?" Zachary asked.

Maria nodded. That was how she told them she got around, wasn't it? She didn't look like she had just traveled the highway all the way from Clintock. But she hadn't said that's where she had been. Maybe she had been staying in Roxboro since they had last talked.

"Things are happening," she said intensely, wringing her hands. "I don't like it. You have to be more careful."

"More careful?" Zachary repeated. "What do you mean? We haven't been doing anything wrong."

"Kenzie was on the TV." Maria pointed at Kenzie's chest insistently. Kenzie felt like she would have pounded her finger into Kenzie's chest to make her point if she thought she would get away with it. But Kenzie wasn't going to be bullied and pushed around, and maybe Maria sensed that.

"I wasn't on the TV. But they *mentioned* me on the TV," Kenzie admitted.

Maria nodded. "I told you they were following me," she said. "You should not have told them anything."

"I didn't tell them anything. What are you talking about?"

"Let's go sit down," Zachary suggested, encouraging them both over to a more secluded part of the park with benches where they could put their heads together and figure out what was going on.

Maria shook her head, but went with them, wheeling her bike along. The back wheel was reverberating, in need of oil.

"We haven't told anybody anything," Zachary told Maria. "What's going on?"

Of course, that wasn't true. Kenzie had talked to Dr. Cook and Detective Samuels, to the shelter and the clinic doctors and nurses, and to the homeless people they had tried to get information from. And also to Dr. Simon, who was still—as far as Kenzie knew—running the mobile clinic. A lot of people knew she had been asking questions and trying to pin down exactly what had happened to Jack Lane. Had word from one of them, or several of them in concert, gotten back to Maria? Or was the leak somewhere else entirely?

"Do you know what he is doing?" Maria demanded.

"Who?" Kenzie asked, as if she didn't know.

"The Night Doctor," Maria hissed, then looked around to make sure they had not been overheard. "It's worse. It's much worse than we ever thought."

"Tell us about it," Zachary said calmly. "We'll do whatever we can to help."

Maria's eyes darted back and forth. "It's worse than you could imagine. Oh," she put both hands over her face, moaning, "You just don't know, Zachary."

"Tell me about it."

"They are taking people's parts!" Maria touched her stomach and poked and prodded at herself. "What if they took my parts when they worked on me? What if they are selling them to someone else, and my parts are in someone else on the other side of the world?" Her eyes were wide. "We can't let them do that."

"No," Kenzie agreed. "We won't let them. There are laws against trafficking in human organs. It's okay. They can't do that. I'm sure no one has taken your organs."

Maria clutched at her body, worried. Kenzie looked at Zachary. Could he now see that she was paranoid and not quite connected with reality?

"You would be able to tell if they had taken your organs," Zachary told her. "They didn't. Everything is still where it is supposed to be." He leaned closer. "Where did you hear that they were in the organ trade?"

Kenzie kept her lips tightly closed. She didn't believe that any of what Maria had to say came from a place of reason and sanity. It was not unusual for a person with schizophrenia to believe that something had been put into or taken out of her body. It was a common theme, like bugs and aliens.

"That's why they are treating the homeless," Maria insisted. "They don't have anywhere to go. They just keep taking more and more out of them. And then… they disappear."

Venice, too, had said that people had disappeared. Kenzie hadn't had a way to look into it. Missing person cases for homeless people were a nightmare. The police didn't like to take them. Unless there was some way to show that something had happened to them and they had not just wandered off or taken a train—or bicycle—to the next town.

"Who disappeared?" Kenzie asked. "Do you have proof of this?"

"I don't have *proof*," Maria scoffed. "That's why they do it!"

"If you can't show us that, there's no way for us to find out where they went."

"You don't really want to know," Maria decided. "You don't

want me to be right. You think if you ignore it, it will just go away. Nobody has to worry about Maria or Ella or any of the homeless folk. You cared once," she turned to Zachary, appealing to him, "You remember when you were on the street, trying to survive? You remember the people who helped you to get a leg up?"

"Of course I do," Zachary said. "Look at me, Maria. I want to help. Don't worry about anything else. Just pay attention to me." He obviously didn't want Kenzie to interfere with his handling of Maria. They didn't need her logical, reasonable comments and questions.

Maria would need a referral to some kind of mental health program. Maybe an intake at the hospital. Kenzie knew a few people there now, thanks to Zachary. They would help her to find the right placement for Maria.

"Is all of this being done by the Night Doctor?" Zachary asked.

Maria nodded vigorously. "Yes. It's him. It's all him. We have to stop him."

"We are trying to. Others have tried to, and he just keeps hiding and doing what he says. Have you seen him? Do you know what he looks like?"

Kenzie felt an electric buzz of excitement. Maria had apparently encountered the Night Doctor more than once. She could describe him and, even better, pick his picture out of a lineup. She could tell them whether or not Evan Hartfield was the Night Doctor and whether he was the one who had given Jack Lane a transfusion the night he had died. Then they could talk to Evan Hartfield and find out his version of what had happened that night and why he had disposed of the body the way he had. He could fill in all of the blanks for them.

"Of course I know what he looks like," Maria told them, looking offended. "I told you he treated me. You think I am blind?"

"Well, it seems like he doesn't want people to know who he is. I thought he might have worn a mask when he saw you. It would be easy for a doctor to hide his face from the people he treats."

"Oh yes, it would be," Maria agreed, obviously forgiving Zachary. "But he didn't. I did see him."

"Can you describe him?"

Maria fiddled with the beads at the end of one of her braids as she considered. "I suppose he is good-looking. Dark hair, blue eyes. Very young." She shook her head. "I can't believe how young doctors are these days. He's got very nice manners. Patients like him."

Kenzie nodded. "That's what Dr. Simon said."

"Dr. Simon?" Maria looked surprised. She glanced around the park as if looking for him. "I know Dr. Simon. He is good too, but not young like the Night Doctor. And he asks a lot of questions." She sighed in exasperation. "*So* many questions!"

"Did the Night Doctor work with Dr. Simon once?"

"Did he?" Maria considered. "I don't know. So many different doctors work with the mobile clinic. Different all the time."

"That's true," Kenzie agreed. One of the problems the mobile clinic faced was that the doctors were changing all the time, depending on who was available. Since it was mostly volunteer positions, they couldn't dictate when people came in.

Zachary was fiddling with his phone. Kenzie wasn't sure what he was doing, but let him work on whatever it was while she talked with Maria.

"Which do you like better, the Night Doctor or the mobile clinic?"

Maria held up her hands, unable to decide. "It's so hard to get a doctor when you need one. They only come into the community now and then. And there were so many people to see. The Night Doctor is much faster. And so sweet."

She probably had a crush on him. Simon had said that he was popular with the patients. But being handsome and popular did not make him a competent doctor.

"Here," Zachary offered. "Do you know any of these doctors?"

He flicked through a few pictures of doctors he had arranged in an album on his phone. Maria made an interested noise and leaned over. She studied them closely.

"I know this one," Maria paused, looking at one of them. Leaning closer for a better look, Kenzie was surprised to see Dr.

Cook's familiar handsome face. She registered his general description, remembering what Maria had just said. Handsome, dark hair, blue eyes. Just like Dr. Cook.

Maria kept flipping through the pictures. "And this one," she paused and looked at another man. Same general description, but not someone Kenzie knew. Those were the only two in the six or eight pictures that Zachary had assembled. Some of them, she suspected, were from stock photography sites.

"Is one of those the Night doctor?" Zachary asked.

Maria looked through them again, frowning. She paused at both Dr. Cook's photo and the other young doctor she had recognized the first time. She flipped through them a couple of times, eventually settling on the other doctor. "This one." She shook her head. "I told you, they are so young!"

Kenzie nodded her agreement. She remembered when she was a kid, how old all of the doctors who treated Amanda were. She had never considered any of them young, even the students. Now, even doctors who had been practicing for a few years hardly seemed to be more than teens.

Zachary took the phone back from Maria, checking the photo she had selected and giving Kenzie a subtle nod, which she took to mean that Maria had, in fact, picked out Dr. Evan Hartfield.

But her thoughts were stuck on Maria also knowing Dr. Cook. How would she know him? He was a pathologist. The substitute medical examiner. Was it just because he and Dr. Hartfield were so similar in appearance? Or was there more to it?

Dr. Cook *had* made it clear to her that he didn't want to pursue the identity of the Night Doctor any further.

Was that just a coincidence?

37

They bought Maria a hot dog for her supper and offered to take her to the grocery store or anywhere else she needed to go before parting company with her. Maria shook her head, patted Zachary on the arm, and said he was sweet, but an old lady like her knew how to get around and get the things she needed. She still seemed somewhat aloof toward Kenzie, despite seeking her out. She clearly favored Zachary. Kenzie couldn't say she blamed her.

Eventually, they said goodbye to her and watched her ride off on her bike. Children laughed and played a game of catch in a field nearby.

"Do you think she's going all the way back to Clintock?" Kenzie asked.

"No, I doubt it. She probably has somewhere to stay here. If she is going back to Clintock, she'll probably hitch a ride with someone with a truck most of the way there and just throw her bike in the back."

That would explain how Maria could appear not to be sweaty and windblown after making her way from one town to the other.

"That's dangerous. Hitchhiking like that. Especially for an old homeless lady nobody will even look for if she disappears."

Zachary nodded his agreement. "But you can't stop people from living how they want to, even if it is dangerous. Just like you can't stop them from drinking or taking other risks."

Kenzie pondered this. It was true. People made their own choices about how they were going to live.

"So what is my next step?" Kenzie asked. "Just reporting to Detective Samuels that Maria identified Evan Hartfield as the Night Doctor? Then let him run with it?"

"I can swear an affidavit with the pictures attached so he can see that we showed her a photo lineup rather than just a single picture. Better for any evidence that has to be admitted to court. You don't want to prejudice a witness by only showing them one picture."

"She hesitated about Dr. Cook. Said that she knew him."

"I noticed," Zachary agreed. "But she didn't say he was the Night Doctor, just that she knew him."

"Yeah. So you think that's okay?"

"She might have run into him somewhere else. She didn't say where, and I didn't think it would be wise to inquire further and cement his picture in her mind."

Kenzie nodded slowly. These were all considerations she never had to worry about in the cases she presented. Her evidence didn't depend on the vagaries of the human mind.

"Will Maria have to testify in court?"

"It depends on what she saw. I don't know yet. We'll need to keep track of her."

"That could be sort of hard, considering her lifestyle. What if, right when we need her, she disappears?"

Zachary shrugged. He was occupied with something on his phone. Some days, Kenzie really found herself annoyed at how easily distracted he was.

"Zachary, I know you know this world better than I do, but some things are outside our control. What if something happens and Maria goes missing? Or decides that she doesn't want to talk to either of us anymore and drops out of sight?"

Zachary turned his phone around and Kenzie saw he had it open to a maps app. She studied it closely for a moment, then saw a triangle Zachary tagged with "Maria 1" and one overlapping it tagged "Maria 2."

"Wait—you put trackers on Maria? Is that what this is?"

Zachary nodded. "Sure. You didn't want me to just let her ride away from here, did you?"

"No! But I didn't think to—I didn't even know you had any trackers on you. How did you get them onto Maria? What if she finds them or changes her clothes? She won't keep the same things on forever."

"One in her bike frame and one in her bag. Either of those could get stolen, but hopefully not both at the same time."

"How did you do that without either of us seeing?"

He smiled. He gave a little flourish like a magician making a coin disappear via sleight of hand and looked smug.

38

Kenzie worked her way through the emails and reports that had come in since she had been in the office last. It was amazing how much they could pile up in just a couple of days. But the office was as quiet as a—well, as quiet as a morgue, as she plowed through the work.

Unlike Zachary, who could not work without background noise to distract one part of his brain and keep it entertained, Kenzie preferred silence. She didn't turn on a radio or something on her phone. She wouldn't have any visitors from the public to talk through filling out forms on a Saturday when the office was officially closed. None of the other employees who drifted in and out performing their various tasks were there. Dr. Cook was in his office, but he had promised to stay out of Kenzie's way, and said she was to pretend he wasn't even there. When Kenzie had peeked in at him, he was hard at work, focused on his computer. The only other sign he was in the office was the fresh coffee in the break room, which Kenzie appreciated and helped herself to.

Her breath quickened when she came to a series of reports back from the lab with the file number for Jack Lane in the email subject line. Even though she knew what to expect, her heart thumped as she opened them up one at a time and downloaded the reports.

Then she highlighted them and opened them all at the same time so she could browse quickly through them and see if there were any surprises.

The toxicology report was no surprise. The BAC on the alcoholic was through the roof. Whatever else had happened to him, he'd at least not been suffering any withdrawals the night he had died. He'd been well-dosed with his favorite medicinal aid and feeling no pain.

Though when she looked through the other reports and remembered the shape his stomach had been in, she doubted that he had been clear of pain. Even the quantity of alcohol he had consumed had probably not been enough to mask the agony of holes burned through his stomach, the membranes of his esophagus tearing with the force of his vomiting, and his dying, cirrhotic liver.

Kenzie read through the various blood tests that they had requested. It was all pretty much as she expected, until she came to the line with the results of the Direct Antiglobulin or Coombs Test indicating the presence of antibodies bound to the red blood cells.

Kenzie sat back, staring at it, her head whirling.

She had not been expecting that.

She read the lines again. She looked through the other reports and came back to it again. The words had not changed. They stood out as if illuminated by a spotlight. Kenzie swore.

Everything had changed in an instant.

She tried to calm her brain down and list the next steps in a logical order.

She called Detective Samuels. She didn't expect to reach him, but had been hoping he would answer even though it was a Saturday and he was not supposed to be in the office. He still had a cell phone and, like Kenzie, could decide whether to take business calls on his day off. But he chose not to, so she left him a brief message to give her a call to go over urgent lab results, and hung up.

Kenzie's first call should have been to Dr. Cook. He was her supervisor and standing in for the medical examiner, and he should have been the one she reported to immediately. But she thought about how he had been so unconcerned about the Night Doctor or Evan Hartfield's possibly unlicensed medical treatments before Lane had died, and she thought of Maria looking at his picture Thursday afternoon and saying that she knew him at the same time as she had identified Evan as the Night Doctor. She couldn't help wondering what involvement he might have had with the homeless.

Had Detective Samuels managed to visit Evan Hartfield and ask him about his treatment of Mr. Lane? Kenzie hadn't seen any reports from Samuels in her inbox, but he might have planned to talk to her in person when she was back in the building. If he had talked to Hartfield, he could be in the wind and they would never be able to catch up with him to see that justice was done.

And if Kenzie went to Dr. Cook with the results of the lab tests, what would happen? Would he do the right thing? Would he cover for his friend Evan Hartfield? Bury the reports? He would make sure they never got to the media; that much was certain. Every effort would be made to keep it all quiet. The report couldn't disappear once it had been issued. There would always be a record of it.

Kenzie reached for the phone. There was only one other person who was as concerned about the integrity of the medical examiner's office as she was. She tapped in the digits she knew off by heart, hoping that he would be around and would answer when he saw her name on his caller ID.

The phone rang a few times, and then stopped.

"Kenzie?" There was the sound of wind and birds in the background. Was he fishing? Playing golf? Kenzie hoped it wouldn't be very long until his hand was fully rehabilitated and he was back at the office. There would be no need to tiptoe around Dr. Cook and to wonder where his loyalties lay.

"Dr. Wiltshire—"

The line was suddenly silent. Kenzie's eyes jumped to the phone screen and she saw Dr. Cook standing on the other side of her desk, his finger on the hang-up switch, handsome face pale.

"What's going on?" he asked.

Kenzie swallowed. There was no threat in Dr. Cook's expression or voice. But he might just be very good at hiding his intentions. If he didn't know about her suspicions, he might just act as if everything was as it should be and not see the need to censure her.

"I just... wanted to discuss the reports that came through on the Jack Lane case," Kenzie told him, keeping her voice as calm as possible.

"You're supposed to discuss them with me," Cook told her. "I am the acting medical examiner, not Dr. Wiltshire."

"He is the medical examiner," Kenzie corrected. "You are the substitute. He still has higher authority than you do."

"That is debatable. What did you find?"

For a moment, they just stared at each other, giving nothing away.

Kenzie couldn't very well keep the results from him. They were probably in his inbox as well. Maybe he had already seen them, and that was why he had walked out to the front to Kenzie's desk so silently, sneaking up on her and then confronting her when she tried to reach out to Dr. Wiltshire.

Kenzie took a deep breath in and released it.

"The Coombs test showed antibodies bound to red blood cells."

Dr. Cook continued to stare at her, then shook his head. He swore quietly.

"That means that the Night Doctor was responsible for his death," Kenzie said. "It was medical malpractice. Mr. Lane would probably have died anyway, maybe within hours or minutes. But he had no chance once the Night Doctor gave him that transfusion."

Dr. Cook did not disagree.

"Evan Hartfield," Kenzie said. "Do you have his number? Know how to reach him?"

Dr. Cook was even more pale than he had been when he had walked up to Kenzie's desk. "Yes," he admitted. "But we'll have to be very careful in how we act. If we do the wrong thing, and he runs away..." His eyes got distant, maybe picturing the other handsome doctor fleeing the jurisdiction. Maybe settling in some foreign country without extradition. Somewhere nice, with a beach, where whatever American dollars he had managed to sock away would last as long as possible. She was sure Dr. Cook would prefer that to seeing his friend on the inside of a cell.

"I left a message for Detective Samuels to call me," Kenzie advised. "Maybe we should just wait for him."

He rubbed his forehead painfully. "Maybe we should. But we don't want to give Evan a chance to run. If Samuels takes too long... he could be off for the weekend with his wife. We might not hear back from him until it is too late. In the meantime... he will still be treating patients."

Kenzie felt a chill at the thought. Dr. Simon had warned her. He had said that the mistakes that Evan Hartfield had made were life-threatening. Simon had managed to save patients that Hartfield had screwed up on while he had been interning. But now, the rogue doctor had no one supervising him. Any mistakes that he made might result in another Jack Lane. Another patient accidentally killed and thrown away, discarded like an empty pack of cigarettes in a dark alley. There might have already been more. Maybe deaths that they had thought to be natural or accidental had been the result of Hartfield's random mistakes. Maybe some of the people who had disappeared, disposed of more carefully than Jack Lane.

"Why didn't you do something before?" Kenzie demanded. "I told you about the Night Doctor. I told you that it might be Evan Hartfield. Why didn't you stop him? Tell him he'd better lie low until this all blew over? Or turned him in for practicing without a license?"

Dr. Cook looked pained. "I didn't think there was anything to worry about. He was doing the same things that we did at the mobile clinic. Cleaning wounds, changing dressings, putting in a few stitches or giving someone antibiotics. Counseling them on lifestyle issues, giving them referrals to rehab clinics or other programs that would help them. We rarely had anything to do with any serious illness; we would just call an ambulance or send them off to the hospital. What Evan was doing on his own wasn't any different; it just meant that we had better coverage, another mobile unit..."

"You worked with the mobile clinic?"

"Volunteered, yes. I put in my hours. Helps to keep my skills sharp. Gives a much-needed service. I do a night or two a week. It's not much, but it is important to the community."

"Why didn't you tell me?"

"It never came up. And it has nothing to do with the Lane case —except that Evan volunteered with the clinic for a while. But he wasn't anymore, so there wasn't any connection with the clinic."

"When did you know that he'd worked on Jack Lane?"

Cook shifted uncomfortably. He gave a little grimace. "I suspected as much from the start. When you reported the IV mark on the victim's arm. It had to be either Evan or the mobile clinic, and the clinic keeps strict records. If he had been there that night, we would have known it right away."

"But you just kept quiet about it."

"I didn't see what difference it would make, other than to cause trouble for Evan. It didn't look like Mr. Lane's death had been caused by any action or negligence on the part of any medical professional. It looked like alcoholism, pure and simple."

"But it wasn't."

39

It had taken some negotiation for Kenzie to get Dr. Cook to agree that they needed to do something before Evan Hartfield could do any more damage. He didn't want to call the police to get ahold of another of the detectives or sergeants they knew in the police department, or 9-1-1. Detective Samuels had already been notified, so they had done everything they were required to with regard to letting the authorities know of the latest developments.

"He's a good guy," Dr. Cook insisted. "And he'll fare much better with the justice system if he turns himself in than if they have to go after him. I'm sure I can convince him to, and then there won't be any more trouble."

Kenzie didn't know Dr. Evan Hartfield but wondered whether Cook was just deluding himself. Hartfield had already been kicked out of his internship and had his license revoked, and none of that had stopped him from practicing medicine. It had not stopped him from continuing to treat patients until one of them had died. Maybe more. And Kenzie had a sneaking suspicion that Dr. Cook was right. One lost patient wasn't going to stop him.

But what was the harm in talking to Hartfield and asking him to turn himself in? In the best-case scenario, he did, and they didn't have to do anything further. In the worst-case scenario, he said no, and they would be forced to take other measures to ensure he was dealt with properly. Call Samuels again. Maybe, at that point, Dr. Cook would be more amenable to calling the police to step in and intervene.

Even if he weren't, that didn't stop Kenzie from making the call herself. She would be alone in her car; she could do it at any time. If she felt like things had gone too far, she had an alternate plan.

"Shall we drive over together?" Dr. Cook offered. "No point in us driving separately. We'll just be coming back here again after."

"No, I'll take my car along too. We don't know what will happen afterward; we might want to go our separate directions."

He looked at her for a moment, then shrugged and nodded. "Fine. We'll take separate vehicles. Let me write down the address for you."

So he could give her the wrong address and send her off somewhere else while he went on ahead to warn Dr. Hartfield that he was in trouble?

"I'll just follow you," Kenzie said. "Are you in the parking garage?"

"Yes."

"We'll go down together, and I'll follow you."

"Of course, sure," he agreed, his smile seemingly effortless. Kenzie had an idea that he wasn't nearly as relaxed about it as he would like her to think.

He went back to his office to get his jacket. Kenzie put her loose papers and folders away in her drawer, which she locked. She locked the screen on her computer as well. By the time he had returned, she was ready to go.

They walked together to the elevator and found they were on different levels in the parking garage. Kenzie told him she would get her car and then join him on the third level so they could leave together.

"I'm easy to see, little red convertible," Kenzie told him. "My baby." They didn't usually attend a scene of death together, but she was sure they had probably ended up in the same place in the last few months. He had probably already seen her car. Even people who didn't know her well usually knew what she drove, having heard about it through the grapevine. But she had no idea what Cook drove.

"A black SUV," he advised. "Eats up the gas like you wouldn't believe. But I can't bear to part with it for some little, energy-efficient car."

Kenzie could relate. Her little convertible was not practical, but she loved it. She was glad to see that Dr. Cook had some human failings after all. Besides trusting too much in his friend who thought he could get away with practicing medicine without a license and no one would get hurt.

They met up in the parking garage and Kenzie followed the big black SUV out onto the street. Roxboro was not a big town and, in a few minutes, they were on the edge of it, passing acreages with houses peeking out from the trees, charming and picturesque. The houses got bigger and grander the farther they got out.

The one that Dr. Cook turned off of the highway at was larger than anything Kenzie would have contemplated buying herself. Not unless she had a much larger family. But it was not as big as Kenzie's family home. Hartfield must have had family money, as Kenzie couldn't see a doctor as young as he was being able to afford such a house. Not with the debts that they had to rack up to get a doctorate in the first place. And Dr. Hartfield had not practiced for long, first losing his internship and then having his license revoked. That didn't leave a lot of time during which to make money. Especially not the fortune it would take to buy that house.

Cook shrugged uncomfortably when he got out of his SUV after they parked in front of the house. "I've only been here once or twice before," he told Kenzie, as if that would excuse the luxury his friend lived in. Or was he telling Kenzie that he was not the same kind of person as Dr. Hartfield?

"It's nice," Kenzie commented.

She didn't gush over it. She had seen bigger, fancier homes in Vermont. Some even larger than her family home. The Wade home, for instance, where she had investigated the tragic death of a child.

She had never been tempted to prove her own worth by buying a big, showy house.

And that wasn't the reason she drove the little red sports car, either. That had nothing to do with social status.

She paused and waited for Dr. Cook to lead the way up to the door. His friend. He could make the approach.

There were no other cars parked in front of the house, so Kenzie had no idea if there was a full staff or if Dr. Hartfield lived by himself. Or something in between, just an executive assistant there during the day and a cleaning woman once or twice a week. Or maybe he was married and had three kids, but no one had mentioned it to her. There wasn't really any reason Dr. Simon or Dr. Cook would have needed to fill her in on Hartfield's family life.

Dr. Cook rang the doorbell, but he also pulled out his phone and dialed a number, presumably to tell Hartfield they were there to see him. An anonymous doorbell ringer might be ignored otherwise. People liked their privacy.

But neither the phone call nor the doorbell was answered. The house seemed silent and empty. Kenzie walked up to the windows and tried to see inside, but she couldn't see anything that told her whether it was unoccupied or if they were just being ghosted.

"I don't think he's here," she said eventually. "What do you want to do?"

"Well, he must be working," Dr. Cook said eventually, "or maybe out running some errands. He's not answering the phone, so it must be something he has to focus on, or doesn't want to be interrupted from. I can just leave him a message, and then when he calls back…"

"I thought he was 'the Night Doctor,' so why would he be working right now, during the day?"

"Well, he does other work as well. That isn't the only thing. Obviously, volunteer work doesn't pay anything, and a place like this requires maintenance."

"It's not family money?"

"Well, it probably is, but he is still expected to work and support himself and contribute something."

"What else does he do? Do you know where to find him?"

Kenzie wasn't that much older than Cook, but she was older, and she was trying to get him to step up and take responsibility when he clearly would rather just forget about it and leave it to someone else to take care of. She felt like a mother telling her teenager he could not go out with his friends until his homework was finished.

"I know a couple of places," Cook admitted reluctantly. "I don't know where he is most likely to be, though."

"Let's just go to the next one on the list, then," Kenzie told him, trying to sound cheerful and collected, not forced or stressed about it. They just needed to keep looking. For as long as Cook had any idea of where he might be.

40

D r. Cook sighed and turned away from the house.

"Okay," he agreed. "There is a counseling center where he does some work."

"Let's check that out. What kind of counseling?"

Dr. Cook shrugged. "Just... outreach kind of stuff. Addiction, youth runaways, job training, whatever people need."

"And he doesn't need a license to do that?"

"No, I don't see why he would. He is just counseling them, not prescribing drugs or doing psychotherapy. It could be done by a layman." He glanced at Kenzie. "Layperson."

"Okay, let's go see if he is there, then, or if anyone has seen him today or knows where he might go." Kenzie blew out her breath. "We'll find him sooner or later. I would have been happier if he had been home, but... he hasn't left town, right?"

"Not that I know of."

"Have the two of you talked? Does he know that the ME's office was investigating the death of Mr. Lane?"

"We haven't talked," Dr. Cook said curtly.

Was that because Dr. Cook thought Hartfield was involved and didn't want to compromise the case? Or because he was didn't want to face the fact that his old friend might be knee-deep in something pretty nasty?

Dr. Cook again led the way to the counseling center, which bore a name that Kenzie found vaguely familiar. She ran it through her head a few times, wondering whether it was another organization that the Kirsch family foundation sponsored. Another charity that bore the mark of her family. She hoped they were not mixed up with the Night Doctor even more deeply than she had thought.

They must have looked like quite the pair—two shiny, expensive vehicles driving in together and parking in the potholed, glass-strewn parking lot of the small, one-story community building. Kenzie wondered if she should be worried about someone stealing her car while they were inside. She looked around but didn't see anyone who was obviously watching her or waiting to jack her car. Zachary would probably have laughed at her for her suspicion. But he also would have checked at least three times to make sure that the doors were locked and the security system armed.

Dr. Cook apparently caught wind of her nervousness about leaving the car in the parking lot.

"There's a security camera," he said, pointing to it, "and they pay a guard who patrols the parking lot every few minutes to make sure there's no trouble brewing."

But she still couldn't see the guard even when she looked for him, so she wasn't much reassured.

"Okay," she told him. "But let's make this quick. Find out if he is here."

In the time it was taking them to get out of their cars and into the building, Evan Hartfield might have fled the building and be a couple of blocks away. But only if he was watching for them and understood what had gone down without being told.

Dr. Cook did not hold the door open for her, but was the first one into the building, looking around, either for hazards or for his friend.

They were greeted by red carpet worn through to the floor, narrow halls, and the smell of curry and body odor. The building was small, so it didn't take long for them to talk to the few people who were there, preparing for tutoring sessions, counseling, and a support group. The counselor shook his head when they asked about Hartfield.

"He was supposed to be here, actually, but he asked me yesterday if I would take the next few days and cover for him. He thought he was coming down with something and wanted to make sure that he was well and wasn't going to spread his germs around to everybody else here," Ben, a tall, thin man with a shock of wheat gold hair that stood straight up from his head informed them. "It's such a small building; everybody is always right on top of everyone else, so things spread quickly."

"Did he say when he would be back?" Dr. Cook asked.

"You're that friend of his, aren't you? You've been here once or twice before?"

Cook nodded. "Yes, we were friends. I wish he'd joined me in pathology."

Ben shook his head, looking puzzled. "He was very good at what he did. I know he previously had trouble with some of the technical requirements for practicing, but it's a shame that things like that should keep a very talented man from being able to share his talent."

"Technical requirements?" Kenzie repeated.

"Yes, he told me all about it. That he wished he could have met all of the requirements to be able to keep serving at the mobile clinic but, because of some problems with his license, he'd had to give it up."

Some problems with his license.

Like not having one.

Because of the mistakes that he kept making. The fact that he was an addict and might kill people with his unpredictable performance.

"I'm glad he was able to get into counseling," she said, as if she knew Evan Hartfield and was pleased that he had found his calling. "You must be thrilled to have him here."

"We are," Ben agreed. "He really makes a difference in a lot of lives. We are lucky to have him."

"So, he's sick at home?" Dr. Cook asked.

"Yeah. Sorry about that. I can tell him you were by to see him the next time he's in. Actually, I'll leave him a message, because if he's in, I'm not, and vice versa. Unless it's for a staff meeting or something."

"No, that's okay," Dr. Cook said. "I'll give him a call."

They were back out to the parking lot within five minutes but, even so, Kenzie was glad to see that her car was still there, all of its tires intact, and no graffiti or other vandalism was apparent.

"I only know one other place to look," Dr. Cook said. "I hope he's there."

Did he really? Or did he hope that he had warned Hartfield in time and he was in the wind?

41

Kenzie checked her phone when she got into the car to ensure she had not missed any calls or messages. Still nothing from Detective Samuels. Should she call Sergeant Campbell? Or one of the other cops she had dealt with and knew she could count on to listen to her?

One more place, Dr. Cook had assured her. They would look one more place; if Dr. Hartfield was not there, Kenzie would need to take the situation in hand and call in the police. She understood Dr. Cook's wish that Hartfield be given the opportunity to turn himself in to the police to show his remorse for what he had done.

If he felt any remorse. Or regret. Or any level of responsibility.

She was pretty sure that if he did feel responsible for his mistakes, he would not have kept practicing after he had been told to stop. More than likely, he was like many doctors who saw themselves as being above everybody else. Infallible. Any mistakes that were made were obviously someone else's fault, or the result of things out of his control. An act of God.

"Okay. So where is the next place that he might be?"

She didn't expect to find him there. After all, he had told Ben he was sick and would be at home, but he was not.

"A soup kitchen," Dr. Cook told her.

"Oh, of course. What is it with this guy and serving the homeless and underprivileged?"

"Don't you think that is a *good* thing? Why are you making it sound like something is wrong with him or there is something sinister about him wanting to serve the poor and marginalized? A lot of people consider that positive."

"You can't tell me that he is making any money to support himself on that big property with the money he makes counseling or working in a soup kitchen."

"Well, he isn't just serving soup; he is helping to manage it. But like I said, it's not just his own money paying for the property. He believes he needs to make money on his own no matter what circumstances he was born into. And he believes he should be giving back, serving the community."

It all sounded very virtuous. Kenzie wasn't sure she could believe a word of it.

She climbed back into her car and again followed Dr. Cook a few blocks to another dilapidated, low-slung building with peeling paint and a crumbling front stairway. A sign on the front door directed people around to the back.

People were already gathering, and the smell of a hearty broth and onions hung in the air outside the building. Kenzie glanced over the queue of homeless for any familiar faces, but she didn't see Maria or any of the people she and Zachary had made contact with in Clintock. There were a lot more young people and families than she had expected.

"This is probably not the best time for us to show up," Dr. Cook said, looking at his watch. "They serve lunch at noon on Saturdays."

"We just need to see whether he is here. That's just a minute in and out."

He nodded. They walked past the line of people, some of whom catcalled or accused them of trying to budge in at the front of the line. Kenzie ignored the comments and kept going. It didn't matter what anyone thought she was doing. The ones who had called out probably didn't even think she was planning to stay there for the hot lunch. She didn't exactly fit the profile of the soup kitchen's usual patrons.

The interior of the building was humid and the smell of the dinner so thick she could practically swim in it. Kenzie's stomach growled, even though she would have said before that point that she wasn't hungry. She could hear voices and the clink of silverware and dishes in the kitchen.

Dr. Cook took a hallway that led away from the kitchen and main hall to a series of small offices where Dr. Hartfield had apparently worked.

One of the offices was occupied, but there was no sign of the rogue doctor.

"Can I help you?" asked a stern-looking woman with a pencil in her bun. "I'm Tara. I run this program."

"I was hoping Evan would be here," Cook told her. "I'm an old friend and… there is something I need to ask him about. Do you know… is he coming in today?"

"No, I don't think so. I saw him here earlier, but things were a little disrupted and, when I looked for him, he was gone. I guess he must have just been in here to finish something up and then left again."

"Do you know where he was going from here?"

Tara pursed her lips and shook her head. "I really have no idea. Home, probably. But he is involved in so many different things, and I have trouble keeping track of them all. That's the problem with people like him; they have so many projects going on at one time, you never know where he is going to be or when he's going to be back."

"People like him?" Kenzie repeated.

The woman studied her for a moment before responding. "People with that kind of intelligence, that kind of drive. Always with their fingers in ten different pies. Jumping from one thing to another."

Zachary had wondered whether Dr. Hartfield was dyslexic. Tara's description sounded like he might also be ADHD. And probably gifted as well. Neurodivergent was the word coming into popularity now. And the addiction? Simon had said he thought Hartfield also had a substance abuse problem. He had been sure about it. Kenzie assumed that meant he had seen Hartfield using, or seen his stash or track marks. Mix all those things together, and they ended up with a very unpredictable and volatile ex-doctor.

"That woman might know."

"Who?" Kenzie looked at Tara, confused.

"There was a woman with him. A client. I've seen her around here a few times lately; I don't think she's from Roxboro. She came here looking for him, said that she knew him and he needed to talk to her, explain something to her."

Dr. Cook was already heading for the exit, but Kenzie wasn't ready to leave. Maybe there was enough information to lead them to Hartfield, or at least give them some idea of where he might be.

"A client. You don't know her name?"

"She might have told me, but honestly, I'm not the best with people. And she was kind of... ranty. I thought he would just throw her out, send her on her way."

"Can you describe her?"

Tara shook her head. "Older black woman. Corn rows. I don't know."

"Maria?"

"Might have been. I don't know for sure."

"And Dr. Hartfield talked with her? How did he react?"

"I don't know. I didn't hear their conversation. She quieted down a bit, but I still got the feeling that she was upset with him and wanted him to do something about it."

"But she wanted to be with him. She didn't act like she was afraid of him?"

"Afraid of him? No. But she was... agitated, like I said. He was trying to calm her down, but she didn't want to be handled. She wanted him to go with her, and he was trying to just get her to relax."

"Do you think he would have gone with her? That maybe he did go with her?"

"I don't know. Maybe. I didn't see him after that. But he didn't ask for any help with her."

Dr. Cook's body language told Kenzie that he was impatient to get out of there and didn't think there was any point in pursuing the conversation. But he hadn't been privy to the happenings Thursday afternoon. If it had been Maria, and it sounded like her, then they might have an easy way to find Dr. Evan Hartfield. If he had gone with her, they might just be able to find him, even if he didn't intend to be found.

42

Kenzie waited until they were out of the soup kitchen before explaining to Dr. Cook who Maria was.

"I'm sure I've seen her around," he acknowledged. "But I don't remember anything about paranoia and conspiracy theories. That is concerning."

"If it's a new development, yes... but my point is, if Evan is with Maria, we might be able to track him down."

"He hasn't been in any of the places I thought he might be. I'm fresh out of suggestions."

"I'll give Zachary a call."

Cook looked puzzled. "Does Zachary know this woman?"

"Only casually. We've talked to her a couple of times. But Zachary is a private investigator, and he has his ways of figuring things out." Kenzie smiled. She looked around. "But we'd better find somewhere we can sit down and sort it out. This isn't the best situation."

"There is a coffee shop a couple of blocks away that is very good. Would that do?"

"Sure."

Cook gave her directions in case they got separated, and Kenzie returned to her car—still undamaged—and followed him there.

They settled into a booth in the back corner of the coffee shop, and Kenzie called Zachary on speakerphone. She kept the volume as low as she could, and they both leaned close to hear it. She should probably have found a private dining room. Or stayed at the soup kitchen and asked if they could use one of the unoccupied offices.

"Kenzie? How's it going?" Zachary sounded concerned. Kenzie looked at the time and realized it was quite a bit later than she would typically have called him. Or she would have gone home after a couple of hours. She didn't usually put in full days on Saturdays. But she had been away from the office for several days and had a lot of catch-up work to do.

"Well, there have been some interesting developments. I'm actually not at the office at the moment."

"I noticed."

Kenzie's face warmed. "Oh, I guess I should have told you when I was going out." He had probably been quite worried about her, watching her travel all over town looking for Dr. Hartfield.

"You don't have to tell me every move you make. That's the whole point of sharing locations. We can carry on throughout the day, and if we need to know where the other person is, we can check."

"I guess." She still felt a little guilty for not checking in with him at least once during the day. It was slipping away from her quickly. They had better pick up sandwiches while they were at the coffee shop to keep them going. "So, I got some tests back from the lab, and we are trying to track down Dr. Hartfield to ask him a few questions about his treatment of Mr. Lane the night he died."

"Uh-huh? Something unexpected?"

"Yeah. And I didn't tell you I've got you on speaker with Dr. Cook. We're out in public, so we can't say too much. But yes... things are not looking good for the doctor. We are hoping that he will talk to the authorities voluntarily."

"But it doesn't sound like you are having much success."

"No. We've checked his house and a couple of places where he works. But at the last one, it sounds like he was there earlier today and was talking to an agitated black woman with cornrows..."

"You think it was Maria?"

"It sounds like her. And we know she has been worrying about the Night Doctor and what he might be up to. I think they might have left here together."

Kenzie didn't want to think of why Hartfield might have left with Maria. Hopefully, it was just to go somewhere more private to talk. Maybe to evaluate her and talk to her about trying an antipsychotic or adjusting the meds she was already on.

"Ah!" There was a lift in Zachary's tone, a note of excitement over being able to help them with their investigation. "Give me a second, then…"

"What's going on?" Dr. Cook murmured to Kenzie, watching the phone.

"Just wait, you'll see."

Zachary took a moment to check his trackers app and then reported to Kenzie. "Interesting, the two trackers are no longer in the same location."

"Really? Which one is where?"

"One is near your location. The other is nearly back in Clintock. On the move."

Kenzie considered. Was the bike on its way to Clintock and the bag still at the soup kitchen? Or was the bike at the soup kitchen and Maria's bag was traveling back to Clintock?

"If she's with Hartfield, then the bike must still be here," Kenzie said slowly.

She didn't like to think of the alternative. If Maria's bag was still at the soup kitchen, then chances were, she was too. Or her body. She did not want to find Maria's body in a nearby alley. But why would Hartfield kill her and take her bike? That didn't make any sense. Nor could she see Maria biking back to Clintock and leaving her bag behind.

"We need to look for her bike," Kenzie told Dr. Cook. "It's probably still parked at the soup kitchen."

"You have a tracker on her?" Cook questioned, still lagging behind the conversation.

"Two of them. One on her bicycle and one in her bag. But they're not in the same place anymore."

"Well, if one of them is headed to Clintock, isn't that the one we need to follow? We already checked the soup kitchen."

"Yes. I just want to make sure that..." Kenzie looked around uncomfortably. She didn't want to say the words aloud, as if they might jinx the situation. She wasn't normally superstitious, but...

"That she is still ambulatory," Zachary filled in. He, too, avoided using words like 'dead' or 'body.'

"Exactly," Kenzie agreed. "We just need to make sure she's okay, and then we can follow the tracker and hopefully find the two of them together."

"So, back to the soup kitchen." Cook sighed heavily. "Do you think we could stop and get something to eat? That soup smelled really good, and I don't think I can go back there without having something to eat first."

Kenzie grinned. "Yes, definitely. I don't think we have time to stay in line waiting to be served."

"And they didn't seem to have much tolerance for people trying to jump the line."

"No," Kenzie admitted, "they didn't."

He stood, patting his pocket for his wallet. "What do you want? Anything special?"

"Sandwich, pastry, maybe some milk."

"Milk?" Cook repeated. "I don't think I've ever seen you drink milk."

"Well, I figure I'll need something to dilute the coffee we're going to take 'to go,'" Kenzie laughed.

"Ah," he nodded, "now that makes more sense."

"Besides, it will go with the cookies or whatever you get me for dessert."

Cook nodded and went over to the counter to buy their meals. Kenzie smiled and watched him go. She picked up the phone, turning off the speaker.

"Just me now."

"Is everything okay?"

"Yeah. We'll have a bit to eat and then see if we can find Maria's bike at the soup kitchen. Uh… do you remember what it looked like? I didn't really take a good look at it."

"Schwinn 14-speed road bike," Zachary said promptly. "Red. She had a DIY box on the back to carry gear in."

It became more clear in Kenzie's mind. She could remember the box on the back. She would know it when she saw it again.

"Right. Thank you."

"I want to come with you."

Kenzie didn't think they needed another person in the convoy going after Hartfield. Maria, Dr. Cook, Kenzie, and now Zachary? At some point, they were going to need to call the police, too. She was pretty sure at this point that Hartfield was not going to be talked into turning himself in to the police voluntarily. He was on the run. He wasn't at home or at his places of work; he was on the way back to Clintock with a woman who thought he was illegally harvesting organs. Kenzie gave a shudder at the thought. She had a bit too much experience in the world of gray market and black market organ transplants.

"I don't know, Zach. I think if we get too many people following him, he'll bolt. Right now we can track him if he's with Maria, but if he gets spooked, I don't know. He might dump her, and then we won't know where he is."

"*You* can't track him," Zachary pointed out.

"Well, but if you tell us the location of the tracker…"

"I will. If I'm with you. I'm not going to do it blind."

Kenzie hadn't anticipated this. But she couldn't see any way around it. Zachary was about as stubborn as they came. It made sense that he would want to be there to see any hazards and know that he wasn't walking them right into a trap. If he wanted to be in on the operation, there wasn't much she could do about it.

"Uh, how are we going to swing this, then? You want to join us here? At the soup kitchen?"

"You come back here, leave your baby in the garage, and we take my car."

That would keep the convoy shorter. But Kenzie didn't want to garage her car. Zachary could come in hers.

"Your car is not good for covert surveillance," Zachary pointed out. "If Hartfield is at all suspicious—and we know Maria already believes she's being followed—one of them will see you."

Kenzie hated to admit that he was right. Zachary's car, intended to be unobtrusive, was a middle-of-the-line white compact, which would blend into any other traffic. Kenzie's would stand out like a beacon.

"Dang it. Okay. We won't be long. We'll just have a bite to eat and then see if we can find the bike. Then we'll come get you and head out of town."

"What does Dr. Cook drive?"

"A black SUV. Nothing too fancy, as far as I can tell. Just a regular old soccer-mom SUV."

"Good. That shouldn't be a problem. Do you want to come get me first? I can help you to pinpoint the location of the bike with the locator program. And you can eat while we drive."

"No… we'll try finding the bike first, rather than going across town and back again. It shouldn't be that hard to spot. Can you tell which side of the building it is on?"

"Appears to be the east, but sometimes signals bounce around. I could come to you and we could leave from there, but then you would have to leave your car behind, and that's not the best place to leave it."

"No. I'm not leaving my car here by itself. It's been through enough trauma today, being left in some of these parking lots."

Zachary chuckled. "Okay. Well, I'll be ready when you get here. Don't spend a long time looking for the bike. If you can't find it right away, it will be faster to pick me up and go back there with the locator program than to spend your time wandering."

"Got it," Kenzie agreed. Roxboro was a small town. It wouldn't take a long time to do the extra driving around. But she thought they would be able to spot the bike without help.

"How is Dr. Cook?" Zachary asked, his voice low so it wouldn't carry if Dr. Cook had returned with the food.

"He's... struggling with this. He and Hartfield are friends. Dr. Cook knew he was probably the Night Doctor. But he didn't think he would actually do any harm. Now... I think he still wants Hartfield to redeem himself. He thinks he can get him to turn himself in. But I don't know. The fact that he already is running or behaving erratically doesn't fill me with confidence."

"No," Zachary agreed. "And from what your friend Simon said... he doesn't seem like the kind to admit wrongdoing and throw himself upon the mercy of the court."

Kenzie grunted her agreement. Dr. Cook headed back to the booth with a tray full of food. "Here comes Dr. Cook. I have to go."

"See you soon."

Kenzie disconnected the call.

43

As they got closer to the soup kitchen, Kenzie tried to control her breathing. She was feeling more and more anxious, worried that they were going to find something other than Maria's bike. It was silly for a medical examiner to be worried about finding a body, but she was. She didn't want to discover that the Night Doctor had progressed from accidentally killing someone out of incompetence to intentional murder to cover his tracks. She liked Maria and didn't want her to be dead. She wanted to talk about the case in the future with a light heart, knowing that Maria had been able to get out of the street life and was stable and happy.

She did not want to be dissecting the woman on her slab, where Jack Lane had lain just days ago. She was glad she had not met him in life.

Unsurprisingly, there were a lot of bikes and shopping carts parked around the soup kitchen. And people did not like them driving by slowly or getting out of the car to examine them. Kenzie repeated several times that she was looking for Maria or Maria's bike, but people still eyed her and scowled, not liking it. When she asked them about Dr. Hartfield and whether he had been there earlier, and whether he and Maria had been together or knew each other, people liked it even less. They clammed right up about the doctor, as if knowing his secrets, they knew he had to be protected even more closely than Maria or the other homeless people.

"There it is!" Kenzie quickly pulled her car over and dashed to the red Schwinn leaning against a wall behind the soup kitchen. She ran up for a closer look, looking at the box on the back and trying to picture it as she had seen it in the park that day, Maria wheeling it along while she talked to them and then mounting it and riding away.

"That it?" Dr. Cook asked.

"Yes. Definitely. This is Maria's bike."

"Let's put it in my truck; we can give it to her when we find her. Save her having to hitchhike or bus back here to get it."

Kenzie hesitated. Was it a crime scene? Was it a piece of evidence? And if it were, didn't she have the responsibility of preserving it rather than leaving it on the street where someone else might steal it? She couldn't definitively tell the police that it had any direct connection with a crime. Maria might have left it there while she willingly went with Hartfield for medical treatment. There was no way Kenzie would get a couple of cops out there to look at the bike and document its presence there.

Kenzie stepped back from the bike and took a few pictures with her phone. She started a voice memo and dictated the time, date, and location to go along with the photo.

"Don't touch it," she warned Dr. Cook, and he nodded his agreement.

Kenzie returned to her car to get a pair of gloves from her small scene of death kit, dialing Zachary's number again as she walked.

"Find it?" Zachary asked. "It looks like you're right on top of it."

"Yes. Just collecting it now. But I wanted to document it before we do anything else. Can you take a screenshot from your locator program showing its location? Preferably with time and date stamp. And do you have breadcrumbs? Something that shows where it has been the last few hours or since you put the tracker on the bike?"

"Yes. I will preserve that data in case there is any need for it."

"Great, thanks. We'll be home in a few minutes."

She tied an evidence tag to the bike and filled it out. She took a picture of it again with her phone camera, zoomed in on the tag and took another, then looked at Dr. Cook. "Anything else? Am I missing anything?"

"No, I think you've done everything."

Kenzie looked down at the pavement. No dirt and, therefore, no tire tracks or footprints showing who had parked the bike there.

"Okay, let's put it in your truck."

Dr. Cook had cleared space for it. They loaded the bike in, and Kenzie looked around once more. "We should just do a quick scene survey," she told Dr. Cook. "I want to be sure that... we haven't missed anything."

They walked around the site in widening spirals, checking the ground for anything that might have been dropped, poking around in garbage cans, and checking the nearby alley and dumpsters especially thoroughly to make sure that there was no body dumped out of sight. Kenzie took comfort in the fact that the other tracker was still showing up on Zachary's phone and appeared to be heading to Clintock. Maria had her bag with her. The tracker had not been discovered and destroyed. Her bag had not been left in a garbage or sewer or been left with her bike. Maria had been willing to leave her bike behind, at least for a while, but not her handbag.

"Okay, I'll see you there," Kenzie told Dr. Cook as they returned to their respective vehicles. "You have the address if you lose me?"

He nodded. "I do. See you there."

Zachary was eager for Kenzie to arrive. She could see him standing at the living room window when she drove by and, when she entered the kitchen from the garage, he was standing too close, not giving her any space to breathe.

"Everything is fine," Kenzie told him, giving him a quick hug and then nudging him back. "I haven't even seen Hartfield; there is nothing to worry about."

"I still worry," Zachary said, with a quick look toward the front window, through which she could see Dr. Cook's black SUV waiting at the curb behind Zachary's car.

"Dr. Cook wants to find Hartfield as much as anyone," she told Zachary. "Maybe more. Other people might not care that much about what happened to the victim. He died a few minutes or few hours earlier than he would have otherwise because Hartfield made a mistake. It's hard to get riled up about that. The guy really seems to have a savior complex. Not just working in the mobile clinic or as the Night Doctor, but volunteering with counseling and the soup kitchen. Like he has something to make up for. So it's easy for people to give him a pass. The mistakes he makes along the way... I think people are willing to forgive him because he is so earnestly eager to help people."

Kenzie had nearly lost the thread of where she was going with this.

"But Dr. Cook wants to find him to make sure that he doesn't get thrown in jail. He doesn't want Hartfield to be shot in some police takedown or to serve time for killing someone in what was an accident."

Zachary grunted. He didn't sound too enthusiastic about it, but he was willing to take her at her word. They headed toward the front door without discussing it further. They both knew the next step. Zachary grabbed a bag of equipment from the hallway, and they left through the front door. Zachary turned to listen to the bolt slide into place and the two-tone notification that the burglar alarm was armed. He tried the door handle.

"It's locked," Kenzie confirmed. "Let's get on our way."

He tried twisting the door knob one more time, then conceded that it was, in fact, secure and walked down the sidewalk to his car. He waved at Dr. Cook, threw his equipment in the back, and slid into the driver's seat. He placed his phone in the holder on the dash and brought up the locator app map on the screen.

"All set."

"I guess we get to be lead car, since you're the one who knows where we are going." Kenzie put her seatbelt on, and they pulled out.

44

Kenzie spent the first part of the drive catching Zachary up on the details of the investigation and their search for Hartfield. She was surprised to find that he had been watching her all morning, so he already knew where she had been.

"Nice house?" Zachary questioned. "Couldn't see much except the size from the satellite picture. No street view camera, and I couldn't find anything online for it."

"Yeah, it's a nice place. Not huge, but certainly nice. I guess he has family money. He wasn't just a starving medical student."

"Yeah. I found a little bit of history. His parents passed when he was a teenager. A car accident. He has been largely on his own since then. A guardian, financial advisors, maybe some staff, but no parental figure. He was too old already."

"Is that supposed to excuse his lack of a moral compass?"

Zachary laughed. "Don't know, you'll have to ask him."

"I'd really like to know what makes him think he can keep practicing medicine without a license. What makes him think he can save everyone and do all this good when he just keeps making mistakes? *Serious* mistakes. Does he think everyone is just picking on him, and he could have saved those people if Simon had let him continue? Does he think that Jack Lane was the only serious mistake that he made?"

"And have there been others that he won't admit to?"

"I was thinking about that earlier. Whether I have seen any of his other victims. I will have to review earlier records to…. make sure we haven't goofed up on anything, calling it an accident or natural causes when it was something Dr. Evan Hartfield did."

"Yeah. Something to think about."

Kenzie looked at the map on the phone. "Is he still moving? Where is he?"

Zachary glanced away from the highway for a moment to check. "Looks like he has entered an industrial area. Not sure whether he has slowed down or stopped. Watch it for a minute for me."

Kenzie nodded, watching the little triangle with Maria 1 in tiny letters beside it.

"He might be getting close to his destination. He has slowed down quite a bit."

"Can you tell anything about the location? You can zoom in and tap to try to identify locations."

Kenzie took the phone out of the holder to be able to see and handle it more easily.

"It looks like maybe… it might be a self-storage lot." She shook her head and looked at Zachary. "Does that make any sense?"

"I'm not sure." Zachary bit his lip, considering the question.

Kenzie ran through scenarios in her mind, none of them very nice. Everything seemed to end with Maria getting hurt. Or maybe she was already hurt. Kenzie couldn't help thinking that a self-storage unit would be a good place to get rid of a body for a while. People might complain about the smell, but would probably think it was just a dead mouse or squirrel, and it would make perfect sense that there would be rodents in a place like that. There would be privacy while he continued to pay for the unit. And eventually, when the flesh had either dissolved or mummified, making disposal a much simpler task, he could clean it out, let it air out for a few months, and then end his rental contract.

Kenzie rubbed her forehead.

"We don't know that anything has happened to her yet," Zachary said. "Or that it will. Don't jump to conclusions."

"I think we should call the police."

"Yeah… that might be a good idea. If they're ready to move in, it would probably be helpful."

Kenzie grimaced. Not only was she going to have to call in the police to help them with the apprehension of Hartfield after agreeing to let Dr. Cook try to handle it himself first, but she was going to have to explain why she hadn't called them earlier if she was so sure now of what he had done and that he might be a danger to the public—or at least one member of the public.

But she didn't want anything to happen to Maria. If she were still safe, Kenzie wanted to make sure she stayed that way.

"Dang," she said under her breath. "Dang, dang, dang."

"You can swear," Zachary told her. "I won't be offended."

Kenzie chuckled. "I'm just trying to keep myself under control." She took a few deep breaths. "Okay. I left a message for Detective Samuels earlier. Do I try him again or someone else?"

"Do you think he will come himself?"

"Uh… no, I wouldn't count on it. I've tried to keep him in the loop from the start, but he hasn't seemed interested in the case. Even with the possibility of the Night Doctor practicing medicine without a license. And Clintock is out of his jurisdiction, so he probably wouldn't want to come."

"And you already left a message for him."

"Yes. He's probably got kids or something like that. A weekend away, maybe. Cops are allowed to have lives. Take a weekend off now and then. Detectives, anyway."

"Really?" Zachary cocked his head comically. "That doesn't seem right."

"Apparently, they are. So I should call someone else instead? A different detective or Sergeant Campbell? Or someone else? I could just try 9-1-1 and we get whoever we get when we arrive."

"Try Campbell. He's usually pretty easy to reach. He will probably just refer us to someone in Clintock."

"Okay." Kenzie returned Zachary's phone to the holder and took out her own. She called Sergeant Campbell's cell, though she felt a little guilty doing so. Shouldn't she just leave him alone? Didn't he have the right, like Samuels, to a little personal time on the weekend?

The phone only rang a couple of times before Campbell picked it up.

"Dr. Kirsch. How are you doing? I didn't hear that we had any callouts for you."

"No, this is related to that one a week ago. Jack Lane."

"The homeless guy. Has something come up? I thought you put it to bed."

"Well, I thought I had. It appeared to be natural causes in the beginning."

"Okay. How can I help you?"

"Well, I already passed this on to Detective Samuels, but maybe he's away for the weekend..."

"Some cops are better than others at maintaining boundaries," Campbell said wryly.

Kenzie laughed. "I take it you need a little more practice?"

"Unfortunately, I do. But fortunate for you. What do you have? I take it things have blown over after that, er, media exposure."

"Well... there may be some more coming." This whole thing was going to shine a lot more light on the Jack Lane case and some of the problems inherent in the current system.

"What's going on?"

Kenzie steeled herself. She would have to tell him the details and stop dancing around it.

"It *wasn't* natural causes. I got lab tests back today showing it was medical malpractice." Kenzie sighed. "The doctor who treated him—or former doctor, as he'd had his license revoked—definitely caused his death."

"You are sure of that?"

"Yes."

"Okay. The name of the doctor—former doctor—who administered this treatment?"

"Evan Hartfield."

Campbell repeated the name as he wrote it down. "And you know that for sure?"

Kenzie thought of everything she had. "I have a witness, or apparent witness, who said she saw him administer the treatment. And there were others there at the time. He treated a number of different people."

"Of course he did. Why would the man stop seeing patients just because he'd had his license revoked?" Campbell questioned, his voice heavy with sarcasm.

"Yes. Apparently, he had a differing opinion on the matter."

"I'll make sure Samuels got your message and looks into it on Monday."

"Well... actually, there have been developments. Dr. Cook knows Hartfield personally, and he thought he might be able to talk him into turning himself in."

"Well, it's always nice when they police themselves. I'm sure someone can take his statement."

"As it turns out, I think Hartfield caught wind that we were coming to talk to him, or at least that we were getting closer to the truth."

There was a silent pause from Campbell. "And what exactly has happened?"

"He is on his way to Clintock. There now, actually. We think he has the witness who talked to us about him, and... we're worried she might be in danger."

"Does he know she told you what she saw?"

"I don't know. ... when we saw her a few days ago, she was quite paranoid and thought he was following her. But I don't think he was at that point; I think it was just... a break. But she was seen talking to him earlier today and might have said something to tip him off."

"And he's with her now? How do you know that?"

"Zachary has a tracker on her. We're following it now, and she is back in Clintock."

"And how do you know she is with Hartfield?"

"Well… that part is just speculation, I guess," Kenzie admitted. "They were together earlier and then both dropped out of sight. Maria rides a bicycle, but we found her bike still in Roxboro, so someone else gave her a ride. There is no guarantee it is Hartfield… but we've been looking for him all day, and we think he's brought her to Clintock."

"Why would he do that?"

"Well… he's pulled into a self-storage lot. I'm worried that…"

Campbell did not stop at "dang." Kenzie grimaced and waited to see what he had to say about it. He clearly was following the same line of thinking as they had.

"Have you had any contact to indicate what kind of shape she's in?"

"No. We haven't been in contact with either one."

"Does your witness have a cellphone?"

"She might, but I don't have her number. Dr. Cook has Hartfield's number and tried to reach him, but he didn't answer."

"Dr. Cook is there with you?"

"He's following in his car."

"How close are you to this self-storage lot?"

Kenzie looked at the ETA on the phone. "Twenty minutes out."

"We'd better get some cops from Clintock out there. Have you called them? Tried 9-1-1?"

"I didn't know if they would take me seriously."

"You're the assistant medical examiner. I hope they would."

"I hope so too, but it's kind of a scattered story. I wasn't sure anyone would think it was anything serious."

"Well… maybe if I didn't know you, I wouldn't be sure whether to be concerned. You've made a lot of assumptions in your chain of logic. But better to take it seriously and find out you were wrong than to do nothing and let this woman be harmed."

"So you'll get someone from Clintock over there?"

"Yes. Give me the address and a description of your parties. Do you have pictures of either of them?"

"I have one of Hartfield. Maria is an older Black woman with cornrows, not exactly a common demographic here in Vermont."

"Send me the picture. I'll get someone on this, and I guess… I'll hear from you later."

45

"Campbell is going to get some cops over there," Kenzie confirmed to Zachary. "They'll probably get there before us."

Although she probably should not take the ETA on Zachary's map as gospel, since he was going significantly over the speed limit. Zachary saw her looking at the speedometer and touched the brake, slowing slightly.

"I figured it was an emergency," he defended himself.

"Well, it sort of is, but let's get there in one piece."

He grinned and didn't comment. Zachary always thought he could get away with breaking the speed limit without fear of tickets or accidents. And so far, she had to admit he'd been correct on that score. As fast as he drove, she'd never seen him come close to having an accident. It was one of the ways that his ADHD was beneficial. He could be totally focused, his reflexes like lightning. He saw and processed everything around him instantly and responded accordingly.

"This might be a case that calls for a little more speed," Zachary suggested.

"I don't think we should get there ahead of the police. It will take a few minutes for Campbell to convince them to get people over there, and time for them to arrive and assess the situation."

"If we get there first, we might have everything under control by the time they do."

"I'm not willing to bet Maria's life on it. Are you?"

His smile disappeared. "No. I guess not."

Kenzie looked over her shoulder at the black SUV following them.

"I'd better talk to Dr. Cook about what is going on," she told Zachary.

He glanced at her and then back at the road. "You don't think he will be happy about it?"

"Uh, no. Hartfield is his friend. He was hoping to talk to him before the police got involved."

"Well, that was before things escalated and Maria was apparently taken."

"Yeah. He probably won't be happy that I called the police without discussing it with him."

"Probably best that you did. Better not to give him a chance to talk you out of it."

Kenzie grunted an acknowledgment. She considered her phone for a minute before putting the call in. It would be easier to just continue on to the storage lot and let Cook find out what she had done when they got there, but she couldn't treat him that way. They had been working together for several months, and Kenzie respected the serious young doctor. He didn't deserve to be ambushed.

She took a deep breath and tapped his number on her phone.

"Kenzie," Dr. Cook sounded both amused and out of breath. "Zachary's a bit of a speed demon there."

"Uh, yeah, sorry about that!" Kenzie glared at Zachary, and he touched the brake, slowing the car just slightly. "I thought I'd better fill you in on developments."

"Developments? What happened?"

"It looks like Hartfield is going into a self-storage lot. We are concerned about Maria's safety and what he has in mind. He could... intend to harm her and leave her there, where no one would know what happened to her."

"Evan wouldn't do something like that. I'm sure he has a good reason for taking her to a storage unit. You don't know what supplies he has there that she might need."

"Have you been to it before? Do you know what he keeps there?"

"No, but he must have a place to keep medical supplies handy. He doesn't have an office. And I know from working with the mobile clinic that it's hard to keep everything you need in a van. We have to restock every day."

Kenzie hadn't thought much about the logistics. It *was* possible that Hartfield simply needed to get medical supplies to treat Maria. If so, Kenzie's call to Campbell might have been entirely unnecessary.

"Well... yeah, I guess that's possible. But it is also possible that he is planning to do something we might regret. We felt it was necessary to get the police involved in... making sure that no one comes to harm."

"You don't know Evan."

"No, we don't. So, we need to treat this as a volatile situation. No one wants Maria to get hurt."

"Of course, but I don't think you need to involve the police when we don't know anything yet."

"I've already called them," Kenzie disclosed.

Cook's growl of frustration was audible over the phone. "Dr. Kirsch, I expect you to consult me before—"

"This is not a situation in which you have any authority over me," Kenzie cut him off. "I have responsibilities to see that the public is not put at risk and that the law is enforced. I am a medical doctor, and that means I have a code of ethics to follow. I can't ignore the possibility that Hartfield could hurt Maria, or might have already."

"I know Evan. This is ridiculous. I know that he wouldn't hurt anyone. He has always been very focused on helping those who are... part of vulnerable populations that slip through the cracks here. Do you really think he would do anything to hurt someone in one of those populations?"

"I don't know what he would do. I just know where he is, and that worries me. Things could go terribly wrong at this point, and I don't want to take the chance."

"You're wrong, Dr. Kirsch. You've got it completely backward."

"If it turns out to be a mistake, I'll happily admit it."

46

Zachary and Kenzie were quiet as they approached the location on the phone screen. Zachary slowed down when he took the ramp off the highway and navigated through the side roads, going past various warehouses, car lots, and other light industrial buildings on their way there.

Kenzie heard the distant wail of a siren. She looked in her mirror, and then turned to look back over her shoulder. It was a minute before she could see the lights of a couple of police cars as they approached. The road was quiet with no other traffic, so it seemed a fair conclusion that they were the cops sent by Campbell. As the cars approached, Zachary slowed and pulled to the side of the road to let them pass. He never actually stopped the car, but kept traveling at a slow speed, even while they passed him. Then he pulled back in behind them and hit the accelerator. They were over the speed limit, but what were the police going to do about it? Stop and pull them over? Their eyes and minds were ahead, focused on the man who might have taken a hostage or have a dead body with him that he had intended to conceal.

She and Zachary would probably face some opposition when they got to the site. At least Kenzie was nominally involved in law enforcement. But the cops would certainly not want to have anything to do with Zachary, a private investigator. He would have to do some pretty quick talking to get them to listen to anything he said or allow him close to the crime scene or suspect.

Zachary had been detained or arrested in the past for showing up at a crime scene where the police didn't want him or were worried he might interfere with a situation.

They didn't need the GPS of the locator app anymore, but just followed the police in. Kenzie kept an eye on the app, in case it had gotten Maria's location wrong while they were still a distance away, and she was actually in a warehouse next to the storage unit or some other nearby location that they would be able to identify now that they were close by.

The police cars pulled into the front of the storage lot, where there was a small parking lot and a business office. An electronically controlled security gate kept them from driving into the lot. The woman at the business office came out, frowning.

Zachary grabbed his phone and hopped out of the car, not hesitating about whether to jump directly into the midst of the situation. That was Zachary. What was it he always said? Impulsivity was the hallmark of his ADHD. That was what the psychologist's report had said when he was first put into foster care, and the family and school were trying to determine what was wrong with him and how to manage his erratic behavior.

As if they had not been able to figure out that a child raised in an abusive home, who had just been through the horror of his house burning down and being separated from his family might have been traumatized and have difficulty sitting still and focusing on the work at school. But there had been additional problems; they had been right to do a psycho-educational assessment when one had not previously been done for Zachary. ADHD, dyslexia, PTSD, and probably a smattering of other issues that were not yet fully understood but would continue to plague him throughout his life.

Kenzie wasn't quite as quick to jump into an unfamiliar and potentially explosive situation as Zachary. She got out of the car slowly and watched the police to make sure they did not object to her movements. Behind her, she heard Dr. Cook's car door slam.

Zachary held the phone flat in front of him to show the cops the map showing where Maria was in the storage lot.

"Do you have surveillance cameras?" he asked the woman from the office. "Something that would show what is going on in this aisle?"

"Well, we don't have anything that points inside the storage units. We try to give clients their privacy about what is stored in their units. You don't want staff getting curious about what is in the units or its value. Sometimes people are storing things worth tens of thousands of dollars. We had one client who stored his Lamborghini..."

So much for not knowing what was in the units. Kenzie could understand wanting to avoid tempting staff with what looked like an easy score. A pair of bolt cutters on a night when the surveillance video mysteriously blinked out would make it simple. The theft might not be discovered until weeks or months later when the owner of the unit came around and found the hasp of the lock on the unit severed.

"What cameras do you have in that aisle?" a mustached cop asked the owner firmly, undistracted by the tale of the Lamborghini and what else might be stored in the units.

"Uh, come into the office."

The woman led them into the business office. It was a tiny, cramped room, which would have been full with just two people inside. Kenzie and Dr. Cook stood outside the open door, not speaking to each other, behind two of the cops. The room was extremely crowded with the employee, Zachary, the mustached cop, and his partner. They huddled around a computer while the employee went through the feeds to find the one pointing at Hart-field. Kenzie was not in a position where she could see what was on the screen or hear what they were discussing.

47

Eventually, Zachary, the woman, and the mustached cop came back out of the office, leaving the other cop stationed in front of the computer, watching the surveillance camera.

"Hartfield and Maria," Zachary confirmed succinctly to Kenzie. "She's alive and appears to be unharmed. The police are going to get close and then walk in, hoping to catch him off guard and not escalate the situation."

"Is he armed? What's going on with him and Maria? Are they fighting?"

"Ma'am?" Closer to him, Kenzie could see that the mustached cop's name was Bleaker. "Sorry, and you are…?"

Zachary opened his mouth to answer, but Kenzie raised her hand to stop him. She needed to be independent, for Bleaker to see her as a separate entity, capable and professional. A member of the law enforcement team. Not associated with the private investigator who would probably get kicked off the scene now that they knew where Hartfield was.

"Dr. Kenzie Kirsch," she pronounced slowly, putting her hand out to shake. "Medical Examiner's Office in Roxboro. All of this…"

She motioned toward the storage lot, "is related to a death I am working on."

Bleaker raised an eyebrow. "How?"

"Dr. Hartfield's actions resulted in the death of the victim."

"He killed your victim?" The cop looked toward the other two who were getting ready to enter the lot, frowning. Walking up on a suspect who might have coerced an old woman was different from approaching someone they knew had violently murdered someone.

Dr. Cook shook his head. "No!" Kenzie could see by his scowl that he wanted to tell her *this was exactly what he had been talking about.* He didn't want his friend getting hurt or killed because the police thought he was dangerous.

"Not like you are thinking," Kenzie explained. "Not violently. Medical malpractice. But he still defied authority when he had been told he was not allowed to practice anymore, and continued to treat people when the medical board had decided he was a danger to them."

Cook continued to glare, but didn't say anything else.

Bleaker nodded, looking a little more relaxed about this. He headed toward his car.

"No one else is to get any closer than they already are. We don't want any civilians getting close to the subject."

Kenzie nodded. She had no intention of following them into the lot. She hung on to Zachary's arm, trying to get his full attention while his eyes followed Bleaker.

"Tell me about what is going on," Kenzie urged. "You could see him on the camera? Was he armed? Was he threatening? Could you tell what was going on? Why are they here?"

Zachary's eyes were slowly drawn back to her face, and his smile grew as her questions continued. "I can't answer most of those. Couldn't see any weapon, but also couldn't tell what was going on between them. Hartfield was unlocking and opening his unit. They don't look like they're arguing, but they don't exactly look happy, either."

Kenzie couldn't hear all of what the cops said to each other as they climbed back into their cars. She could hear more sirens in the distance and wondered whether they were additional backup, or something completely unrelated.

The woman punched a code into the electronic keypad beside the gate for them, and the door swung slowly open to admit the two police cars. It stayed open rather than closing again automatically. Zachary paced back and forth, watching the police vehicles disappear behind one of the long, low buildings that housed the storage lockers. He looked down at his phone to confirm to himself that Hartfield and Maria had not moved.

They all strained their ears and waited with a mixture of eagerness and anxiety, hoping to hear something reassuring, and not a series of shots that would end in tragedy.

"He didn't have a weapon?" Kenzie repeated.

"Might have. Couldn't see one," Zachary confirmed.

"Of course he didn't have a weapon," Cook asserted. "He would not do anything to hurt anyone. He swore the Hippocratic oath. He is sworn to protect human life, not to take it."

Kenzie pressed her lips together and didn't point out that he had been the cause of the loss of at least one human life already. There had been other near-misses when he had interned with Simon and worked with him in the mobile clinic. Who knows whether there had been other tragedies when he had decided to go out by himself as the Night Doctor. She immediately started mentally reviewing the cases of various homeless people she had autopsied in the past year and what their causes of death had been. Was it possible more of them could have been victims of the Night Doctor as well?

But she understood what Dr. Cook was saying. Hartfield hadn't set out to kill those people. He had never intended that they would be his victims. It wasn't like he had stalked them and shot them with a gun. That was a different kind of killing.

As they waited, other emergency vehicles started to arrive. As well as a couple more marked squad cars. There were some dark unmarked cars and an ambulance which parked at the entrance of the parking lot so it wasn't boxed in by the other vehicles. The various cop cars filled the lot quickly and started to pull up onto the grass verge and an adjoining street.

They ignored the civilians for the most part. A couple of detectives went into the office to watch the surveillance feed and returned. They talked back and forth on radios and phones. The tension was building, with nothing to relieve it. Kenzie wished they were back in Roxboro, where there would at least have been some familiar faces amongst the law enforcement agents.

Zachary stopped pacing for a moment, standing beside Kenzie. "Obviously, just walking in there and talking to him didn't accomplish what they were hoping," he pointed out. If Hartfield had been cooperative, they would have returned by now. Hartfield and Maria in tow, telling everyone the reasonable explanation for what he was doing there with Maria.

"Yeah, you're right," she admitted. "I guess... he isn't cooperating."

"I need to talk to him," Cook said, hearing Zachary's and Kenzie's assessment. He looked around for the proper law enforcement officer to talk to. "Excuse me. Excuse me! I need to talk to someone. Who is in charge?"

The cops he spoke to barely gave him a glance, irritated, moving quickly to take care of their appointed duties, but motioned toward a plainclothes cop in a collared shirt with the top button open and blazer. No tie. Did that mean he was a rebel who refused to dress up as a sergeant or captain should? Or had he had one on earlier and pulled it off when he grew too irritated to put up with it anymore?

Cook approached him. Kenzie followed, even though she was pretty sure Cook did not want her to be any part of the conversation.

"Sir? Are you in charge here? I need to talk to someone."

The man ran a finger around the neck of the collar as if it were choking him. He scowled at Cook. "You must be Dr. Kirsch, then?"

Cook glanced over at Kenzie with a little shake of his head. "No, this is Dr. Kirsch—"

"And who are you?"

"Dr. Cook. I am the Medical Examiner in Roxboro, but more than that, I am a friend of Dr. Hartfield's, and volunteered with him at the mobile clinic. I know him well, and you're going about this all wrong. He isn't a dangerous person. All of this is just going to escalate things…"

"Come over here." The man pulled Dr. Cook to the side to a slightly quieter piece of the pavement. "I'm Captain Morrison," he introduced himself curtly. "*What* do you know about what is going on here?"

"Well, I don't know why he came here, other than… maybe to get Maria something she needed? It was Dr. Kirsch who called it in. I just wanted to talk to him. I'm sure I could get all of this straightened out."

"Because you know this Mr. Hartfield? You think you could convince him to give up his hostage and turn himself in?"

"Hostage?" Cook repeated. "Maria isn't his hostage. She's just… a patient. Someone he's treated before. We've both treated her. She's had some difficult conditions to manage, especially living on the street. But she's in transitional housing now and—"

"Dr. Cook," Morrison said sternly, "I need you to focus here. If you think Mr. Hartfield would talk to you, we can give it a try. We won't have a negotiator here for a while and are just trying to keep things calm for the moment."

"Well, yes, I'm sure if I could just talk to him, we could sort this out. It's just a misunderstanding." Cook shot a look at Kenzie. "People jumping to conclusions. That's not the way it is at all."

"Wouldn't that be nice," Morrison said, in a tone that clearly communicated he didn't think it was too likely. "Come with me. You too." He pointed at Kenzie. His eyes flicked to Zachary, but he quickly disregarded the short, scruffy-looking man and didn't even ask him who he was.

Kenzie cast an apologetic glance at Zachary and didn't try to explain to Morrison who he was or to try to get him included in the discussion. She was surprised at Morrison agreeing to talk to either of them.

48

Morrison led the two of them to a black van, and they all entered the cramped quarters where Dr. Cook and Kenzie finally had a close-up view of Hartfield on the large monitor, apparently being broadcast by Bleaker or his partner.

Hartfield was handsome, but looked a little worse for wear. He was not coiffed and wearing his blue scrubs, as he had been in the picture Kenzie had seen of him, the handsome soap opera version of Dr. Hartfield that had been fed to the media. But he also wasn't the nightmarish dark figure that had haunted Kenzie's dreams since hearing of the Night Doctor.

He was dressed in a plaid flannel shirt and khakis that looked like they had been worn for a few days. Maybe he hadn't had the energy to change since he realized that they were closing in on him. Or maybe he had been depressed by his failure to save Jack Lane. Did he even realize Jack's death had been his fault?

"You have his cell number?" Morrison asked.

Dr. Cook nodded. "Yeah, it's on my phone."

"Great. Give him a call. Put it on Bluetooth, and we will be able to hear it on the headsets." He put on a headset and handed similar devices to Kenzie and Cook. The technicians in the van were already equipped.

Cook just stood there for a moment as if waiting for someone to give him more detailed instructions or maybe to tell Morrison that it was a bad idea and that Cook shouldn't be allowed to call his friend after all.

Eventually, he pulled out his phone and woke it up. One of the technicians walked him through connecting it to the headset. Then he tapped and swiped it a few times until he found the contact record for Evan Hartfield and initiated the call.

Kenzie expected it to go to voicemail. Hartfield wasn't likely to want to talk to anyone, even his friend. She heard it ringing on her headset, and then a change in tone as it was picked up.

"Jeffrey?"

"Evan," Cook said eagerly, and then stopped suddenly, unsure what to say next, how to approach the conversation that loomed before them.

"Are you here?" Hartfield asked. His voice was stringy and high. Anxious. He sounded vulnerable. On the screen, he looked around uncertainly and wiped his forehead. "What's going on, Jeffrey? Why are you doing this?"

"It's not me. We're just investigating the death of Jack Lane. You treated him, right? That's all I'm involved in."

"You called the police about that? Had me followed here? How did you know where I was?"

"I didn't follow you. There was a private investigator... he followed Maria, not you. Never mind, don't worry about that."

"Don't worry about it? There are all of these cops. I heard sirens, there are more of them here. How can I not be worried about that? They're setting me up. They think that I did something I didn't and they're going to shoot me down."

"They're not going to shoot you. They're just worried about Maria and making sure she's safe. And she is, right? No one has to worry about her? Where is she?"

"She's with me."

They couldn't see Maria on the monitor, but Kenzie assumed the police knew she was safe. Zachary had said that she was fine when he had seen them on the security camera.

"Just let her go, Evan. They think you're holding her hostage."

"She stays with me. If I tell her to go, they're going to shoot me."

"No one is going to shoot you. They just want to talk to you. Get this all straightened out about Mr. Lane. If you just let Maria go and tell them what happened, everything will be fine. We know it was just an accident. You didn't intend to hurt anyone. You were trying to save Jack."

"You weren't there, Jeffrey. You don't know what it was like. Everything happened so fast. There was nothing I could do to save him."

"He was an alcoholic," Cook said. "That was what killed him."

Kenzie knew that wasn't true. But it was pretty close, and that might be what Hartfield needed to hear. She wasn't going to correct Dr. Cook. Arguing would only intensify things and make the situation worse. And she suspected her mic was probably muted anyway.

"He was an alcoholic," Hartfield echoed.

Kenzie remembered Simon's assertions that Hartfield had abused drugs. Did the mention of Lane's alcoholism make him feel more guilty because of his own substance abuse problems? Had *he* been drunk that day? Was that why he had made the mistake he had? Kenzie couldn't imagine how he had made such a mistake otherwise. It seemed impossible.

"Yes," Dr. Cook told him soothingly. "Let Maria go and tell us about what happened. Get it off your chest."

"People don't understand how hard it is to be a doctor. They think it is just knowing a lot of facts. They think everything happens the way they see it on TV, when you come into the hospital, get a diagnosis and the proper treatment, and go home. And everything is fine. They don't see how hard it is to diagnose problems properly, and then you treat it and the patient has an adverse reaction. They have allergies and side effects, or the treatment just has no efficacy. You have patients who would get better if they would stay on their medication, but they don't."

"No," Dr. Cook agreed. "They don't do the things you tell them to. They think they know better, or it is too hard, or they don't believe you and keep looking for another doctor who will tell them what they want to hear."

"On TV or in a good book, the doctor would tell the alcoholic what he is doing to his life and how it is going to affect his health and relationships and lifespan. And he would *get it*. They would send him to rehab, and he would go, and he would get better and not relapse."

Dr. Cook agreed. "He wouldn't keep drinking until he was bleeding all through his digestive tract, and his liver, spleen, and kidneys looked like something out of a horror movie."

Hartfield nodded on the monitor, relieved that someone understood what he was talking about. "Yes," he agreed in a choked voice. "Do you know how many times I had talked to Jack about doing something about his drinking? I talked to him as a doctor and as a friend; I begged him, but he would just smile and say that when it killed him, it killed him. No one would be able to stop it, and he would be at peace when he was gone. Until then, the only way for him to get any peace was by drinking, and at least it wasn't hard drugs." Hartfield shook his head. "Hard drugs would have been kinder. He would have been gone faster."

"How is Maria doing?" Cook prompted.

"I told you Maria is fine."

"Where is she?"

They watched the screen intently. The cop whose cam they were watching got the message and turned slightly so that his camera focused on Maria, a little behind Hartfield, slightly sheltered in the open doorway of the storage unit.

"Can I talk to Maria, Evan? Make sure she's okay?"

"The cops can see she's okay. Would she still be here with me if she wasn't? She would have left long ago."

"I just want to make sure."

Hartfield scowled. He looked around, but then decided abruptly to do what his friend asked, and reached toward Maria with the phone. She flinched back when he moved, but when he offered her the phone, she took it from him.

"Hello?"

"Maria? Hi, this is Dr. Cook. Do you remember me? I volunteer for the mobile clinic sometimes. We've met before."

"You're the other doctor," Maria said brightly. "I saw your picture."

Kenzie winced, hoping Cook wouldn't ask Maria where she had seen his picture. She didn't fancy telling him they had shown Maria his photo in a photo lineup. Even though they had never intended for her to identify him.

"Yes, I'm another doctor," Dr. Cook agreed. "How are you doing, Maria? The police are a little concerned about you."

"I'm fine! Just leave us alone. We don't need any help."

"Is Dr. Hartfield keeping you there against your will? Is he doing anything to convince you to stay?"

"We came here to get a bike," Maria told him. "Dr. Hartfield said he had a bike for me."

It was just plausible. Dr. Hartfield turned back to Maria to get the phone back from her. It wasn't until then that they could see the scalpel in his hand.

49

D r. Cook swore. But he did it before Hartfield got the phone back up to his ear, so he didn't hear it.

"You have a knife?" he demanded when he had Hartfield again. "It's no wonder the cops are worried. What are you doing with a knife?"

"It's a scalpel," Hartfield said, turning his hand to look at it. Sunlight flashed off of the blade. "Tools of the trade. It isn't a weapon. It is a tool. It is used to heal, not to hurt."

"Yes. When used correctly. But when the police want to talk to you, having one in your hand isn't a good idea. Just put it away and talk to the police. We'll explain what happened, and Maria will tell them that she can leave whenever she wants, and we'll be able to put this whole thing to bed."

Hartfield seemed to be somewhere else. He stared off into space. Everyone waited, tense, for his next move, but he just stood there, his expression flat, not moving.

"Evan," Dr. Cook prompted, trying to nudge him into a response.

"I just want it to end," Hartfield groaned. "I just want it to all be over. This whole thing is ridiculous."

"It is, isn't it? Why don't you just drop the scalpel? We can all sit down together and talk."

"You weren't there. It was terrible. Oh." Hartfield covered his face with both hands. "It was the kind of thing I would only connect with a field hospital on the war front."

He swore to himself. Kenzie wondered what he was seeing in his head. Whatever flashback he was living was pretty traumatic.

She put her hand around the headset mic to muffle her voice in case it was not muted. "Try an anchoring exercise with him," she told Dr. Cook. "Do you know how?"

Cook shook his head, frowning.

"Ask him for five things he sees. Five things he hears. Five things he smells. Focusing on the concrete will help him to anchor to the present instead of getting stuck in flashbacks."

Dr. Cook nodded. "Evan. Tell me five things you see."

"What?"

"Just do it. Look around. Tell me five things you see."

"The... sky. Maria. The storage unit." He manipulated the scalpel in his hand, looking down at it. "My shoes. How many is that?"

"One more."

"Uh... the ground. The pavement."

"Tell me five things you hear."

Hartfield shook his head. "What is this?" he asked irritably. "Don't try to 'handle' me."

"Are you okay? I just want to help you end this."

"You need to know what happened, that it wasn't my fault. I need you to know."

"Okay... why don't you tell me about it?" Cook suggested.

Kenzie shook her head. She didn't think it was a good idea for Hartfield to get into the details of what had made him so agitated and had him holding Maria hostage at knifepoint, even if he denied that was what was going on. She looked at Morrison to see what he thought of this. He should be trying to manage the situation until they could get a professional negotiator there.

Morrison just shrugged. He must have had experience to get to the position he was in, but Kenzie didn't see how he could have gotten that far without some idea that the situation they were in was dangerous and Dr. Cook might be throwing gasoline on the fire.

But what was said was said, and no one jumped in to try to back it up. As long as Hartfield was talking, that was good, wasn't it?

"Jack was in pretty bad shape when he came to me," Hartfield related. "I had a bunch of people to treat; he wasn't the only one. But someone told me that he was spitting up blood, so I figured I'd better see what was going on and if I could get him to agree to go to the hospital."

"You know Jack," Maria singsonged.

Hartfield rubbed his forehead. "You know Jack," he agreed, "he hated the hospital. He would never go, even when things were serious. I think he was afraid they would admit him to the psych ward, and he wouldn't be able to get any booze."

"So you tried to treat him," Dr. Cook said.

"I thought... maybe he had some bloody sputum. Coughing too hard or pneumonia. I didn't realize he was throwing up blood."

"When you realized, why didn't you call an ambulance?"

"I couldn't. He wouldn't go with them. I already knew that. They wouldn't take him unless he was unconscious and, by the time he got to that point, it would probably be too late. His blood pressure was dropping, so I wanted to get some fluids in him while I figured out what was going on and if I could find a way to stop or slow the bleeding."

"So you inserted an IV."

Hartfield nodded. "I know you told me not to. That it could get me in trouble. But it's hardly practicing medicine to insert an IV. That's just... palliative support..."

So Dr. Cook *had* tried to stop Hartfield from practicing medicine, trying to get him to limit himself to procedures that could be considered first aid. There was so much that the homeless needed help with, and a lot of the medical care was just basic first aid and counseling, things he could do without a medical license. Ways he could help without breaking the law.

"But that isn't all you did," Cook said, his voice low, not wanting to have the conversation in front of anyone else. "You didn't stop with just giving him fluids."

"I couldn't. He was… it was getting worse by the minute. He was throwing up so much blood… it was like a dam had burst. I had to do something to replace it, or he was going to die for sure."

Kenzie swallowed, her throat feeling constricted.

"What did you do?" Cook asked. "Use your own blood?"

"Of course not. I'm not the right type."

"You knew what blood group Jack was?"

"Of course. *A-positive*. He confirmed it. I just needed to find someone close by who could do a direct transfusion."

"Without any testing?" Cook demanded, his medical training getting the better of him. No screening for blood-borne diseases or compatibility?

"It was an emergency. I didn't have any choice. The amount of blood coming out of that man…" Hartfield's voice was choked. "I had to act immediately. Any hesitation, and he was going to die. I knew that. He was already as pale as death. I had another patient there who was O-positive. So I asked whether she would make a direct donation, and she was happy to help. She could see what was happening to Jack; everybody there could see that he wouldn't last if we couldn't replace some of the blood."

"The donor was O-positive?"

"Yes. And it was working. I could see him getting some color back. I still needed to get him to the hospital. But maybe with some blood in him, he would at least survive until I could get him there."

"The donor couldn't have been O-positive," Dr. Cook said. "Jack suffered hemolysis because of an incompatible donation. That means the donor was either AB or B."

50

"That's not possible!" Hartfield looked around wildly. His voice was panicked. "I checked. I made sure they were compatible!"

"How?" Dr. Cook demanded. "Did you test it? Did you even have a test kit?"

"I made notes of everyone's blood types," He insisted. "I kept a record so that I couldn't make a mistake. You can't rely on recollection in the midst of a crisis."

"You didn't have everyone's medical records."

"I kept my own notes." Hartfield patted his chest and pulled a notepad from the small pocket in his shirt. "Look, it's all right here." He flipped through the notebook. "Jack Lane. Type A positive."

He turned more pages, squinting at the handwriting on the pages. Remembering Zachary's question about whether it was possible Hartfield had dyslexia, Kenzie hoped he didn't also have dysgraphia like Zachary. It was a learning disability that made writing difficult or painful. The result, in Zachary's case, was nearly impossible-to-read handwriting unless he took an extra-long time to carefully write each letter neatly. Half the time, Zachary couldn't even read something he had jotted down. Was Hartfield's writing that bad? Could he read it?

"And the donor was…" Hartfield flipped pages. He stopped and mouthed the words on the page, then shook his head. "No, this isn't right. I looked that night. I checked and made sure that they were compatible. There were only a few people there to choose from, and I checked to see who was compatible. I had it right here."

He flipped back and forth through pages, desperately searching for what he had read that night, what it was that had made him think the two blood types were compatible. He made a choking noise. "The two names are very similar…" He closed the notebook again and tried to slide it back into his pocket, but couldn't seem to find his shirt pocket to put it away again. Eventually, he stuffed it into his pants pocket. "I looked it up," he protested again. "I couldn't make a mistake." He wiped sweat from his forehead.

Dr. Cook didn't say anything. Kenzie looked at him, waiting for him to come up with something to reassure or calm Hartfield. Cook shook his head and rubbed his forehead.

"Evan, let Maria go and turn yourself in. The police just want to talk to you about what happened. You know I need to document exactly what happened for the final medical examiner's report. We will need to outline exactly how you treated Jack and what happened. People make mistakes, and we need to document it to help prevent the same thing from happening again. Just like a morbidity and mortality conference at the hospital."

"That's why I kept records," Hartfield said, aggrieved, "So that I wouldn't make any mistakes."

"A notebook is not a proper medical record."

"But I didn't have an office. I couldn't keep standard records. And you know that they're not complete. They go to different places for treatment, and the records are never complete. I had to keep my own notes and rely on those…"

"And you mixed up two patients."

"It was… you don't know what it was like. There was so much blood. Jack was dying. The only way to save him was to get more blood into him. There was no way he was even going to make it to the hospital without a couple of units."

"He was very sick, even before he started bleeding," Dr. Cook reminded him. "We all knew he didn't have much longer. The cirrhosis would have killed him even if you'd managed to stabilize him. He should have been in a hospice until the end."

"But he wouldn't. We have to have a way to serve people who live on the street."

"Vermont has one of the lowest rates of unsheltered homeless in the country. We're doing better than most states."

"But they still don't get the medical care," Hartfield exploded. "Sleeping in a shelter instead of in the rough doesn't solve the problem!"

"No," Dr. Cook admitted. "But we're not going to fix that today."

"I couldn't have made a mistake like that," Hartfield insisted.

"We got the lab tests back. The Coombs test. It clearly shows blood type incompatibility. Your records were wrong, or you looked at the wrong page. But you knew you were not going to save him. And you knew that giving a direct blood transfusion without any testing was improper."

"I just wanted to help him."

Kenzie sighed. Everything she heard about Evan Hartfield indicated that he was sincere in his desire to help people, especially those in the homeless population or those who were marginalized. But one man could not save everyone and, even if it were possible, Hartfield was not that man. He was too prone to misjudgment, to making unpredictable mistakes that no amount of training seemed to be able to cure.

"Let's end this now," Cook urged. "Put down your scalpel and end this standoff."

"I'm not threatening anyone."

"Well, put it down so no one feels you are a threat. The police just want to talk to you."

Hartfield shook his head sadly. He looked down at the scalpel in his hand. He looked briefly toward the camera, the cop who was closest to him.

He reached back toward the storage unit and set the scalpel down inside the door, back in whatever kit or surgical tray he had picked it up from.

Kenzie breathed a sigh of relief. It was all over.

51

The cops started closing in on Hartfield. Maria darted forward with a cry. A collective gasp went up as she grabbed the scalpel and brandished it at the approaching law enforcement officers.

Unlike Hartfield, who had never directly threatened anyone in the time Kenzie had been watching, Maria waved the knife and yelled, warning them to stay back. Hartfield's phone was still connected, picking up her voice.

"This is the Night Doctor," Maria told the police. "You can't hurt him. He is under my protection."

Kenzie would never have predicted that Maria would be the aggressor, that she would stand there with a knife and threaten to hurt anyone. It seemed so incongruous, yet it was happening.

Maria had been paranoid; she had been running away all the time, afraid of people following her. Did she think she was cornered so, like any threatened animal, she was now defending herself and her territory, her doctor? Did she see him as part of her chosen family on the street?

She had thought for a while that Hartfield or his minions were following her, but he must have told her something that made her change her mind. He said he had brought her to the storage locker to get her a new bike. Maybe that had been enough to convince her that he could be trusted.

Morrison swore. He picked up his radio and gave his men various instructions, having them back off and give Maria and Hartfield more space again. He didn't want an incident on his watch. He was willing to wait it out.

"Maria," Hartfield sounded surprised. "What are you doing? You can't do this."

"They want to take you away. I'm not going to let them. You are the only one who cares about us. We need you."

"I know," he told her sadly. "But I won't be able to be here for a while. You'll have to trust the other doctors. Doctor Simon and Doctor Cook. You know them. You know they'll help you out."

"Not like you!"

"They're good doctors. Better than I am." He said it with sadness and regret. He had done the best he could. He'd been persistent. No matter what roadblocks were thrown up in his way, he still tried to get around them, overcome them all, and continue doing what he was driven to do.

But he knew that he had failed. He continued to make serious mistakes. Mistakes that would kill people if he kept doing what he was doing.

"Let me have that." He reached for the scalpel in Maria's hand, and she slashed at him wildly.

Kenzie flinched back as if she could protect Hartfield by protecting herself. But that didn't work. A bright red line appeared across Hartfield's arm. He looked down at it in disbelief.

"Maria!" He again reached for the scalpel, and Maria slashed at him again. The cop whose camera they were watching moved forward, closing in on the threatening woman. Kenzie's heart was in her throat. She knew that the protective vests the police wore were not stab-proof and that, if necessary, the cop would protect himself by firing on the threat.

"No!" she burst out. "Don't escalate it. Give us a chance to calm her down. Please, she's an old woman and is mentally ill. She is paranoid. Give us a few minutes to work with her, and she'll calm down."

Morrison spoke into his radio, telling the officers to pull back again. On the monitor, Hartfield was looking at the slash in his arm as he gradually seemed to realize that he was hurt and needed medical treatment. He applied direct pressure to control the bleeding and spoke calmly to Maria.

"It's okay, Maria. I just need to go with the police to talk with them. They're not going to hurt anyone. Not you. Not me. They're just here to help."

"They're the ones who have been following me around! I know it now. They're the ones who have been after me."

"No, the police are here to help. They aren't going to do anything to hurt you. Just put the scalpel back where it was so I know where it is when I need it, okay?"

"You're with them? You're together on this? I trusted you!"

"No, no one is threatening you. You're safe. We're all going to keep you safe, Maria. You're just feeling anxious. It's been a hard day. Let us take care of you, and you'll feel better."

"No! I see you for who you are now."

52

"We're going to have to do something if she doesn't calm down," Morrison warned. "We can't just let her keep threatening people with a weapon. We already have one injury. She could go after him again or injure one of my officers."

"Maria knows Zachary. She went to him for help before. She might talk to him."

"Zachary?" Morrison looked at Dr. Cook.

"No, not me. He's still out there."

"He's the one who tracked her here," Kenzie explained, "because we were helping Maria and he wanted to keep track of her."

"He's outside? He's here?"

Kenzie nodded.

It was a big vehicle, but it was getting pretty crowded when Zachary was brought in. He was reluctant to put on one of the headsets when offered one. "I can go talk to her face to face. She'll be a lot more responsive that way. It's pretty hard to convince someone that you are a safe person when you're just a voice in her ear. Especially if you're competing with a lot of other voices in her head."

"I can't send you in there in person," Morrison said. "That would be totally against regulations. We have to keep civilians out of dangerous situations, not put them in."

Zachary conceded and put on the headset when he saw that Morrison wouldn't let him communicate with her any other way.

Hartfield was still holding the phone in his hand, away from his body as he tried to keep pressure on the cut the scalpel had caused. He wasn't listening to it and, even though they could hear whatever Maria and Hartfield said as long as they were loud enough, there was no way for Maria to hear what Zachary was saying even if he shouted, unless she put it up to her ear.

Morrison spoke over the radio to one of the officers.

"Tell Hartfield to give the phone to Maria. There is a call for her."

The officer repeated the instruction. Hartfield looked in surprise at the phone in his hand. He held it up to his own ear rather than handing it to Maria.

"Hello?"

"I need to talk to Maria. Tell her it's Zachary."

"Zachary?" Hartfield looked at Maria as if he still didn't think it was the right thing to do.

"Zachary?" Maria repeated. She looked at Hartfield. "Who is Zachary? Where is he?"

Hartfield offered her the phone. "On the phone, for you."

"Oh!"

Maria took it. Hartfield reached for the scalpel as if it were an exchange, but Maria jerked it back. "No! You don't get that."

Hartfield withdrew and again put pressure on his wound, shaking his head.

"Why don't you step back from her, sir," suggested the cop.

Hartfield looked at him. "So that you have a clear shot? No, I don't think so."

"I'm just trying to ensure your safety, sir. Step back from the woman to where you are safe. Just a couple of steps would be beneficial."

Hartfield stubbornly would not, but stayed right with Maria, where he was well within range if she decided to start slashing. Kenzie didn't think Maria would go wild and start hurting anyone close to her, but she didn't know for sure. Maria's behavior was unpredictable.

"Hello, Zachary?" Maria queried, her voice warbling a little. "Are you there?"

"Yes, it's me," Zachary agreed. "Are you okay, Maria? You must be scared."

"No, no. I'm not scared. Everything is under control here."

Kenzie couldn't help exchanging a smile with Zachary over Maria's brave declaration. She was holding people she believed to be dangerous to her at knifepoint but claimed that everything was under control.

"So everything is okay? I was wondering about Dr. Hartfield. Do you think he could come and talk to me about something?"

"What? No, he's going to stay here. He was following me, Zachary. He had someone following me around. That's how they knew I was here. And now they are not letting me go. I know that. They are going to put me in some locked room somewhere. I don't want to be in one of those places."

Had Maria ever been in an institution due to her mental health? Was that what she was remembering? Or was she thinking about times she had been in jail or something she had seen on TV?

"I'm close by, Maria. I heard you were in trouble, so I came to help."

"You're a nice boy," Maria said. "Ivy said that you are a nice boy. You always were."

"Well, Ivy has been around for a long time. We've known each other for a lot of years. She knows that I would never do anything to hurt you or anyone else."

"Yes. You are a nice boy," Maria repeated in a singsong.

"Has Dr. Hartfield been taking good care of you?"

Maria turned and looked at Hartfield, who towered over her. He was holding his arm, which was dripping blood and starting to look alarming, though Kenzie knew there wasn't enough to be concerned about.

"Oh, doctor," Maria said sadly, looking at him. "You are hurt."

"I don't think it is serious, Maria," Hartfield assured her. "But I should probably get it looked at. Might need a few stitches."

"Physician, heal thyself," Maria said, and laughed. She motioned to the storage unit. "You have supplies here."

"Yes. But I can't do it myself. I'll need a couple of extra hands."

"No hands in there?" Maria teased.

Kenzie sincerely hoped that there were not any body parts in the storage unit, but she couldn't shake the feeling that the reason Hartfield had brought Maria there was to dispose of her. She supposed those morbid thoughts came naturally to a medical examiner, forever dealing with human remains collected from very diverse locations.

"Maybe you'd better give the scalpel to one of the cops," Zachary suggested. "You trust them, don't you?"

"Trust the police?" Maria laughed. "No one trusts the police."

"Then maybe that's who you *can* trust," Zachary suggested. "If no one trusts them, they can't do anything wrong without being caught."

For a moment, it seemed as if this twisted logic appealed to Maria, but then she shook her head. "You can't trust the cops."

"Who do you trust? Can we get someone here that you trust, so we can straighten everything out without anyone getting hurt?"

"Zachary is a good guy," Maria offered. "Always a good guy."

"Do you think you can trust me? Do you think you could give me the knife, and then we could help you with whatever other errands you need to do today?"

"Hmm." Maria hummed. She looked around her thoughtfully. "Why am I even here? I didn't want to come up. I was in Roxboro. You live in Roxboro."

"Yes, I do."

"But not in Clintock. Not for a *long* time." She stretched the word out.

"You're right," Zachary agreed. "I moved away from Clintock as fast as I could."

She giggled. "Did you run?"

"Well… maybe not the whole way," he teased. "But I didn't want to stay there, and I didn't want to be reminded of all the bad stuff that happened here." He paused, staring at Maria on the screen, trying to discern as much from her face as he could. "But you like Clintock, right? That is your home."

"Yes, I would not want to run away."

"It was nice of you to come to Roxboro to talk to Kenzie about Jack Lane. You remember that?"

"I'm old, Zachary. I haven't completely lost my mind. I remember."

"Did you come to Roxboro to see the doctor? Before Jack died?"

"Sometimes he is in Clintock, and sometimes he is in Roxboro. Sometimes in another town." She looked at Hartfield. "It's very hard to keep track," she told him sternly.

"Well, you seem to be able to figure out my schedule," he said with a smile.

Kenzie tried to evaluate his face from the video feed. He was pale, but it was hard to tell if that was just his natural complexion or an artifact of the video feed. It didn't appear that he'd lost enough blood to be concerned about him, but he seemed frail.

Maybe it was just his thinness. He was a tall, slim person, and his slenderness seemed exaggerated on the monitors.

"I came to see the doctor," Maria agreed in answer to Zachary's question. "A long way to bike. But it only takes me a day."

"You must be in really good shape," Zachary said admiringly.

"There are lots of things wrong with me, and sometimes I am in a lot of pain, but I can still bike."

"Better than me. I try to get out and walk, but I spend too much time sitting at my computer staring at the screen. And too much time driving from place to place in the car when I could be walking or biking."

Maria shifted her grip on the phone. She seemed to be tiring of the conversation or of having to stand there without anything being resolved.

"You were in Roxboro when Dr. Hartfield treated Jack," Zachary suggested.

Kenzie caught Zachary's eye and shook her head. He hadn't been in the room when Hartfield had told his story, and Kenzie didn't think it would do them much good to hear it again, from Maria's or Hartfield's perspective. It was best just to let that rest now.

Zachary covered up his mic, cocking his head to the side. "What?"

"We already got it from Hartfield," Kenzie whispered. "It will just wind her up again."

Zachary nodded.

Morrison was looking at his watch, scowling. "I don't like to let this go for too long," he warned. "I know you can't rush negotiations and, for the moment, she is quiet and compliant, which is progress, but…" He pressed his lips together, looking at Hartfield on the screen. "You're a doctor," he said to Kenzie. "Maybe not the kind we want in this situation, but… am I right in thinking that the doctor isn't looking too good?"

Zachary looked back at the screen. Kenzie nodded. "I was thinking that too. Maybe that wound is deeper than it looks, or he is getting woozy. We don't want to leave it too long with him needing first aid. Maybe it is nothing, but I do think he is getting paler."

Zachary nodded. He uncovered his mic.

53

"The doctor needs some attention," Zachary told Maria firmly. "You remember Kenzie? She's a doctor."

"A mortician," Maria said, then corrected herself, "A medical examiner."

"Yes, but she still can be handy with live people, too," Zachary said with a chuckle. "And she's worried about the doctor. She wants to come and give him first aid. You wouldn't want anything to happen to him."

Maria turned to look at the doctor, frowning and turning her head this way and that.

"What is going on here?" she mused. She started to lower the phone from her ear and then caught herself, as if she were falling asleep on the bus and then waking herself up abruptly. She blinked and put the phone to her ear.

"I think the doctor isn't feeling very well," she observed. "Maybe someone should take a look at him."

"I think you're right," Zachary agreed. "Why don't you put his scalpel down with the other stuff, and Kenzie will come over and have a look at him."

Once she put it down, Kenzie would probably not be allowed

anywhere near the scene. But if the doctor needed attention, she might be called upon. Zachary was just saying whatever he needed to. He needed Maria to put down the knife. That was the only real point at the moment.

Maria looked around her as if she wasn't quite sure about this action, then she nodded and set the scalpel down.

The police didn't yell or rush her. Bleaker and his partner, Kenzie assumed, were the closest ones, and they were watching the body cam of one of them. The camera view closed in slowly as the cop slowly approached the woman. He did not tackle her and take her to the ground, but put his hand on her arm. "We'll just take you out this way," he advised, and Maria went with him quietly. The other cop was Bleaker; Kenzie saw his face as he approached Hartfield and took him into custody. But he didn't shove him around and immediately frisk him either. They were trying to keep things from blowing up. They were quiet and deliberate and, Kenzie assumed, would ensure they both got medical attention immediately. Hartfield for his laceration, and Maria for a mental health assessment.

Both could face charges, but Kenzie hoped they wouldn't charge Maria. It was clear that she was not in control of her faculties and had only attacked because of her instability. If they could get her compliant on a drug that would minimize her symptoms, then hopefully she could live an easier life. She was already in transitional housing, so that meant she had access to a fridge if she needed one, and had a place where she could leave her things instead of carting around all of her earthly possessions with her all day. Kenzie was happy to know that her family foundation was helping Maria already and that they were doing something that would make a difference in her life.

She and Zachary stood outside the van, breathing the fresh air and watching the first responders dealing with the situation. Kenzie was feeling a definite chill from Dr. Cook. He was clearly upset with her for calling in the police, even though, at this point, it should have been evident to him that it had been required. If they hadn't called the police… who knew what would have happened. Kenzie was glad that everything had been resolved peacefully without anyone getting hurt. Or at least, not getting hurt by Hartfield. They had not foreseen the hostage becoming the threat. Cook talked to the police about what would happen to Hartfield and where he would be held. Then he headed back to his SUV without a word to Kenzie.

Zachary was watching Cook's departure as well.

"There's going to be trouble there."

"Yeah. I feel bad. I didn't mean to make things strained between us, but we had to do what we did."

"Hartfield was his friend. There's nothing you could do to make him feel better about it."

"I guess not. But I wish there was. I didn't do it because I wanted to get Hartfield in trouble. But… someone had to stop him."

"Yeah," Zachary agreed. "You couldn't let him keep operating when he was putting people in danger. I can't believe Dr. Cook would let it go on without doing anything about it. I mean, he could get in trouble for that, couldn't he?"

"Knowingly letting someone else commit malpractice?" Kenzie asked. "Yeah, I would say so."

Zachary nodded. He looked at his phone. "Time for dinner?" he suggested.

Kenzie looked at her own phone and was surprised her stomach hadn't been rumbling. It had been a long time since she had eaten a sandwich at the coffee shop. Everything had taken much longer than she had thought it had. It seemed like the events of the afternoon had rushed by, everything happening quickly. But it had not all happened in a few minutes like she thought it had.

"Yeah, for sure. We'd better have something before we hit the road back."

"What do you want to get?"

"I actually have no idea what's good around here. You're from Clintock. Are there any must-see dining places?"

Zachary shook his head ruefully. "I never had money to eat anywhere when I lived here. I was in foster care or living on soup kitchens and what I could afford at the convenience store."

He didn't say he had been eating out of garbage bins, but Kenzie suspected panhandling and dumpster diving had not been outside Zachary's experience.

"Okay, well, do you want to find somewhere nice, or just a drive-thru?"

Zachary looked at the time again, considering.

"I'm not working tomorrow," Kenzie told him, "if that makes any difference to you. If you want to stay out late, it's not a 'school night.'"

"Well, it might be nice to sit down, relax, and have a date night before heading home."

"Okay, why don't you check the map and see what is around that we might be interested in? I just want to check in with Morrison before we leave, make sure he doesn't need anything else…"

Zachary nodded and bent over his phone to see what he could find that they might be interested in.

"I didn't want to leave without talking to you," Kenzie told Morrison. "I feel like we kind of threw a wrench in the works for you guys today. I appreciated you not making a big deal of us making the call and being in the way here."

Morrison shrugged. "Campbell had good things to say about you, said it was a legitimate call, so we didn't sweep in here thinking it was a crank call or ready to take some civilian's head off. This guy was a murderer." He shook his head. "Some of these strait-laced guys can really fool you. You think you've got it all figured out and they are the type who would never put a foot wrong. And then you find out they're really rebels who would never listen to the rules of the game."

Kenzie didn't know if she would classify Hartfield as a murderer. He had certainly never intended to kill anyone, as far as she knew. He seemed devoted to being a healer. He just wasn't as good as he thought he was. A doctor who was that erratic and who you could never trust to perform under pressure could be more dangerous than any intentional murderer.

"I'm glad to get him off the street," she admitted. "It's lucky that Dr. Cook got a confession out of him. That will help."

"It's on the record," Morrison agreed. "Unless some lawyer figures out a way to get it thrown out."

"Then we've still got Maria. She said she was there and that Hartfield gave Jack Lane a blood transfusion, and the lab reports show that he died from being given an incompatible blood type. So even without his confession, we've still got enough. Hopefully. I mean, I'm not the detective on the case, so I'm speaking out of school…"

"I get it," Morrison said with a nod. He hooked his thumbs over his belt and watched the activity of the other cops as they finished up their various duties. "We're talking about evidence that *should* be admitted and *should* show that his treatment resulted in the victim's death. Even if things don't always turn out the way we expect…"

"Yeah. So before we head out, do you need anything more from us? Dr. Cook already left." Kenzie motioned to where his SUV had been parked. "Zachary and I are going to get some dinner before we head back to Roxboro."

"I know where to reach you, so if I need any statements from you, I'll just contact your office. Your detective will be in touch from his end. We'll let him coordinate everything."

Kenzie nodded. "Okay. Thanks again. I appreciate you being here to support us."

He gave her a little salute. "You bring me the murderers and I'll lock them up."

Kenzie smiled and returned to Zachary's side. "I'm done here. Let's head out."

He walked alongside her, apparently navigating by echolocation, since he never looked up from his phone. "What do you feel like? Anything in particular? There's an Italian place with good reviews."

"I could do Italian." Kenzie smiled. "Do they have garlic bread?"

Zachary grinned without looking up. "With five-star reviews, apparently."

"Italian it is."

54

She expected Zachary to be completely relaxed when they sat down. They had sorted everything out, done everything they could, and now it was time to enjoy the fruits of their labor. Or at least the fruits of the olive tree. But Zachary was still hypervigilant. He sat with his back to the wall and his face to the door to evaluate anyone who might come in while they were there. His head was constantly turning, checking out everyone present. He startled at a crash of crockery in the kitchen and was turned around and halfway out of his seat before he caught himself and forced himself to sit back down again.

Kenzie didn't comment on his anxiety until they had both made it halfway through their meals, and he'd consumed a considerable amount of garlic bread. With the calming effect of the complex carbs at work and no longer on edge from the stand-off, he should be more relaxed, but he still seemed to be just as wound up as he had been for days.

"So, what's going on?" Kenzie finally asked. "You said that the only reason you've been so paranoid and vigilant lately is because of Maria's concerns. Thinking that she was being followed. But now you've seen how unstable she is. She was being paranoid. There was never anyone following her."

"There wasn't?" Zachary repeated. "She said that she had been followed since she had been treated by the Night Doctor. And today, we saw her being held hostage by the Night Doctor. After he tracked her to Roxboro to get her and bring her back here."

Kenzie opened her mouth, trying to find the words. She shook her head. "That's just spin. She wasn't being followed. Hartfield just found her because… they met up by chance at the soup kitchen. And he didn't exactly take her hostage. I'm not sure how to describe what happened out there today, but it wasn't exactly a hostage-taking."

"They just coincidentally ran into each other?"

"Why would he follow her?" Kenzie asked reasonably.

"Because she had seen him kill someone and he was afraid that she would talk about it… which she did."

"You don't believe that he'd been following her that whole time, from the time Lane died until today."

"Him personally? No. She said people. More than one person. He had friends, colleagues, people who believed in what he was doing and were helping him out somehow. There were street people networked together to help coordinate his appearances, where he would be, when, and what time he would be able to see everyone. He was moving from town to town, so he had people all over the area, not just in Clintock. Could he have had a few people following her and keeping an eye on what she was doing to report back to him? Or even just watching for her in the usual places? You don't think so?"

"Well, I suppose," Kenzie admitted. "There might have been someone… keeping track of where she was. Loosely. Or people in the community that gave him a heads-up when they saw her. But not… spies on her tail, watching her every move. That just doesn't seem believable."

Zachary shrugged. His eyes shifted to the door as someone came in, then eventually back to her again.

"But even if someone was following Maria, that's over now," Kenzie pointed out. "They have the Night Doctor in custody. It's all over."

"Maybe."

"Maybe? He is in custody."

"Doesn't mean he'll stay there. The chances that they'll keep some doctor in jail until he's tried for malpractice are… pretty low. And he still has this network on the outside. We don't know who is involved and how deeply. We don't know if people will be really upset that he was arrested and retaliate."

"Retaliate for what? He's the one who made a mistake. Nothing was done intentionally. I'm just doing my job, following up on how Lane was killed and who was responsible."

"That's not necessarily how everyone will see it. People were real fans of the Night Doctor and what he was accomplishing. Even Maria admired him and said he was a better doctor than any of the others. Half the time, she was worried about the people following her, and half the time, she was worried about him and making sure that he could still operate."

Kenzie considered this uneasily. She didn't like to admit that Zachary had some good points. She had seen not only that Maria admired the disgraced doctor, but also how Dr. Cook and Dr. Simon felt about him. They both said that he was a good doctor. They both talked about how committed he was to helping people, especially the homeless. He was one of the few doctors she had met who was committed to finding a solution to treating the homeless and ensuring they got regular, consistent care. He didn't want them to slip through the cracks of the system, and that wasn't just ego. It was something that was deeply ingrained in his makeup.

People recognized that, and they didn't want to lose him as a doctor.

But that didn't mean that Zachary and Kenzie faced any threat of violence. Hartfield's admirers would understand that he couldn't be allowed to continue practicing without a license, especially when he took extra risks and made serious mistakes in his treatment. Anyone could see that he must not be allowed to continue. Even Dr. Cook.

"I don't think you need to worry that someone is going to come after us here," she told Zachary logically. "That's all I'm saying.

Maybe you're right; maybe there are a lot of people who will be disappointed or angry about the Night Doctor not being able to operate anymore. But I don't think that they're going to come after us. We don't live here and they do not know where we are."

She sipped her water, watching his face and trying to evaluate how he was taking her comments.

"So you can relax and just enjoy the evening. Think about retaliatory action later, when we're home and you've had a good rest and a chance to think about what is or isn't likely to happen. I think you'll decide that the risk is pretty small, and you don't need to spend time worrying about it."

There was an uncomfortable silence as Zachary thought about this, and Kenzie reconsidered how she had worded it. Could she have put it in a way less likely to offend him? She hadn't accused him of overreacting. Not really. She hadn't told him that he was being unreasonable or paranoid. Just that he could relax now and think about it more later.

"You're not a PI," Zachary told her eventually.

"No." Kenzie wondered where this was leading.

"You don't know how easy it is to surveil someone, track them, or predict what they will do next. The people that you deal with are not part of that world. They are either doctors or they are past doing anything. Your patients are not going to track you to try to get back for the way you treated them." He gave her a little smile.

"No," Kenzie agreed dryly. She was glad to see that Zachary was maintaining his sense of humor, no matter how much the situation had stirred things up for him. "My patients are not likely to complain about their medical care."

"That lot was full of cops. But there were other people around, too. The manager who was on duty. The people across the street were rubbernecking, trying to see what was going on, texting and tweeting to each other. Dr. Cook. Who knows how many of the people who were watching to see what went down were former patients of Dr. Hartfield? You know that he arranged things so that he could treat several people at a time. There might have been a number of people there to see him tonight who paid attention to who else was there. You and I were in the van, and the car was unattended. Someone could easily have put a tracker on it."

"With all of the police everywhere?" Kenzie shook her head. "I don't think anyone could have gotten in there unnoticed."

"They may have been noticed, but it only takes a few seconds to attach a tracking device to a vehicle. You kneel down to tie your shoe, lean over on the car, pick up something you've dropped. You act like it is your own vehicle, and the cops will not know the difference. They all had other things to do. They were distracted by the standoff."

"Well… you can check the car for trackers tomorrow."

"You said that they couldn't know that we were here. You said that they couldn't track us to the house." He gazed at her. "But they could. And if they didn't put a tracker on the car, they might have followed us. I watched for a tail, but we only went a short distance. It can be hard to spot a tail in that time, especially if it is more than one car. Or someone could have guessed where we went by what was in the area. It wouldn't take long to check out the favorite and well-reviewed restaurants in the area. Especially if they have more than one person acting in concert."

Kenzie looked around uneasily. Not as worried about Zachary's paranoia now as she was the chance that someone there had been involved with the Night Doctor's network and had followed them there. Or even just been hungry like they had been and gone to the nearest good restaurant, where they might then have spotted Kenzie and Zachary and recognized them from the standoff. She didn't know how much of what had happened was known to the public. Had the police given any information to the public? To the people who had hung around with their phones, trying to get a shot of something interesting?

"You don't really think there is anyone here who intends us any harm?"

Zachary held his hands palms up in a surrendering motion. "I don't know. I've been watching pretty carefully, and I don't see anyone who appears to have recognized us or is watching us. But I don't know if anyone is tracking our movements or waiting for us to go back outside."

Kenzie turned to look out the window. Of course it was dark outside, and it was impossible to tell if anyone was sitting in a car in the parking lot waiting for Zachary and Kenzie to reappear. She and Zachary had once been in an accident after someone had cut his brake lines.

But someone who was upset over their doctor being taken into custody would not retaliate with that kind of violence. That didn't make any sense. Someone upset about their doctor being taken away might shout at her, get in her face about what a terrible thing she had done, about how great their needs were. But they wouldn't resort to violence.

"I think we're fine," she said firmly, hoping to convince both herself and Zachary. "I don't think that anyone would react violently to this. If they want to protest what I have done, it's not hard to find the medical examiner's office and either write a letter or make a phone call. There's no need for anyone to track us."

Zachary shrugged but didn't say that he agreed or disagreed. He obviously had his reservations, and it made sense for him to be careful. They had both been through some tense situations in the past. But she couldn't see anyone reacting violently to what they had done.

Kenzie found that she wasn't hungry anymore, and laid down her fork.

55

Z achary's phone rang, making both of them jump. Kenzie laughed and put her hand over her heart while Zachary fumbled to answer it.

"Sheesh, I hope you don't use that alarm while you're on surveillance," Kenzie laughed.

Zachary chuckled. He swiped the phone screen and answered the call, which surprised her.

"Zachary," he announced himself. His brows went up, and he pursed his lips as he listened.

Eventually, he nodded. He looked down at the phone and then across the table at Kenzie. He covered up the mic and spoke to her.

"Do you mind if we make a stop before we head back to Roxboro?"

"Uh, yeah, if you need to."

If he had to see someone in Clintock, it made more sense to cover it tonight than to return tomorrow or the next day.

"It's just... an old friend. She heard about Maria and is concerned."

Kenzie tried to remember the names Maria had mentioned the first time they had met with her. "Is it... Ivy?"

"Yes." Zachary nodded quickly. "I don't think it will take very long. But she's a friend; I don't want to just put her off, and it would be rude to try to discuss it over dinner." He motioned to Kenzie and the table.

"Yeah."

"Sorry. Be right with you." He spoke into his phone again. "Yeah, I'll be there within the next hour. You're going to be around?"

He listened for a moment, then said a quick goodbye and hung up.

"Sorry," he apologized again. "I know we don't let the phone interrupt dinner, usually... but she's here in town and I didn't want to miss her if she needed something while I'm here."

"Yeah, I get it. Unusual circumstances. We'll finish up here, then, and then head over to..."

"It's a community outreach center. She runs... everything. Takes care of everyone in the neighborhood."

Zachary seemed hesitant to talk about her. She was part of his former life. A life that Kenzie had only caught glimpses of through Mr. Peterson and Pat and the very occasional windows that Zachary opened himself. Kenzie knew that Ivy Shane had been an important part of his past, but didn't know much about her.

"She sounds like a wonderful person."

A smile illuminated Zachary's face. "Yeah. She is. It's amazing what she's done with herself."

"I'm looking forward to meeting her."

Another brief shadow passed over his face. Was he worried that she wouldn't like Ivy? That she would look down on her for some reason? Kenzie came from a very different background from Zachary and Ivy. Zachary had seen the privileged life Kenzie had led. But she thought that she had proven herself in the time that they had known each other. He should know that she did not judge people by how they were raised or their poverty or wealth. She got along with the Petersons and with Zachary's siblings, other than Joss, and she did the best she could with Joss.

But this was another test she had to pass. Another part of

Zachary's life that might be opened up to her if she could show him that she was accepting and nonjudgmental.

Zachary looked at the food remaining on his plate and then at Kenzie's. She had already decided that she was finished eating.

"Do you think… we've got an hour to get over there if you are still hungry."

"No, I'm ready to go. And I think you could probably stand to get out of here. You're just a ball of anxiety right now."

But he'd moved on. Now he was focused on getting to the appointment with Ivy and, while he still took a careful look around the restaurant as they stood up and paid for the meals, it was more perfunctory. He was less tense than he had been. Still careful, but not all wound up in it.

56

Clintock was, on the whole, not as wealthy as Roxboro. It had a few newer, more affluent areas, but most of it consisted of houses built in the sixties and seventies without much imagination. There was denser housing with town-houses, duplexes, and row houses. Not much in the way of apart-ments, it still had a rural feel, with few buildings taller than two or three stories.

The area they had eaten dinner in, just outside the industrial park the storage units were in, had been reasonably nice. The restaurant was good for family dinners or dates, not too expensive or fancy, but also not fast food; a place you could sit down and take your time getting to know the person you were eating with and not feel rushed. But within a few minutes of driving, they were in a much poorer, run-down area. A number of the houses they drove by had boarded-up windows. Some were occupied, and some looked abandoned.

Zachary's eyes were alert as he navigated through the area, darting back and forth, watching for movement and dangers that Kenzie was unfamiliar with. If she had been there by herself, she would have gotten out of the area as quickly as possible. She didn't feel unsafe being there with Zachary. He might be small and not carry a weapon, but he was still tough. He'd been through a lot, and he could fight like a wolverine when cornered or when someone he loved was in danger. He wouldn't just buckle under pressure. And he knew how to talk himself into and out of places. Talking would always be his first layer of defense. He could use his brain and his mouth to get out of almost anything.

Kenzie had hoped that they were just driving through the sad, run-down neighborhood but, in a few minutes, Zachary was pulling into a small parking lot behind a low-slung older building that had been added onto haphazardly, resulting in a number of dangerous-looking dark corners.

Zachary parked in the pool of light below a streetlight. He got out of the car and looked around. He bent down to look back into the car at Kenzie. "Looks okay. Let's go in."

"This isn't the best place to be at night. Are you sure... maybe you could call or video chat with Ivy, or come back here during daylight."

Though she wasn't sure it looked like it would be that much safer in the daylight. It seemed clear that it was a rough area day or night.

Zachary didn't answer, but walked around the car and reached his hand out to her when he got close. Kenzie climbed out of the car and took his hand. Zachary had the key fob in his other hand and locked the doors and set the security alarm. He had a small flashlight on his keychain, and he shone it in the window, checking the position of the locks. He pushed the button a couple more times and looked around.

"You okay with this?" Kenzie questioned.

He nodded. He shone the flashlight around them as they stepped out of the pool of light cast by the streetlight. It wasn't a powerful light, but it did make Kenzie feel a little better. He ran it along the outside wall of the community center in either direction, lighting up all of the pockets of darkness to ensure that there could be no one hiding in the shadows before he reached the door.

Before he could open the door to see if it was unlocked or

whether they would need to knock or phone Ivy, it was pushed open and a tall black man stood there scowling at them.

"Zachary Goldman?" he demanded.

Zachary nodded. "Yes. That's me."

"I wasn't told you would have a guest."

"This is Dr. Kenzie Kirsch," Zachary said briefly, not indicating that she was his girlfriend or the assistant medical examiner in Roxboro. Apparently, this man was not entitled to that information.

He grunted and held the door open for Zachary and Kenzie to enter. When they were inside, he locked the heavy door.

"This way."

The inside of the building was a bit of a maze, having been built onto so many times like it was. Some of the flooring and construction looked like it had survived from the sixties and seventies, and some had been upgraded. It smelled of a mixture of sweat and old food and something Kenzie associated with kids, though she couldn't identify what it was. Throughout the center, there were pictures on the walls drawn by children and teens, and a number of community awards and athletic team plaques were hung here and there. Old and new plaques hung side by side; there didn't appear to be any chronological order.

The man led them to an office with an open door and gestured, but didn't enter. Apparently, he was not part of whatever this meeting was.

"Zachary!" She heard the woman greet Zachary with enthusiasm as he entered ahead of Kenzie, but he blocked Ivy from Kenzie's view, so she could not see the woman until the hug was complete and the two broke apart.

"This is Kenzie," Zachary introduced, stepping to the side so that he wasn't between them. "My girlfriend."

Ivy nodded, her eyes dancing. She was a small, pixielike woman, with short blond hair and an intensity that felt out of place at the end of the day. If she was the director of all or many of the programs at the community center, she must be exhausted at the end of the day, especially at the end of a Saturday, when she must have had programs running all day long. But Kenzie never would have guessed it by her energy level and demeanor.

"Well, come sit down, both of you," Ivy instructed. "We'll try to make this quick. I'm sure you want to get back home early tonight." Ivy's hand rested lightly on Kenzie's arm for a moment as she ushered them into their seats, then squeezed between the desk and the wall to sit back down behind her desk. She looked at Kenzie. "I just have to say… you're a very lucky woman," she told Kenzie. "This kid," she indicated Zachary with a tilt of her head, "is a very special guy. You know he saved my life once?"

Zachary flushed red and waved his hand to dismiss this. "I didn't save her life. I just helped… get her out of a fix when the police thought she had done something she hadn't."

"I would have gone to prison," Ivy said. "I was looking down the barrel of an armed robbery charge, and it would have been the end for me.'"

Zachary was still shaking his head, still blushing. "She always tells people that. But if they had sent her to juvie, she would just have taken over the block there. She would have been telling the COs and matrons what to do and have everything whipped into shipshape in a few months. It wasn't the end of anything."

Ivy grinned in appreciation at his words and settled into her seat.

Most people did not consider Zachary a catch. Kenzie's friends wondered why she had gotten together with him, why they had even dated in the first place, let alone started a long-term live-in arrangement with him. Her parents liked Zachary, for the most part, but still didn't understand how they had gotten together or how the relationship worked. Too many people saw it as Kenzie helping Zachary out when that was far from the truth. She was not his mother or his babysitter. She got just as much out of their partnership as he did. Though when they were going through hard times, she sometimes needed to be reminded of the fact. She liked Ivy and the fact that she thought Zachary was a good catch and still made a big deal of what he had done for her all of those years ago.

Ivy was a few years Zachary's senior, but not a lot, which made it difficult to figure out what their relationship had been all of those years ago and how Zachary had helped Ivy stay out of juvie. If she had been a juvenile, then he had too. Even younger than she was. Mr. Peterson had said something about it one time. It had been something to do with Zachary and some photos he had taken.

"You'll have to tell me about it sometime," she told Ivy. "I think Zachary's too modest."

"I will," Ivy promised. She folded her hands on her computer desk. "Now… what I was hoping to hear was what happened to Maria." Her bright smile disappeared, and she looked serious and concerned. "Things were going really well for her, and now she's been arrested?"

57

"I don't know if she's been arrested," Zachary disagreed. "She was being taken into custody after a... a situation with the police. I think they were probably going to take her to the hospital rather than detention. She was acting very... agitated and anxious. She thought that someone was going to harm her. I don't know if anyone was really trying to follow or hurt her. Although..." he sighed. "Then there was this thing with Evan Hartfield. Do you know him?"

Ivy nodded, her lips pressed together. She did not announce that he was the Night Doctor nor that he had been doing anything out of the ordinary.

"Well, he was there too," Zachary fumbled. "And he *was* arrested, I guess." He looked at Kenzie.

"He was practicing medicine without a license," Kenzie said. "Holding himself out as a doctor when he wasn't one any longer. And he caused the death of one of his patients. That will come out in the next few days."

"No, really?" Ivy shook her head. "That's terrible. I'm so sorry to hear it."

She didn't defend Hartfield, at least, or say that it couldn't possibly be true. Kenzie appreciated that.

"He took Maria hostage this afternoon," Zachary resumed. "We don't know if that was his intention from the start. It seemed like... he might have wanted to get rid of her as a witness because she had seen what had happened and was talking about it."

Ivy nodded slowly. "I told her she should reach out to you," she explained. "I don't know Dr. Kirsch, but I know you, and I knew you wouldn't turn her away without hearing her out."

Zachary nodded. "Everybody else was keeping quiet. Shutting us out because we were strangers. It was really helpful to have someone come to us who would talk about what had happened."

"You're not a stranger," Ivy said. "They just haven't been around long enough to know you."

Zachary smiled.

"Something has been going on with Maria," Ivy said, frowning. Lines ran from the corners of her nose to her mouth, making her look older than she had appeared at first. "I wish I knew exactly what. But... if the police are taking her for evaluation, maybe the doctors will be able to figure it out."

"What do you mean?" Kenzie asked. "Has she been behaving differently than usual?"

"Absolutely," Ivy said emphatically. "I don't know how she behaved with you, but when I saw her... she was being very erratic, very anxious. Almost paranoid."

"She was definitely acting paranoid today," Kenzie agreed. "She doesn't normally?"

"No. No, she has always been very stable. She was on the street because of physical illness and losing her job, not because of mental illness or addiction. That had never been part of it before."

Kenzie remembered Zachary saying something to that effect. She frowned. "What physical illness? She seems to be able to ride long distances on her bike."

"Uh, honestly, I don't remember..." Ivy trailed off.

"Asthma and arthritis," Zachary advised.

Kenzie turned to look at him, surprised. "She talked at the gala," Zachary said, shrugging. "I remember her story."

"Well, I guess they'll do their evaluation at the hospital and see what they can find out," Kenzie said. "I'd be surprised if it was late-occurring schizophrenia. Maybe bipolar. Maybe a medication side effect. Seniors can sometimes display very bizarre behaviors due to a urinary tract infection. Treat it, and their behavior goes back to normal."

"Then what would happen with the police? With charges, I mean," Ivy said. "If she was mentally ill because of a UTI and did something like this... is she going to jail?"

"I don't think anyone wants Maria to go to jail. I don't think Hartfield himself would want her going to jail. He was trying to help her. He knew she wasn't acting normally."

"But that doesn't necessarily mean she won't be charged with anything, does it?" Ivy asked.

Kenzie shrugged, conceding. "No. It isn't up to the victim. But I don't think anyone wants to put this woman in prison."

Neither Ivy nor Zachary appeared to be particularly reassured by Kenzie's gut instinct. They had lived on the street and seen things that Kenzie had not. The justice system did not work the same for an indigent Black woman with no permanent address as it did for someone in the Kirsch family's social circles. A scenario that could easily be taken care of by placing a phone call to the right person or making a donation to the policeman's benevolent fund if Lisa or Kenzie were the woman involved could result in a devastating, life-changing ordeal for someone like Maria.

"Okay," Kenzie said. "I don't know that. I will follow up with the police and see if I can find out how it was disposed of and if we can keep Maria from being charged with anything in this. I certainly don't want to see her punished for something that was clearly out of her control."

Ivy smiled. "I knew you would see things our way."

Kenzie smiled back. "Of course. I'll do what I can to ease this through. I don't want anything to happen to Maria either."

Zachary looked at them both and nodded his agreement. "And what about the men who were following her?"

"We don't know that anyone was," Kenzie offered. She couldn't prove it, but Maria had not had any evidence that she *was* being followed either. All they had was her word for it. The word of a clearly delusional woman. But, as Zachary would tell her, just because she was paranoid, that didn't mean someone *wasn't* out to get her. "I don't think there was." She considered her answer before going on. "If she was being followed, then wouldn't they have done something? Made her disappear? Found a way to silence her? She told you that someone was following her?"

Ivy nodded.

"She told us someone was following her. She told us about what had happened to Jack Lane. If she was being followed by someone in the Night Doctor's network, then would they have been content to let her keep talking about what had happened and seeking out help?"

Zachary nodded slowly. "Yeah, maybe not," he admitted. "Although they might just not have moved very fast."

"If they thought the Night Doctor was in danger of being identified or exposed as having been the one to kill Jack Lane, wouldn't they have acted quickly?"

Again, Zachary and Ivy both seemed to concede that this was likely.

"I really don't think anyone was following Maria. I think it was just paranoia."

Ivy Shane leaned back in her chair, making it creak. "Okay," she agreed. "Thanks for coming to talk to me and let me know the details. I just hope that Maria is okay. I would hate to see her lose her housing because of this. Or to be slapped into an institution or jail. There have to be better ways to take care of her, even if she is mentally ill."

Kenzie got the feeling that Ivy knew something about the fact that the Kirsch family foundation had helped to fund the program that had provided transitional housing for Maria. She nodded her head. "I'll talk to my mother. See what I can do."

"Excellent. I think... Zachary was very lucky to find you, too."

Zachary looked at Kenzie, his ears getting red.

"I think so too."

58

"Let me have John walk you out," Ivy said when they got up to say their goodbyes.

That was one service that Kenzie was not going to decline. She glanced at Zachary. He did not seem inclined to be macho about it and reject an escort out to the car either. She was glad he wasn't inclined to be that way, acting aggressively and trying to show how tough he was. Despite his background, he didn't seem to feel the need. About the only "macho" thing he did was to pretend that he wasn't in any pain when he clearly was. She always had to be on the lookout for any injuries or emotional traumas that he didn't want to disclose.

John, the tall black man who had opened the door for them and led them to Ivy's office, walked them back through the rabbit warren of hallways to the door they had come in through.

"Will you be here until Ivy leaves?" Zachary asked him.

"Yes. One of us always sticks around until she leaves for the day."

"Good. I know she's tough and can protect herself, but…"

"Call me sexist," John said, "but I don't want any woman here alone at night. It's just not a good idea. We make sure people know that she is never alone."

"She seems like a really special lady," Kenzie told Zachary. "I'd love to hear more of the story about what happened when you were kids."

Zachary blushed again. He turned his face away from her. "She makes a big thing of it. But it wasn't that big of a deal."

"It obviously was for her. Didn't Lorne say something about it being your first case?"

Zachary nodded. "It was after that I started thinking about being a PI. Finding out what training I would need and what the process was to get certified so that I could be an investigator. I might not be able to sell my pictures to earn a living, but I could make money from photography in other ways."

"Surveillance pictures instead of art."

He nodded.

John gave Zachary a brief look, but then his expression closed as he obviously decided it was none of his business and didn't say anything about it. He unlocked the door and stepped out, reaching out an arm to bar Zachary or Kenzie from following him. He looked around outside, body tense, listening and alert. He had a large flashlight, much stronger than the one on Zachary's keychain, and shone it around the parking lot. There wasn't any movement. He stepped out farther and repeated the process. He looked back at them and nodded.

"All clear."

Kenzie released her breath. She hadn't realized how tense her muscles were and that she had been holding her breath in anticipation of John finding an intruder.

Zachary clicked his key fob before stepping out of the building. The car lit up inside and out and didn't reveal any sinister figures.

"Okay," Zachary breathed. "Looks good." He stepped out ahead of Kenzie, looked around, and then allowed her out with him. They got into the car. "Last time I was here, looking for Robby... things were a bit exciting."

Kenzie didn't know any of the details, but that investigation had ended up being rife with danger and had re-aggravated a lot of old trauma for Zachary. She was glad that everything had worked out and Zachary had been safe. She knew he was still dealing with some of the memories that had surfaced, though he did not detail them for her, and she didn't know if he had brought them up with Doctor B in his individual sessions.

He locked the doors and started the engine. John retreated back into the community center. Kenzie looked at Zachary. His eyes were wide, and his respiration rate elevated. "Are you okay?"

"Yeah, I will be." He sounded somewhat strangled. Kenzie was glad that they were heading home. It was about time. And she was glad for the highway drive before they reached home. It would give Zachary a chance to recover. Highway driving always helped to relax him. She decided she would *not* talk to him about anything related to the day's events or any danger that anyone had been in, whether today or during a past investigation. She would keep everything light and calm and let him recover.

Sunday was a free day. No work. No trip to see the Petersons. No dinner with either of Kenzie's parents. She wasn't on call for the medical examiner's office. That meant she could sleep in as long as she wanted to, have a lazy mid-morning breakfast, and spend the day any way she wanted to. Which probably meant running a few errands that she had neglected earlier in the week.

It was a nice way to celebrate the resolution of the Jack Lane case. When she went to work on Monday, she could put the finishing touches on the preliminary report she had issued and hopefully go final on it. It was always a relief to get to the end of a difficult case.

But Kenzie found that she could not sleep as late as she would have liked to. By the time she passed her normal wake-up time, her mind was already worrying over the details around Maria, and her brain would not let her settle back into sleep.

Eventually, she got up, had a cup of the coffee that Zachary had already brewed, and looked up the phone number for Captain Morrison in Clintock. She didn't think she would reach him at the office on a Sunday, but hoped that her brain would calm down and let it go if she left him a voicemail message and could tell herself that she had taken the necessary steps to follow up on Maria's case as she had promised Ivy.

"Morrison."

"Oh," Kenzie was surprised to hear his voice in her ear. "Captain Morrison, it's Dr. Kirsch. I actually wasn't expecting to find you in and was just planning to leave you a message."

"Busted," he told her. "Not going to get away with a hit-and-run voicemail today."

Kenzie smiled. "I guess not. I was just following up on Maria. I have been worrying about her and what was going to happen. I assume... well, I didn't think that you would put her in jail, so I was just wondering if she is being evaluated at the hospital, or if she was sent to another facility..."

"Yes, she was transferred to the hospital for evaluation and possible treatment," Morrison agreed. "She can stay there however long she needs to; I'd rather not have her behind bars. When she's released, the DA will have to decide whether to charge her for her assault on Dr. Hartfield with a deadly weapon. We will recommend against it, but I can't make any promises."

"Good, I'm glad to hear that. And... do you know how they will deal with Dr. Hartfield?"

"He's in the hospital right now too. I don't expect he'll be there long, but the same is true... when he gets back, the DA will need to decide how to proceed. Of course, in his case, we are hoping for a strong response. He has been warned not to treat anyone in the past and has continued to act with reckless disregard. If released, I am sure he would continue to do the same."

"Yes. I suspect so. What was he taken to the hospital for? I didn't think the cut on his arm was bad enough for hospitalization."

"Not the cut," Morrison agreed. "We could have had that stitched up quickly enough for him to be back in our cells last night. But the paramedics were concerned about possible complications. Something to do with his heart and blood pressure. They took him to the hospital to have it all checked out. Doctors say he is fine, but they would keep an eye on him overnight just to make sure there were no issues."

"Maybe a vagal response," Kenzie suggested. "He did look pretty unsteady in the end yesterday. Good thing he didn't faint on us."

"Might have ended things more quickly. I imagine Maria would have given up pretty quickly to get him medical aid."

"Maybe. But you always have to worry about someone hitting their head when they faint. We had a case a few months back where —" Kenzie cut herself off. Morrison had things to do. He wasn't interested in hearing about her interesting and unusual cases. "Sorry. I like my job. Thanks for taking the time. You have a nice day off."

Morrison chuckled. "You too, doctor."

59

When Kenzie disconnected the call, she realized that Zachary was hovering near the doorway, waiting for her to get off the phone.

"Hey. I guess I should have put that on speaker so you could hear. I didn't know you were there. Maria is at the hospital in Clintock for evaluation. They're happy to recommend medical treatment instead of having to prosecute her for something that was caused by mental illness. So hopefully, everything will be okay on that end."

He nodded, rubbing his dark-whiskered beard. "Good. And what about Hartfield? It sounded like you were talking about him, too."

"He was also taken to the hospital. Some people have a reaction when they get hurt or in other circumstances, called a vagal response. Heart rate slows, blood pressure drops, and they might faint. That's probably why he was looking so rough at the end. I didn't think it could be from blood loss because it didn't look like that much."

"Unless he'd been donating blood."

"What?" Kenzie looked at him. "You think he was the donor for Jack Lane? I don't think so. He would have known his own blood type. He wouldn't have made the mistake of giving Jack the wrong type if it was his own. If he had dyslexia, like you suggested, then he might have read the wrong patient record in his notebook. Two similar names, and he's in a panic because Jack is losing so much blood, so he ends up looking at the wrong page in his book and thinks he's got a compatible donor. But he didn't."

Zachary nodded. "Easy to make mistakes."

"A doctor can't afford to make mistakes like that. Not when he's making life and death decisions with no one supervising or checking his work."

"Yeah. By the way, you should talk to your mom."

Kenzie blinked at the abrupt change in subject. "Uh, okay. Of course I will. I should catch up with her today."

"I was talking to Tyrrell..."

Zachary's brother worked at the administrative office for the Kirsch family foundation. It was a good fit for him, and Kenzie was proud of herself for having helped place him there. And, as it turned out, it could be nice to have a spy in place, too, when Tyrrell was in a position to overhear something that Kenzie should be aware of or look into further.

"Oh, okay. What's going on with my mom?"

"There's been quite a bit of trouble with the board over the possibility that the foundation was funding an organization that had caused a death with so much negative publicity."

Kenzie rolled her eyes. "Why are they jumping on the bandwagon without knowing anything about what happened? I haven't even issued my report yet. What are they doing, assuming they know the details when they don't?"

"You might want to fill her in."

"Yeah, for sure," Kenzie agreed. She looked at the clock on the wall. But it wasn't like Lisa would still be in bed. She was always up early, finding it much easier than Kenzie to get up in the morning. Even on a Sunday, she wouldn't have slept past six-thirty or so. And if she had a brunch fundraiser to go to, she might have gotten up even earlier. "I'll give her a call."

Kenzie took a few large swallows of coffee to fortify herself. She had been working with the family foundation more closely for over a year but still didn't fully understand how it worked. She was often embroiled in an investigation when they wanted her to review an organization or make a decision on some policy change. As much as she could, she just let the rest of the board make a majority decision, assuming that they had done the research necessary. But there had been several decisions lately that had seemed like they had been rushed and due consideration had not been given to all of the aspects of the case. Blaming Lisa for the decision to fund the mobile clinic was unfair when the entire board had approved it.

Kenzie tapped her mother's name on her phone favorites and waited for the call to go through.

"Mackenzie," Lisa purred into the phone. "It's lovely to hear from you. How are you this fine morning?"

"I'm pretty good. Taking things easy this morning. How about you? I hope you aren't getting any grief over the publicity about Jack Lane's case."

There was a beat as Lisa considered what to tell her about it. "Well, as you might have guessed, they are concerned about the exposure. But I know a lawsuit hasn't been filed, and things have been quiet in the media since the original release. It has been tapering off."

"But the board is still concerned?"

"It is their job to be concerned with the foundation's reputation and how people perceive it. I have been getting some backlash about the shift in focus to mental health, addiction, and homelessness. They are saying we should not be getting away from 'hard science' in favor of... well, a lot of nonsense about how people need to help themselves and that mental health issues place an undue burden on society..."

"If they aren't taken care of, yeah. Do they think they are going to be better off if we *don't* treat people with mental illness and worry about other 'soft' social issues?"

Lisa laughed. "You're very blunt, dear."

"Somebody needs to knock a few heads together."

"Perhaps. Sometimes, when people spend too much time sitting around pontificating about the ills of society instead of getting out into the trenches, they can... get some very strange ideas about how to solve the problems we are facing."

"Well, they need to get their heads out of... the clouds and see how the real world works."

Lisa continued to chuckle. "Well, I'm happy to have you on my side, dear. I don't suppose you have any information on Mr. Lane's death that might help to... redirect the concerns of the members of the board?"

"Well, actually, yes."

60

Kenzie paused to gather her thoughts.

"The media reported that the mobile clinic had treated Mr. Lane and must have missed something or not treated him properly, because he died."

"Yes."

"The doctors at the mobile clinic knew about Jack's alcoholism and the serious medical conditions he was suffering as a result of his drinking. But you can't just take someone off the street and send them into rehab. They have to make that decision for themselves. They did the best they could to make him comfortable."

"Was it that dire? And they knew it?"

"Yes, they knew he was getting towards the end of his life. That he was on his final days or weeks."

"He should have been in the hospital. Or a hospice of some kind."

"Would you have forced him to?"

"Well, I don't suppose there was any way I could have forced him," Lisa admitted. "If someone refuses treatment, they have to let him go. Even from the hospital."

"Yes. Once a patient refuses treatment, there's little you can do about it."

"So that was what happened to Mr. Lane? He refused treatment, and his illness took its natural course?"

"No. He was treated by someone else. Someone who called himself the Night Doctor."

"The Night Doctor. That sounds rather romantic."

"I guess he saw himself as a hero figure. A savior of all of the homeless."

"But he was not able to save Jack."

"No. He ended up killing him. He was practicing without a license, and he made a mistake. Gave him the wrong blood type."

"And that killed him?"

"Yes. Very quickly. He would have died almost as quickly if he had not been treated, but there was no chance once he had been given the wrong blood type."

"But it wasn't the mobile clinic. They didn't do anything wrong or fail to find something they should have."

"Exactly."

"Well, that's good news. That should help to calm the sharks a little, at least."

"This doctor had once been working with the mobile clinic. But they fired him because he was not competent to practice medicine."

"A positive and a negative," Lisa mused. "Bad that he was working for the mobile clinic, but good that they recognized him for what he was and fired him before he treated Mr. Lane."

"Right," Kenzie agreed. "Once his name is released, I'm sure the reporters will investigate whether he worked for the mobile clinic, and they'll find a trail there."

"Knowing ahead of time will give us a chance to do damage control. I'll get in touch with counsel and our communications consultant, and we'll start crafting a statement. How sorry we are about Mr. Lane's death, that this highlights the need for vigilance and for awareness of the problem. To ensure we have highly qualified doctors treating the indigent and are not just scraping the bottom of the barrel."

Kenzie nodded to herself. This was Lisa's wheelhouse. She would put together a press release that hit all the right notes, promoting the foundation while expressing sympathy for those who had known Jack Lane. Rather than being an indication that they were putting their money into the wrong thing because a man had died, it would show that there was even more need for funding in the area and encourage people to donate to a very important cause.

"That sounds good, Mom. I'm sure it will all turn out okay."

"I'm not sure it will satisfy all the naysayers; but then, nothing ever does. There will always be detractors. Pessimists and dissemblers. There are always people who try to pull down instead of building up. But you and I are builders, aren't we? We're not going to let them do that."

"No. We'll get it all sorted out." Kenzie smiled at her mother, including her in the statement. She did not see herself like Lisa in very many ways. But Lisa was right about that; Kenzie was always trying to build and move forward, not to tear down what everyone who had gone ahead of her had done.

"How's Dad?"

"He's fine. You should give him a call. I'm sure he would like to hear from you."

"I will."

It was just another confirmation that her parents were leading separate lives, even if her father was back to living in the mansion again. It was big enough to accommodate several families. There would be no problem with Walter and Lisa each leading separate lives that only occasionally crossed paths in the entry hall or the kitchen.

But she could be wrong. Lisa might just be at the foundation offices and Walter at home, so Lisa could not call Walter to say hello to his daughter while they were on the line together.

"I have a question for you, Mom."

"Yes, Mackenzie?" Lisa adopted a formal tone.

Kenzie realized that her statement might have come out sounding stiff and made an effort to sound more natural and friendly.

"Do you remember the woman who you had to speak at the gala? Maria?" There had, of course, been more than just one speaker that night. There had been a whole parade of individuals from all walks of life.

"Certainly. I remember Maria."

"Did you meet her personally? Was she... what do you remember about her? Was she... clear when she spoke to you?"

"Yes, she was quite clear and well-spoken. Not necessarily the type of person you expect to find homeless. It makes you stop and reconsider your personal biases about the homeless."

"She didn't have any odd ideas or seem... *out there?*"

Lisa laughed. "Goodness, no, certainly not. She was just the type of person you would expect to find working at an accounting firm or boutique store. Very well-organized and professional. As I said, she was well-spoken. I don't know what else to say about her."

"Because when I talked to her, she was very different. Erratic. Paranoid."

"When you talked to her at the gala?"

"No, no. This past week. She came to me because she knew me from the gala and knew I was the medical examiner who had worked on Jack."

"And *they* knew each other," Lisa said. "Ah, that makes sense. She wanted to know what had happened to him and thought that you would be able to help. She must have been acting differently because of grief. That can affect people quite a lot, you know."

"Yes, I know that. But I would not expect it to make her act so paranoid... she wasn't very coherent."

"That does *not* sound like the Maria I know," Lisa said firmly. "Something must be wrong. That doesn't make any sense."

"I'm hearing the same thing from multiple people, so I guess it must be true. She's been admitted to the hospital. Hopefully, they will be able to find out what's going on and get it straightened out."

"She's been admitted?" Lisa repeated. "What for? Where?"

"In Clintock. She was... involved in an incident with the police yesterday and is being evaluated. It was pretty clear something was going on with her yesterday."

"I will go see her. Do you think I'll be able to? Will they let me in?"

"Possibly not within the evaluation period. You might want to call ahead to find out what the rules are." Kenzie was impressed that Lisa knew Maria well enough to be concerned with her and want to be at her side. Maria was not just some "face of the homeless" that Lisa had plucked off the street and knew nothing about. She was not being exploited for what had happened to her, but was, hopefully, actually someone who wanted to spread the word about the good the foundation was doing and how they needed more funding if they were going to continue working with the homeless and other underserved communities in the future.

"Thank you for letting me know. I don't imagine the hospital would have called me. I will make sure they know who I am and that I stand at the ready to help in any way I can."

"I'm sure that will help," Kenzie agreed. Lisa would see that no expense was spared. Whatever evaluation and treatment Maria needed, she would get it.

61

Kenzie didn't manage to fit everything she wanted to into Sunday. But then, she never did. There was always more to be done than she could possibly fit in.

But at the end of the day, at least she had felt like she'd caught up on a few things. She was calmer and more relaxed and, although she wasn't looking forward to returning to the morgue on Monday, she at least felt like she had caught up on her sleep.

She knew she was going in to finish the medical examiner's report on Jack Lane's autopsy. Then she would try to get caught up on the other reports, emails, and various tests that needed to be coordinated.

"Are you worried it will be awkward with Dr. Cook?" Zachary asked over breakfast.

Kenzie nibbled on her toast, trying to ignore the knot of anxiety twisting in her stomach. She dreaded facing Dr. Cook, knowing what she now did about him. How he had known when she first went to him that his friend was practicing medicine illegally and had not told her or the authorities. Maybe he had talked to Hartfield and tried to convince him to stop, but he had to know at that point that talking wouldn't get him anywhere. As Morrison had said, they had ample evidence that no matter who tried to stop

Hartfield from practicing, he was going to go on and continue to treat people until he was physically stopped. Dr. Cook should have gone to the police or the medical board. He'd had a responsibility to do so to ensure that Hartfield was not able to injure or kill anyone.

"It's not going to be easy," she admitted to Zachary. "He's been a good boss while Dr. Wiltshire has been gone. Different, but still good, and I have learned a lot from him. He was always respectful of my space, and friendly and helpful. But... he should have talked to someone before Jack was killed. And he should have talked to someone after."

Zachary nodded his agreement. He swirled a spoon around in the yogurt container and then put it in his mouth.

"But I'll manage," Kenzie said. It would be awkward, as Zachary had suggested, but she could look beyond that and focus on the working relationship. He was still the same doctor as he had been the week before. She would learn what she needed to from him, get his approval on reports he needed to sign off on, and otherwise stay out of his way.

Kenzie's phone rang. She looked down at it and, even though they normally did not answer phone calls during mealtimes, she swiped to accept the call. She tapped the speaker button. "Captain? You've got me and Zachary."

Morrison's voice came through the speaker. "Did you enjoy your day off?"

"It was good," Kenzie told him. "I suspect I got more rest than you did."

"You are probably right," he admitted. "I was here or somewhere else taking care of this case for most of the day."

"Did you need something more from us? I will hopefully have the medical examiner's report on Jack Lane to you today."

"I actually have information for you."

"On Jack Lane?"

"On Maria. Normally, we are not allowed to pass on private medical information, even to the medical examiner, unless it is about your victim. But in his case, Maria explicitly authorized us to talk to you and tell you what the hospital found."

Kenzie leaned toward the phone. "Great! I'm glad to hear they found something. Does that mean she is feeling better?"

"I'm told it will be a while before she recovers. It took a while to build up, and they will need to taper off gradually."

"It was a medication?" Kenzie discerned.

"Apparently, Dr. Hartfield prescribed corticosteroids for Maria's asthma and arthritis. She had an adverse reaction. I guess there is a well-documented link between paranoia and corticosteroids."

"I'm not familiar with it, but it's not surprising. There are a lot of drugs that can have adverse reactions, some of them common and some of them not. Hartfield shouldn't have been prescribing anything, of course, but he wouldn't have known she would react that way."

"Unless it was a reaction she had previously experienced."

"Of course, but—" Kenzie realized that the captain was telling her Maria had, in fact, reacted to the class of drugs before. "She had? He should have learned that when he took a medical history or checked her records."

"Unless he skipped over that part," Zachary contributed. "I'm guessing it's another demonstration of the fact that he doesn't do very well at record keeping." He had another spoonful of yogurt, thoughtful. "She said *they* started following her after she first saw Dr. Hartfield."

"She did, didn't she? Were there *any* records in that storage unit?" Kenzie asked.

"Hardly any paper at all. Some personal records. Aside from that, he had a couple of bikes and plenty of medical supplies, a lot that he shouldn't have been able to get without a valid medical license. Some personal belongings that… did not belong to him."

"Didn't belong to him?" Kenzie frowned at the phone, then glanced at Zachary's face to see what he made of this news.

"At this point, we don't know who they belonged to. Apparently, he knew better than to hang on to their IDs. But he had clothing, jewelry, and other personal possessions from unknown individuals."

"The patients who disappeared," Kenzie realized.

"What's that?" Morrison asked.

"When we started making inquiries about the Night Doctor on the street, we were told that some of his patients had disappeared."

There was a short silence as Morrison considered this. "There were no human remains in the storage unit. We will... do our best to identify who they belonged to and look into where they went. These items may be all that is left of them."

62

The most recent discovery had Kenzie even less eager to go to work as usual, but she steeled herself and did what she had to.

The office was quiet when she arrived, and no coffee had been brewed in the break room. Dr. Cook was almost always there ahead of her, so she was surprised but pleased to be the first one in and be able to work through her weekend emails and correspondence before having to see him. It would be almost like when Dr. Wiltshire had been there.

She lost herself in her work, eager to get as much administrative work done as she could before Dr. Cook got in. It was some time later when she heard the elevator down the hall and knew that he had arrived.

Kenzie looked up as footsteps rounded the corner and came down the hall. Her jaw dropped, and her eyes opened wide.

"Dr. Wiltshire!" She stood up.

"Dr. Kirsch. How has your morning been so far?"

"Quiet. I've just been catching up on the weekend influx and my report on Jack Lane. But what are you doing here? Did you need to pick something up?"

"Actually," he had a mischievous twinkle in his eyes, "I am here to work."

Kenzie's eyes dropped to his hand. No longer in a cast or any type of support. There were some ugly scars from the repair work that had been done, but the dark bruising from when he had initially hurt it were long gone. His fingers appeared to be straight. Looking at each digit and each knuckle, she could not spot anything that seemed out of place. He'd had one of the best surgeons in the country in to repair it, hoping that, despite how badly it had been broken, he would one day be able to work again.

"Is it completely healed?" she asked. "What level of functionality do you have?"

"I would say eighty percent. With lots of physio to do to gain the last twenty."

But Dr. Wiltshire's eighty percent was better than most people's one hundred.

"So, Dr. Cook…?"

"Dr. Cook has been thanked for his service substituting here while I was out of commission."

"And that's it? He's gone?"

She had been expecting a transition period. A slow return to duty by Dr. Wiltshire, a day or two a week and gradually increasing as he was able to take on more. But it would seem that he expected to start back full-time today, and Dr. Cook was out. There would be no awkwardness as she tried to do her work to her standards without questioning everything Dr. Cook did and wondering whether he had other friends she should know about or if there were other things he was keeping from her and the proper authorities. He'd had plenty to say about Dr. Wiltshire, but it turned out he'd been the one with moral issues.

"He will find another position elsewhere," Dr. Wiltshire confirmed. "We won't concern ourselves with that. If there were any issues with his work here, please let me know and report it to the medical board."

"His work was always good," Kenzie said. "He was a good doctor and a great helper. I never had any problem with that.

But… I do have concerns about him knowing that Evan Hartfield was still practicing medicine when he shouldn't be, even when I had concerns that he was involved in the treatment of Jack Lane. Dr. Cook shouldn't have been involved in the autopsy, and he should have told the police what he knew, even if he wasn't willing to do anything to stop Hartfield himself."

Dr. Wiltshire nodded. "I will review all of the autopsy notes, recordings, and evidence and confirm your findings. We will add an addendum about his conflict in the case and that all findings have been independently verified."

"Okay, good. And I did report everything to Detective Samuels as it came up, even though Dr. Cook didn't really… encourage it."

"I've talked with Detective Samuels. Everything appears to be in order."

Kenzie let out a long sigh of relief. "And you're not rushing things too much coming back now? You weren't planning on returning today, were you?"

"The best thing for me and my rehabilitation right now is to get back to work and start using my hand again. I won't build up the dexterity I need if I can't see the areas that need improvement and strengthening. No, I think today is the perfect time for me to come back."

"Well…" Kenzie held her hand out to him, and after a moment, Dr. Wiltshire took her hand in his and they shook. "Let me be the first to welcome you back, doctor."

"Thank you. I'm thrilled to be back."

Did you enjoy this book? Reviews and recommendations are vital to making a book successful.

Please leave a review at your favorite book store or review site and share it with your friends.

Don't miss the following bonus material:
Sign up for mailing list to get a free reader bonus
Read a sneak preview chapter
Other books by P.D. Workman
Learn more about the author

DON'T MISS A THING! GET THE LATEST NEWS AND A FREE EBOOK

PDWORKMAN.COM/SIGNUP

PREVIEW CHAPTER 1

Kenzie was starting to yawn, a sign she had been up for long enough and it was time to head to bed. She and Zachary had been watching an Unsolved Mysteries marathon, challenging themselves to come up with clues, investigative paths, and possible solutions to the various crimes. They skipped over the ones about UFOs, psychic events, or other paranormal mysteries, sticking to the missing persons, murders, finding long-lost relatives, or exploring family history.

But Kenzie was beat. She was past the age when she could party all night long, or even wanted to. After midnight, she was ready to turn off the TV, put their dishes in the dishwasher, and brush her teeth. Her bed was calling.

Zachary noticed her smothering a yawn and raised his brows knowingly. "Last episode?" he suggested.

Kenzie nodded. "Yeah. Sorry about that. I'd love to watch more, but... my body has other ideas."

Zachary rubbed his thick five o'clock shadow, bristles rasping. "We'd better solve this one, then, wouldn't want to go to bed on a failure."

"Well..." Kenzie covered another yawn. "Since the entire Cincinnati police force was not able to solve it in ten years, I think we can be forgiven for not being able to solve it based on a ten-minute summary and reenactment."

"So, you don't think that it was—"

Kenzie's phone began to ring.

Not just the regular ringtone, but the loud, klaxon blare assigned to the police dispatcher that was designed to wake her from even the deepest sleep. Both of them jumped at the sudden loud alarm.

That meant there was a body to deal with, and Kenzie would not be going to sleep for a couple more hours. She rubbed her eyes and sighed before picking up the phone to get the details.

Zachary waited until she was back off the phone before asking, "You want to watch the end of this one before leaving?"

There was another two or three minutes left, and staying that much longer wouldn't make any difference to either the police or the woman who had been killed, but Kenzie's attention was no longer on it.

"You can watch the end of it, or we can rewatch it tomorrow. I'm going to head out."

Zachary hit the stop button. "No problem. Do you want me to drive you?"

"No. I'll see you later."

"You're not too tired to drive?" he persisted.

She had been yawning, so Zachary could be forgiven for pressing the point. Kenzie shook her head, her dark curls bouncing around her face. "No. That alarm got the adrenaline pumping. I couldn't go to sleep now if I wanted to. It's only five minutes away. I won't have time to get drowsy."

He nodded slowly. "Okay. I'll see you when you get back."

She didn't bother telling him to go to sleep without her. He would wait up no matter what she said. And he slept little enough that waiting for her wouldn't make any difference to his schedule. He would watch TV or putter away at a case on his computer until she returned.

Kenzie hated changing out of her comfortable jammies into day clothes, but she wasn't going to show up at an accident scene looking like she'd just rolled out of bed. She changed into a business-professional outfit, reapplied her bright red lipstick, and grabbed her purse. Her small scene-of-crime kit was already in the car, and it didn't sound like she would need anything more specialized for the scene she was going to.

+++

The accident scene was only a couple of blocks from the police building, which happened to house the medical examiner's office in the basement. They wouldn't have far to transport the body. With a gurney, Kenzie could easily have walked the body to the morgue.

It was a spectacular wreck. Kenzie's stomach clenched when she saw it. She had been at enough accident scenes before that it shouldn't bother her, but the sight of the smashed, upside-down vehicle still affected her.

"Dr. Kirsch," the young cop in charge of the scene, probably recognized Kenzie by her red convertible and he didn't require her to show her badge. "Looks like she managed to hit the center median at a pretty good velocity. It acted as a ramp, launching and spinning the car so that it landed on its roof." He indicated both the place that it had hit the barrier, leaving bits of metal and glass behind, and then the car itself, which Kenzie didn't need pointed out.

"Okay, thanks. Paramedics have examined her?" There was an ambulance standing by, red lights flashing. One of the paramedics was in the driver's seat, and the other was leaning against it, smoking. Obviously, there was nothing for them to do; they were just waiting for Kenzie to officially declare the death and send them on their way.

"Yeah. Head injury from being thrown around. Maybe a broken neck. There wasn't anything they could do for her when they got here."

Kenzie signed her name to the log, put on booties and gloves, and walked over to the lone car, upside down like a ladybug in the middle of the street. The streetlights reflected eerily off the road. Firetrucks stood by. There was no smell of gasoline, but the car was pretty wrecked, and they were probably waiting to cut the door free so that the victim could be removed. As it was, Kenzie had access through the shattered driver's side window. She reached in and touched the woman's throat, probing for a pulse.

As expected, there was none. The body was still warm. Not an hour had elapsed since the driver had been speeding down the street toward her doom. Kenzie didn't smell any alcohol, which surprised her. An accident like this was usually the result of drinking and driving.

Kenzie withdrew her hand and surveyed the rest of the vehicle, looking at the damage to the body, the deflated airbag, and the unfortunate woman with a mask of blood.

Kenzie's first reaction to the accident was visceral, a flashback to the accident she and Zachary had been in after their first date. While the cops had initially speculated that it was the result of drunk driving, Zachary had not had anything to drink that night, and rarely did due to possible interactions with his medications. He didn't take his anti-anxiety prescription or sleep aids every night, but knew that he couldn't combine either of them with alcohol, so he rarely drank in case he would need to take one of them later.

Rather than being the result of drinking and driving, *that* accident had been caused by someone tampering with Zachary's car. It, too, had landed upside down. Kenzie's memories of getting her seatbelt undone, extricating herself from the wreck, calling for help, and trying to comfort Zachary, who was in and out of consciousness, were astonishingly clear. It had taken a long time, in very cold weather, for the police and firefighters to arrive and cut Zachary free. His injuries had been much more severe than Kenzie's. She had some scrapes and bruises that had been sore for a few weeks, but he'd had a spinal injury and concussion that had made for a couple of scary days before it became clear that the spinal cord had only been bruised and not permanently damaged.

"Everything okay?" the young cop, hovering behind Kenzie asked.

She turned and looked at him, pulling herself away from the flashback and focusing on the present. She looked at his name bar to remind herself who he was. Though she had seen him around the police station or parking garage, they had not worked together. *Daniels.*

Even while dealing with her emotional reaction to the crash and the memories that forced themselves into her consciousness, she also maintained a sense of the dispassionate, clinical distance that was required to analyze the scene and the woman's body and to start to build a picture of the mechanics of her death.

The victim was a tall, thin, white woman with dark hair pulled back in a bun. She wore a dress and simple jewelry and had probably been out on a date or at an event.

"Yes. Everything is fine. Do you have an ID on the victim? She looks familiar."

One of the problems with living in a small town was that Kenzie sometimes did know the victims who ended up on her table. She was sure, looking at the limp, bloody figure hanging upside down in the car that she knew this woman. They had met previously, though Kenzie wasn't sure where. It was sometimes difficult to recognize people in death; faces obscured by blood, facial bones broken, with no animation. She sometimes had to work at it to find the similarities to the person she had known in life or was trying to identify from a picture.

"License plate is registered to a Mariya Markov. Haven't been able to verify she is the victim, but the picture on her driver's license looks close enough."

Mariya Markov.

Kenzie knew the name immediately. They had met more than once at fundraising events for the Kirsch family foundation. Kenzie had attended several galas at the behest of her mother, Lisa Cole Kirsch, and Dr. Markov had been an honored guest.

"Dr. Mariya Markov," Kenzie told Daniels. "She is a preeminent nephrologist." She shook her head. Her mother would be shocked to hear of Dr. Markov's passing.

"A kidney doctor?" Daniels asked tentatively.

Kenzie nodded. "Yes, exactly. She was a great surgeon and researcher, at the forefront of kidney disease research and transplants."

Daniels nodded gravely. "I'm sorry to hear that." He looked over the wreck with fresh eyes, considering. "What do you think it was? Asleep at the wheel?"

That seemed more likely than drinking and driving. Dr. Markov might have been tired after putting in an eighteen-hour day or performing an eight-hour surgery.

"Could be," she admitted. "We'll have to see what the accident reconstruction guys and the autopsy show." She sighed. "This is a great loss to the community."

PREVIEW CHAPTER 2

D r. Markov's body was transported to the morgue as soon as it was freed from the vehicle, but Kenzie did not start on the autopsy that night. There was no need to rush into it, and when she had already put in a full day of work, she didn't want to take the chance of making any mistakes due to fatigue. She would do the postmortem when she was fresh and could be sure not to miss anything.

Kenzie arrived at the office an hour later than usual, having intentionally slept in to try to make up for her late night. But it had taken her a while to get settled down for sleep once she was home, and then she had slept fitfully, her mind working away, analyzing the details she already knew about Dr. Markov's accident.

Eventually, there hadn't been any point in trying to sleep any longer. Kenzie would feel more tired from struggling to sleep and dealing with her thoughts, instead of feeling more rested. She had a couple of cups of coffee to get her motor running and headed into the office.

Because she was late, Dr. Wiltshire was there ahead of her. Unlike Dr. Cook, who had substituted while Dr. Wiltshire was healing from a broken hand, Dr. Wiltshire usually arrived after Kenzie, allowing her time to get things organized and the morning emails and reports processed before he got in. Dr. Cook had always been there disconcertingly early, making Kenzie feel like she was running behind when she wasn't.

"Morning, Kenzie," Dr. Wiltshire greeted, smiling pleasantly. "How are you doing this lovely morning?"

Kenzie thought back to the weather as she had driven in. It had been a bright, clear, warm day, but she hadn't even noticed it. Her mind had been far away.

"Good," Kenzie told him. "Took a little extra time for sleep this morning, so I'm ready to go."

"Excellent. I'll let you get yourself together, and when you are ready for the autopsy, just let me know."

"Thanks." Kenzie sniffed the air. "You got coffee going?"

"I did remember how to start the machine," he said wryly.

"See, you're polishing up your skills already," Kenzie told him.

Dr. Wiltshire had been doing physiotherapy to rehab his broken hand, but he figured nothing would help him regain his dexterity as quickly as getting back to work.

And the good thing about working on dead patients was that it wasn't nearly as much of a problem if you accidentally nicked an artery during a procedure.

Dr. Wiltshire smiled and shook his head. "I'll be at my desk if you happen to need me for any other complex tasks."

+++

After processing the daily influx of emails, interoffice mail, and packages she had received, Kenzie finished the last of her coffee and let Dr. Wiltshire know that she was ready to begin the postmortem.

"Did you know Dr. Markov?" Kenzie asked as she gowned up and made the final preparations to begin the postmortem on the body waiting for her.

Dr. Wiltshire shook his head. "We have probably met at some point, but not that I remember. We ran in different circles. She must have been in town for a function, since she operates out of Burlington."

"Yeah, that's what I figured too. I don't remember hearing about anything going on last night, and I usually do if it is related to kidney disease, but there must have been some reason for her to be in Roxboro."

Once they were ready to start, Kenzie tapped the button on the floor to begin recording, then tapped it again to stop and looked at Dr. Wiltshire.

"Sorry, I'm just jumping right in here. You are the senior doctor; you will want to run things."

He dismissed the idea with a wave.

"Not necessary," he told her. "Go ahead. I'll let you run the first few until I'm sure that these old fingers are going to perform the way they are supposed to. If I need a break partway through, it's better if you are dictating, rather than having to switch partway through."

"You're sure? I can take a break anytime you want to, to maintain continuity."

"Just go ahead, Dr. Kirsch. I'll run the next one if I feel up to it."

Kenzie nodded, sure that it was what Dr. Wiltshire wanted and she wasn't stepping on his toes. She tapped the record button again, dictated the date, file number, patient name, and her and Dr. Wiltshire's names. They began with the gross examination of the body, as always.

George had taken swabs of the skin for any trace evidence, being sure to get samples of blood or other bodily fluids or contaminants before washing the body in preparation for the postmortem.

Kenzie noticed again the deformity in Markov's face from a broken nose and eye sockets. There was a laceration down the side of her head from where it had hit the window or frame of the car during the rollover. Given that Markov was unresponsive when the first report came in and deceased upon the arrival of first responders, Kenzie would not be surprised to find some severe damage to the neck and spine. Markov had not had time to bleed out, especially not from that head lac, and there was no impalement, amputation, or other serious tissue injuries.

Kenzie dictated the injuries she could see for the recording, taking pictures of each. They would do full X-rays of the head, neck, and torso to see what other fractures had been caused by the accident or the airbag.

"This is odd," Kenzie said, examining the bruising around Markov's shoulders and upper arms. "Perimortem bruising. It had a chance to set in before she expired, so it was not from injuries sustained in the accident."

Dr. Wiltshire leaned in to examine the bruising more closely, then brought the magnifying lens in for further examination. He nodded. "There is inflammation, which would not be the case if it was sustained during the accident. And the location of the bruises is not consistent with a seatbelt or airbag injury."

"They look like restraint bruises."

As if someone had been holding her still. Both by grasping her upper arms and by holding or pushing against her shoulders.

"We should check for any other indications of assault."

Dr. Wiltshire agreed.

There were no other unexpected bruises or injuries apparent on the external examination. Rather than putting on a lead shield, Dr. Wiltshire left the room while Kenzie took a series of X-rays. He returned, and they reviewed the various fractures apparent on the monitors.

"Ribs and wrists from the airbag as well as the nose and orbits," Dr. Wiltshire observed. "That is all to be expected."

"And here," Kenzie pointed to the vertebrae in the neck. "There is damage to the C4 and C5 from the rollover. She must have been going pretty fast. The competing forces from the rollover resulted in cervical spine fracture."

Dr. Wiltshire agreed. He used the mouse to mark each of the breaks on the X-rays, and they looked for any other fractures that might have occurred during the accident or concurrent with the perimortem bruising. Everything seemed to be straightforward, with no other unexpected injuries.

Death's Charm, Book #13 of the *Kenzie Kirsch Medical Thriller* series by P.D. Workman can be purchased at pdworkman.com

ABOUT THE AUTHOR

P.D. Workman is a USA Today Bestselling author and multi-award winner, renowned for her prolific output of over 100 published works that span various genres. With a knack for crafting page-turners, Workman captivates readers with everything from cozy mysteries like the Auntie Clem's Bakery series to gripping young adult and suspense novels.

A prolific reader and writer since childhood, P.D. Workman crafts emotionally powerful stories that don't shy away from hard topics. Her books tackle mental illness, addiction, abuse, and trauma with raw honesty and compassion, giving voice to the often unheard. If you crave authentic, character-driven page-turners that hit deep and stay with you long after the final page, you're in the right place.

With each new release, fans eagerly anticipate another thrilling blend of thought-provoking storytelling and relatable characters that define P.D. Workman's brand as an author of unforgettable page-turners—gripping tales that leave a lasting impact long after the last page is turned.

> P. D. Workman, does not shy from probing the deep psychological scars of childhood trauma, mental illness, and addiction. Also characteristic of this author, these extremely sensitive issues are explored with extensive empathy, described with incredible clarity, and portrayed with profound insight.
>
> — —KIM, GOODREADS REVIEWER

Some of Workman's titles have been translated into Spanish, French, Portuguese, German, and Italian.

Workman began writing at an early age and is a prolific reader as well as writer. She is also passionate about teaching and learning, expresses her creativity through art and cooking, and loves exploring the Calgary parks and green spaces where the Parks Pat Mysteries are set. She was a legal assistant for many years and has done extensive charitable work.

Workman was born and raised in Alberta, Canada, and is married with one adult son.

Please visit P.D. Workman at pdworkman.com to see what else she is working on, to join her mailing list, and to link to her social networks.

If you enjoyed this book, please take the time to recommend it to other purchasers with a review or star rating and share it with your friends!

tiktok.com/@pdworkmanauthor

facebook.com/pdworkmanauthor

x.com/pdworkmanauthor

instagram.com/pdworkmanauthor

amazon.com/author/pdworkman

bookbub.com/authors/p-d-workman

goodreads.com/pdworkman

linkedin.com/in/pdworkman

pinterest.com/pdworkmanauthor

youtube.com/pdworkman

Find P.D. Workman's books at

PDWORKMAN.COM

Scan the QR code below